CIRCLE OF DANGER

Also by Carla Swafford

Circle of Desire

CIRCLE
OF DANGER

CARLA SWAFFORD

AVON

An Imprint of HarperCollinsPublishers

Excerpt from *Circle of Desire* copyright © 2011 by Carla Swafford.

EPub Edition JUNE 2012 ISBN: 9780062117830

Print Edition ISBN: 9780062117847

10 9 8 7 6 5 4 3

To my beautiful daughters, who inspire me every day.

CHAPTER ONE

Arthur Ryker sprang out of bed and immediately stood at attention, feet apart, his scarred hands in the "ready" position at waist level. One hand cupped by the other, restrained but prepared to kill. He shook his head and sighed. Just once he wanted to leave his bed like a regular person and not like a trained monkey.

"A bad dream?" a deep voice asked from the bedroom entrance. With one pierced black eyebrow lifted, Jack Drago leaned against the doorjamb.

Ignoring the question, Ryker walked naked into the bathroom. When he returned to grab some clothes out of the closet, Jack hadn't moved but his gaze had most likely inspected every inch of the room. There wasn't much to see. A king-sized bed sat in a corner while a mirror-less dresser was centered against one wall—no pictures or the usual bric-a-brac to give away the occupant's personality. Then again, maybe it did. Rather stark for a man who owned enough properties and businesses to keep his organization in the best covert weapons money could buy. He didn't care what Jack thought about his bedroom. Except for a few hours of sleep and a shower and shave, Ryker rarely spent time in the room.

"What do you want?" he asked, glaring at his second-in-command.

With cold blue eyes, Jack studied him, and then his gaze shifted away.

Ryker grunted. Not many people could deal with looking at the thick scars down the side of his body, but it was his blind eye that bothered most. White from the scar tissue damaged in a fire so many years ago, he normally hid it beneath a patch. But he'd be damned before he slept with one on. So if Jack decided to make a habit of waking him in the morning, he could fucking well get use to the sight. Considering the man had four visible piercings—and who knew how many hidden—along with tattoos covering one arm, he shouldn't have a problem with his scars. The man understood pain.

With sure, quick movements, he thrust his legs into jeans and yanked on a black T-shirt. After tugging on his boots, he strapped a small pistol at his ankle. With his patch in place, using his fingers he combed hair over the strap securing its position. Hell, he needed a haircut again. Maybe he'd shave his head like Jack. A simple enough solution. If only the rest of his problems could be so easily solved.

"She's in trouble," Jack said in an even tone as if his voice could defuse a bad situation.

Ryker's stomach and chest tightened as if he'd been hit. He knew who Jack referred to without adding a name. She happened to be part of why his life was so complicated.

"Did you hear me?" Jack straightened his stance.

"Yeah." Desire to break someone's neck raced through his body. "Where is she? What happened?"

With a sharp snap, he inserted a snub-nose into the shoulder holster hanging at his side and jerked on his leather jacket. He gritted his teeth for a few seconds to regain his composure. Then he took a deep breath, squared his shoulders, and exhaled.

"Last time Bryan heard from her, she'd entered the target's house in Chattanooga and was downloading information off a laptop. He lost communication with her." Jack quickly stepped out of the way for Ryker to move into the dark hallway. "They believe she's still in the house. If the Wizard sticks to his MO, we'll have about three hours before he takes her away or kills her."

Ryker wasted no time in reaching a massive room with mirrors from ceiling to floor. When the mansion was built in the eighteen hundreds, the room was used as a ballroom. It was empty now, except for a Steinway covered with a white sheet, and the high-sheen hardwood floor sounded hollow as he tramped across it. He used the room for one purpose only—to reach the stairwell hidden behind one of the mirrors.

"Took you long enough to spit it out." Ryker glanced at his second-in-command.

Jack remained quiet, staring straight ahead. Ryker didn't really expect an excuse. The man knew how he felt about that. No excuse for failure, especially when it came to protecting Marie.

Four months earlier, Ryker had moved The Circle compound from the suburbs of Atlanta to an area near the Smoky

Mountains. The mansion was situated in the middle of almost ten thousand acres, which included a large mountain filled with a network of tunnels and bunkers perfect to house the facility he needed. Last year, the final phase of the project was completed and now they were training new recruits in the underground Sector. The nearly fifteen square miles provided the privacy he needed. In a world filled with evil people, his covert organization of assassins came in handy.

Their footsteps echoed in the long, well-lit tunnel. A semi could pass through the passageway without scraping the side mirrors or the tips of muffler stacks.

"Who was her backup?" Ryker asked.

When a few seconds passed without an answer, Ryker stopped and faced Jack.

"They're handling it."

Ryker continued to stare.

His second-in-command sighed. "She went in without a backup."

Jaw clenched, Ryker strode to the iris scan next to a large metal door. A buzz sounded and he slammed the door against the inner wall.

The gripping pain in his belly grew and reminded him of the fear he lived with for years before he took over control of The Circle. She could not keep doing this to him. He refused to allow anything more to happen to her. She knew this and still didn't listen.

The noise level in the basketball court–sized room almost broke the sound barrier with printers running and people shouting or talking to those sitting next to them—or to others on the Internet or satellite phones—along with the clicking of keyboards. Each wall covered with large screens captured a different scene of people living their lives in various parts of the world. In the center of the room, faces bleached white by the monitors in front of them, the supervisors and handlers communicated with their operatives.

Ryker stopped in the middle of the bullpen, searching for his prey.

The balding, whipcord-thin Bryan Tilton stood over a handler shouting instructions and pointing at the screen. Maybe a sixth sense alerted Bryan. He looked up and his eyes widened.

Ryker charged toward him, ignoring the people ducking for cover behind partitions and beneath desks.

"You son of a bitch!"

His fist clipped Bryan on the chin, sending the man sliding across the floor. Desire to flatten the asshole's pointy nose almost overrode all of Ryker's control. Good thing Bryan remained sprawled out on the linoleum.

Standing over the man, Ryker opened and closed his fists. The temptation to punish him further for his stupidity warred with the fear of jabbing the cartilage of the idiot's nose into his brain.

"I swear, sir, I told her to wait until I could get backup in place, but she wouldn't listen." Bryan cupped his jaw and shifted it from side to side. "Two of our operatives are held up in a traffic accident about twenty-five miles from her last location."

"Last location?" Ryker gritted his teeth.

"The target's house, off Riverview Road." Bryan scooted back when Ryker took a step. The man's head bobbled on his skinny neck. "As soon as Phil and Harry reach it, they'll extract her."

Afraid he would crack the man's chicken neck, Ryker turned away and pointed at the nearest handler.

"You! Sal?" Mohawk trembling, the pale man nodded. Ryker said, "Tell Phil and Harry to call me on my cell as soon as they reach the house. Do not go inside! Jack and I will be there in twenty minutes. Have them wait for us. AHH" He turned back to Bryan. "Have the Spirit ready in five minutes." His helicopter could cover the miles quickly and land almost anywhere.

Marie Beltane struggled against the chains restraining her on a cot that reeked of sex and urine. She stifled a groan. No, no, no. Nausea travelled up her throat.

All the beams and pipes overhead felt like they were squeezing the air out of the room. Basements were never among her favorite rooms. The dampness and creepy-crawly things always gave her the willies.

She still couldn't believe she'd been caught. Bryan had sworn it would be an easy gig. Prior surveillance had revealed the man worked each evening at a massive bank of computers. Go in and download a flash drive–load of info and get out. The target always left his house at nine in the morning and didn't return until nine that evening. Breaking into the house when most people ate dinner in the surrounding homes had sounded so easy. Few would look out their windows as they settled down in front of their plates or televisions or both.

Hours would pass before he returned home. But he came back early.

Oh, God, she'd screwed up big time!

He looked like a fourteen-year-old with his cartoon-themed T-shirt and his mop of hair, but she knew from his file he was between twenty-six and twenty-eight. During their surveillance, they never got a clear photograph of him. Whenever he entered or exited his house, he did so through his garage. His SUV had tinted windows, preventing anyone from seeing inside.

The man standing with his back to her had outmaneuvered every defensive tactic she'd been taught. He didn't fight like a kid. Jack was right. She needed to work harder on her moves. If she had, she wouldn't be in this predicament. The nerd had surprised her, taking her down with unexpected ease.

She refused to cry even though she couldn't stop the trembling in her body. Every inch ached from his battery of hits and kicks. For a scrawny man, he'd moved fast and hit hard.

Her head hurt from holding back tears. She'd hoped to never be in this position again, to be under someone's control. No matter how many times she reminded herself this was different from before, the horror of repeating history pushed her to keep her eyes open. Staying aware of her enemy helped to keep her calm.

"You're not very smart. I'm efficient in seven different types of martial arts." His stiff words failed to impress her. He moved, revealing what he held in his hand. The huge syringe with a shiny green substance in the barrel had a needle longer than her forefinger. "Just because I'm a geek doesn't mean I'm unacquainted with ways to defend myself."

Marie stared at the needle. The duct tape covering her mouth muffled her scream. Ever since he jumped her, she'd tried to see a way to escape, while keeping calm.

She tried to be brave. She kept telling herself, screaming would only be a waste of energy. Stifling the panic engulfing her would keep her alive.

"Wait until this stuff hits your bloodstream. I'm told the sensation is similar to that last second before reaching an orgasm. In other words, you'll do anything to get off." He chuckled and lifted her shirt. He tugged at the waistband of her jeans.

She flinched when the needle slid into the soft skin near her hip.

"Perfect for where I'm sending you." He jerked on the jeans until the tips of his fingers brushed her pubic hair. "White American women—especially petite, natural blondes like you—are quite popular in parts of the Middle East and Asia. Virgins are preferred but rare here unless we go much younger." He shrugged. "Then you get into Amber Alerts and they're too much trouble. Anyway, bitches like you are plentiful and disposable."

He pulled harder at her jeans, taking her panties down.

She froze. Her stomached churned with the thought of what he might do next. Then he pushed the needle deeper. The liquid burned, becoming hotter as he eased the plunger down. The pain took her mind off her fear for only a second. When she tried to move away, the rattling chains reminded her she wasn't going anywhere. Tears pooled at the corner of her eyes and she turned her head, refusing to let him see her cry.

"A formula created by . . . a fucking genius! Especially created to use on sneaky sluts like you. The Wizard is a god!" He laughed. The back of his hand grazed her cheek. "I know it stings, baby. Sorry . . . no. I'm not sorry. You have the look of an ice princess. I love seeing an uptight cunt like you suffer. You have no idea what you've gotten yourself into. This wonder drug is highly addictive and from what I'm told, it has long-lasting effects. You'll grow to love it."

The grin on his smooth face terrified her more than anything else he'd done. Her vision blurred. The man leaned over her, his brown eyes dark and merciless. She whimpered. Every cell of her body tingled.

"Do you feel it? It takes a little while to set in. The Wizard said it tingles all over and next, for a small time, you'll feel like you're floating on water. Then you'll get sleepy and then—*bam!*—you'll be like a bitch in heat." He cackled and thrust his groin several times against her leg and the side of the cot. He punched the air with his fist and did a little dance. When he turned his back, he reached for something on a table nearby. "Now let's see what all of you looks like."

Light glinted off the scalpel. He swiped at the air above her as if he wielded a sword. No matter how brave she tried to be earlier, she couldn't stop her limbs from shaking harder and her stomach from twisting. She squealed behind the tape.

The sound of slicing material had her arching away from his touch. *Please don't cut me. Oh, please, God, help.* In seconds, he peeled away her clothes. He rubbed his groin and a lascivious grin marred his youthful face.

"Not bad, though I find the scars a shame, yet rather interesting. It looks like someone used a belt or whip on you. Have you been a bad girl?" He slid his hand down her bare thigh and over a long, thin white scar. "There are clients who would love to add to them."

She turned her head. Swallowing several times to keep from choking on vomit, she concentrated on the number of blocks in the basement wall. She could get through this. It wouldn't be the first time her body had been used. Eventually, she'd find a way out.

Just as she heard his zipper go down, a loud blast shook the walls. Dust sprinkled onto her face. She blinked her eyes. The room looked smoky, choked with plaster powder.

"What the hell?" The man ran toward the stairs as he struggled to pull up his pants. One foot on the bottom step, he stopped, staring at the door.

A smaller blast was followed by shouting and heavy footsteps running across the floor above. Whoever had come a-knocking were making their way through the house.

"Well, babe, you're on your own. I hope they appreciate the gift I'm leaving them." He laughed and disappeared beneath the stairs into a black void.

Her eyelids felt so heavy. Tingling travelling across her torso rushed down her legs and arms, and then a feeling of lightness and floating followed. A strong breeze brushed her naked body. Someone had found the basement. A wave of dizziness pushed her under and she closed her eyes, unable to lift them even when she felt someone fighting with the chains holding her down.

"Damn it, Marie. You better be alive," a deep voice growled.

She smiled. Deep inside, she knew he'd come for her.

CHAPTER TWO

Ryker ignored the tightening of the scars across the side of his face as he grimaced. Although she'd seen his ravaged face often, it'd been years since he'd been this close to her. He steeled himself for when she opened her eyes and they filled with pity.

That was the last emotion he ever wanted from her. He inhaled deeply. Why was he worrying about her feelings? His only concern should be getting her out of here.

Thankfully she kept her eyes closed as he carefully pulled the duct tape off her mouth. The bruise on her cheek and numerous others dotted across her body shot his temper sky-high. Marie would never hurt another human being. He'd tried protecting her the best way he knew how: by placing her in the Information Systems department of his organization. What was the worst that could happen? Carpal tunnel syndrome? He'd ordered Bryan to give her internal assignments. No external data retrieval. But the bastard claimed he'd forgotten. *Forgotten, my ass!*

He slipped out of his leather jacket and wrapped as much

of her as he could. Seeing the dirty sheets, he wanted to tear them off the bed and use the strips to hang the man who'd done this to her.

"Marie, I'll be careful picking you up. Let me know if you hurt anywhere and I'll stop." She felt good in his arms, solid but soft like a woman should. Over the last year, she'd gained a little weight and it looked good on her, gave her a more womanly figure.

Holy shit, he needed to keep his mind on the matter at hand. And not where he would like to put his hands. Shit.

He settled her against his chest, and she released a long groan.

"Are you okay?" he asked.

He stopped near the doorway. His men swarmed around him, searching the house for clues. Refusing to move another inch, he waited for her answer. She rubbed her cheek against his shoulder. Then moss-green eyes opened. Her pupils were unnaturally dilated.

The son of a bitch had drugged her.

"What did he give you?" His jaw shifted when she played with the hair at the back of his neck. His fingers spread wide on her back as he fought the need to squeeze her tighter to his chest.

"I don't know. He injected me with something green and shiny. He just said it was a gift and something about it being addictive." She licked her lips and winced.

"Hang in there and we'll have the doc check you out." With each step he made toward the van, she whimpered. It broke his heart. He'd never felt so clumsy, but he still refused to let anyone take her. No one could be gentler. Yet having her nearly naked in his arms was a temptation he didn't need. His hands shook in fury with himself for the sick thoughts and with the certainty he was no better than the asshole who did this to her.

The shiny green stuff she mentioned was called Blossom Flower. The new drug kept popping up and causing trouble. All the information they'd received so far pointed to the Wizard as the designer. They'd hoped this information would lead them to the psycho's lab. For the past year, Ryker had planned to stop the nut job from killing more women in his area by either running him out of business or destroying his resources in producing the drug, but the game plan had changed when he stripped Marie and hurt her. The asshole's death certificate only needed a signature and Ryker was the one who would provide the ink.

Within moments, he strode across the yard and into the van. He nodded at the driver to go. If he had anything to do with it, she'd never leave Sector again. The farther away she was from psychos, the better.

She shifted in his arms and his cock hardened. Jesus H. Christ! Why couldn't he just hold her without acting like a sex fiend? He looked at the dark circles beneath her eyes and the paleness of her cheeks. What else had the asshole done to her? He squeezed his eyes shut for a couple seconds, trying to escape the thought of her being raped. *Please, no human deserves being treated like that*. He understood more so than most men the horror in being held down and forced to endure. Mental scars often didn't heal like physical ones. There were only a few exceptions to that reasoning.

He looked at the matted skin along his right arm. The

burns had healed years ago but he still remembered the piercing pain. Only a small part of a past he struggled with every day.

His cell phone vibrated. Being careful not to squeeze Marie, he leaned to one side and pulled it from his jeans pocket.

"Yeah."

"The bastard got out through a cellar door. He jumped on a motorcycle and headed north and in less than five minutes we lost him in the mountains," Jack relayed.

So much for capturing the asshole who harmed his woman.

He looked up and blinked. No. Not *his* woman. Never his.

"Tell them to keep looking." Then he pressed a button, cutting short the conversation.

Marie wiggled in his arms. He shuddered from the electrifying feeling of her buttocks rubbing against his groin. After a slight adjustment, he regained control.

"Honey." He needed her to look into his face. "Marie, quit moving around. We'll be at Sector in less than thirty minutes." He wanted her checked over quickly.

Once he stepped into the helicopter, still holding her, he sank into the soft leather seat. The hum of the luxury craft escalated as they took off. His jacket had slipped down a little and one perfectly formed breast with a coral-pink areola peeked at him. With trembling fingers he adjusted the jacket and resisted touching the hard tip. He blinked hard to wipe the sight away and glared at the man talking to him.

"Sir? You can cover her better with this." A crew member

nodded to the dark-blue blanket he held out with a trembling hand.

Ryker rubbed the rough material between his thumb and forefinger. The wool would chafe her tender skin. But she needed the warmth and maybe it would help him regain a little sanity.

Still shaking inside from the thought of someone else mistreating her and the extreme danger she'd been in, he compromised by leaving the jacket on her and wrapping the blanket over it.

He stared out the window watching the landscape change from steel and concrete to trees and mountains. He forced himself to look anywhere but at Marie during the flight. They were in the air for no more than five minutes when her body became limp. She'd dozed off.

As soon as they landed and the door banged open, an EMT reached in for her.

"No. Tell Doc to come to the mansion," Ryker said, snarling his impatience. He sounded unreasonable. Yet he didn't care.

By the time he reached his bedroom, her wiggling and moaning in his arms almost shattered his control. His chest ached with worry. She appeared to be reliving the nightmare of the last few hours as her eyes darted behind closed lids. He kneeled on the bed and placed her in the center.

With eyes wide open, she batted and pushed at the heavy material. "Let me out of this cocoon." She squealed and shoved again, fighting the blanket. "I feel like a thousand ants are marching all over me."

"Wait." Ryker pulled the sheet back. He planned to cover

the temptation she presented, protecting some of her modesty. The least he could do was act like a gentleman.

She burst free from the constraints of the blanket and jacket, slapping away the sheet. Long hair flying around her head, the white of her eyes bright and almost glowing in her fear, she kicked and screamed, "Get them off me!"

"Marie, calm down. I'm trying to help you."

He tossed the sheet back over her, but she immediately rose to her knees and clasped his arms, obviously uncaring that she provided a clear view of every glorious inch of her again, especially the exquisite shaven apex of her thighs. As soon as her trembling fingers touched his skin, she changed from crazed maniac to purring kitten.

Her talented hands massaged his biceps. "Oh, Ryker, thank you for getting me out of there." Her gaze followed the fiery path her hands made from his elbows to the skin beneath his T-shirt's short sleeves. "You feel so good. Hard and hot." She rubbed her chest against his. "I feel funny. Different. Wonderful. Awww, I love your broad shoulders and the way you're so big, so manly." She fingered his nipple through the thin cotton. "So sad. The scars are so sad, but they make you look dangerous. Everything including the patch makes you"—she inhaled deeply, causing her breasts to lift, drawing his attention—"so mysterious, so delicious." The last said almost in a whisper.

All the air in the room disappeared, shutting down his reflexes and allowing her the advantage to shove one hand under his shirt and the other beneath his waistband. His rock-hard erection greeted her warm hand with a jump.

He grabbed her wrists and folded her arms across her

upper chest, a much safer spot to allow him to reorganize his thoughts. "Listen to me. Whatever that guy gave you, it's making you do this. I'll do my best to help, but you've got to help me. You need to fight it."

"No. I don't want to stop. For years, I've wanted this. For too long, I was afraid you would laugh at me. Being this close makes me remember things. The way we were when I was a kid. And then you changed. I was afraid of you. I was afraid of what you would do to me. I don't feel that way now." She used his tight hold to pull up until her tongue glided across his lips. "I mean I'm no longer scared of this with you."

His body, taut and aching from holding back, braced against sinking in her touch. He even smelled her arousal. Who would've thought it possible? The drug running through her bloodstream had to be the reason. Set off some type of powerful pheromones or whatever. Every available inch of her naked body strained to rub his, and her sensual attack made it difficult to resist until one word she said sunk into his bloodless brain.

"What do you mean, you were afraid of me?" he asked in a whisper. A fear he'd tamped down so many years ago reared its ugly head. Was he the monster their master said he was? She'd known him longer than anyone else in The Circle. Why had she been afraid of him?

"I'd belonged to Master and he called you his beautiful monster. No matter how he treated you, he trained you to take his place. You were so above . . . I . . . I want to show you how I feel." She rubbed her cheek in the crook of his neck.

Releasing her hands, his fingers gripped her shoulders

until he found the strength to push her away. She landed on her butt in the middle of the bed.

"Don't talk like that. You never asked to be treated the way Mast . . . Theo treated you." He needed to quit thinking of the perverted man who warped their lives as Master. Time to move on and realize Theo Palmer had been no more than that. An evil and insane man up to the day he died. His control over their lives continued from the grave only if they allowed it.

"Please. Only you can make it stop hurtin'." She licked her lips as her eyelids lowered and she watched him with a lust-filled gaze.

Her pleading jerked his attention back to the erotic fantasy crawling across the bed. Ryker wanted to take her, wanted to thrust the ache away by sinking into her over and over again. But he couldn't. The drug the freak had concocted forced her to act so unlike her normal shy self. Later, she would hate her actions, and him even more, when it wore off. They needed a sample of what she was given in an effort to produce an antidote. Every designer drug had an antidote. At least, he hoped there was one.

Unable to resist one small touch, he brushed the back of his hand against the silkiness of her breast. She smiled up at him, innocent eyes and sinful mouth.

He arched his neck as he threw his head back and groaned.

Her hand cupped his tight balls. She leaned her cheek against his stomach and slid her hand up his swollen shaft. Even with cloth between them, he almost lost control. He shoved her away again. His common sense screamed to leave the room until Doc could give her something to combat the effects of the drug.

Before he moved toward the door, she scrambled to her hands and knees with legs spread wide, looking at him with such hunger. He inhaled her special fragrance again and devoured the sight of her provocative position on the bed.

His chest rose and fell as he worked to regain his composure.

"Oh, it's goin' to be like that, is it?" she teased. The tip of her tongue peeked out as if she tasted his need in the air.

Leaning forward, she arched her back and lifted her buttocks in the air. The two round mounds held high tempted his hands to smack them until they turned a warm, deep pink. She had no idea what she invited by playing with him. Did she understand the danger she asked for?

More blood surged toward his groin so fast he jabbed his knees into the side of the mattress to remain upright. When she climbed up his torso and wrapped her arms around his neck and kissed him, sucking his tongue into her mouth, all thought of protecting her from everyone including himself dissipated.

Ah, hell.

Denying himself her touch was no longer a viable option, especially when she unzipped his pants and pulled him out. He tried to kick-start his brain again. His hands reached for her head, but when he felt her tongue slide from balls to tip, he gritted his teeth as he hissed with pleasure. He needed to stop her before it was too late.

Instead, his hands fisted in her hair and brought her

mouth to his. He growled a dark yearning against her lips. Her tongue darted around his. He answered by devouring her.

Damn, nothing tasted sweeter. Every moan she released set off warning bells in his subconscious, but the hunger he'd denied himself for so long could no longer be put off.

As soon as her back hit the mattress, he forced his hands to gently spread her legs apart. His gaze centered on what he'd craved for so long. Using his thumb, he traced the soft nether lips. She'd shaved recently, so smooth and tender, and he could easily see they were swollen and moist with desire.

She moaned, arched her back, and reached out her arms to him. "Please. I need you in me." Her eyes half closed and her blonde hair mussed, he found her irresistible. "Help me. Make it stop achin'. I need you."

For a few seconds, he stared, taking in every delectable inch of her luscious body. Then he released her.

"No!" Her small fists hit the mattress.

"Shh, you'll get what you need."

He wanted her as much as she needed him. How could he let her suffer? He knew what the drug did. How could he say no to her again? He'd see to what her body needed if it killed him. He understood how the drug drove those under its influence to do whatever necessary to reach their satisfaction.

His fingers clasped her thighs and spread her wider. With fierce, sharp movements, he parted his jeans and shoved them low on his hips, just enough to plunge into her. Tight warmth surrounded his cock. He groaned. Pure lava pleasure radiated from his groin. He pulled back and thrust again as he pushed her knees further apart, opening her so his groin touched hers. She arched her body screaming obscenities, wanting him to keep going.

Someone knocked on the door. He ignored it. No one dared enter without asking his permission. Moist heat squeezed until he became light-headed. Unable to slow, even if he wanted to, he grunted and pounded into her. Out of the corner of his eye, he saw the door swing open. Without turning or stopping his thrusts, he roared, "Get the fuck out!"

The door slammed shut.

The woman beneath him climaxed, massaging his cock in a mixture of pleasure-pain. Sweat trickled down his forehead. He wanted relief too. Damn it to hell! But he knew it was hopeless. What he needed, she wouldn't understand. He started to pull out. She reached for him.

"No! Again. Pleeease."

So he sank back into her warmth and pushed her knees toward her shoulders as he hammered into her. She screamed and climaxed again.

Hell! She felt so good. He had to let go. *Please let it happen this time.*

No matter how he positioned her, his need grew with no relief. He didn't care. Her satisfaction only mattered. Her hands pushed beneath his jeans and travelled over his hips, stroking scars he'd never thought were erogenous until now.

"More," she pleaded.

Panting like the animal he'd been called many times, he did what she begged him to do. She wanted more. He gave her more until his heart felt as if it would burst. Each time he tried to stop—sure she must be raw, if not sated—she'd cry and plead until he entered her again.

His own release denied him unless he showed her his dark side. His thumb pressed into the tight opening near where he thrust into her. Tempted, but a hidden fear stopped him from pressing further. In all likelihood, she would hate him for pushing her too far, too soon.

So he worked at bringing her relief. Not one inch of her body had been missed by his touch or mouth. She screamed his name with another wave of satisfaction but she gripped his thighs, telling him to keep pumping.

He lifted her buttocks and rotated his hips as he ground against her. Their grunts and moans meshed. How long he'd fucked her, he wasn't sure, but when she whimpered at the end of her latest orgasm, he stopped and pulled out. His sore cock remained hard as a power pole. His scarred knee ached like a son of bitch. Kneeling on the bed, he helped her roll to the side. Tears streamed down her face as she whimpered in exhaustion. Wherever his hands stroked in an effort to relax and comfort, her muscles shivered in waves beneath his fingers. Finally, her body relaxed and her eyes fluttered closed as he smoothed her sweat-soaked hair from her forehead.

He wanted her again. But it was useless. She'd had enough.

Truth be told, he felt separated from the act. It had always been that way. As if someone not human inhabited his body as he performed. He hated the feeling. Feeling like a freak, a monster.

Weary to the bone, he moved behind her, spooning her

limp body. His arm wrapped around her waist as he inhaled the tangy smell of sex clinging to her skin. She sniffled and wiggled her butt against his hard groin. She whimpered again. He bit the side of his mouth to stop from her echoing the sound.

"Shh, everything will be okay. No one will hurt you again." Even him.

Tomorrow, he'd feel ashamed for taking advantage of her while she was under the influence of the drug. For now, he would savor the feel of her in his arms until she slept.

CHAPTER THREE

Marie woke to the pain of another needle sinking into her body. Her brain, fuzzy with sleep, slowly registered what was happening, tempering her fear. This time, it was her arm and The Circle's top doctor administering the dose. She looked at the small hospital-styled room located in the medical area of Sector.

"Hey, Doc, whatcha giving me?"

She inhaled deeply. An unexpected ache shot down her ribcage to her groin, cutting off the welcomed fresh air with her cry. Pictures flickered through her memory until one in particular burst to the forefront. Ryker moving above her, fully dressed except for his cock thrusting into her. His hard, masculine face divided by the ever-present black eye patch. Was it a dream? It wouldn't be the first time. Yet this time something was off.

"You'll be okay. It's a sedative to help you rest and heal," said Dr. Cooper.

"How are you so sure it won't have a bad reaction to the drug that creep gave me?" She yawned and blinked, trying to focus on the people in the room. One male nurse stood near the door while another held a box of Band-Aids for Doc to use. The man she wanted to see was nowhere in sight. The only man she wanted to hold her like he had in the helicopter.

"From the blood test we ran, we know this won't be a problem." Doc shook his head and handed the used hypodermic syringe to the nurse and in an efficient, well-practiced movement, wiped the area with gauze and stuck a small, round adhesive bandage over it.

"Will this get the drug out of my system?" She licked her chapped lips.

"No. We have to run a few more tests. For now you need to relax and drink as many fluids as you can. Your body needs time to recover." The last few words sounded strained.

Marie looked up and caught the doctor's cheeks turning red. What in the world could embarrass a doctor?

She struggled to scoot to the head of the hospital bed. A raw soreness throbbed between her thighs. Then she remembered everything. It had been no dream. Her head jerked up, and zeroed in on Ryker as he walked into the room. Broad shoulders, the lean build of a fighter. Oh, my God! She'd finally got him in bed *and* she'd begged him to do her. In fact, she'd pleaded with him more than once. With a fistful of sheet, she ducked underneath the linen and tugged it over her head. She wished she could disappear.

Maybe she was being silly but for goodness' sake, Ryker had seen her at her worst. *Oh, no! I actually begged him!*

Doc released a nervous chuckle. "Marie, you have nothing to be ashamed of. The drug caused you to act unlike yourself. Give it time and it'll surely run its course, if it hasn't already." He cleared his throat. She guessed he spotted Ryker behind him when he said, "Research has several vials of her blood. We should have more details soon. Then we'll know how much and what strength of the drug they gave her. In the meanwhile, listen to me. Do. Not. Move. Her."

Oh, crap. The doctor knew what she and Ryker had been doing. Had Ryker told him? Who pulled her from his bed and brought her to the clinic? She'd never come out from under the sheet ever again.

"Doc, let me have a moment alone with Marie."

She squeezed her thighs. How could she become so moist by hearing Ryker's deep, raspy voice? A sound produced by ruined vocal chords. She'd cared for and wanted him for years but never felt instantaneous horniness by his voice alone. The drug. Her nails burrowed into the mattress. It still lingered in her system. That had to be the reason.

"Marie, come out, please."

Were her ears playing tricks on her? Ryker actually said please. Had she ever heard him say that word to anyone? Maybe she needed to check and see if he was really here.

She stuck her head out of the covers. He looked the same. Stone-faced. Not giving her any idea of what he was thinking. His gaze cold as he watched her every move. Funny, the patch was such a part of him she often had to remind herself it was there along with the scars. Like when someone described a friend and forgot to mention they wore glasses.

Built solid and over six feet with dark hair and an even darker countenance, he easily frightened everyone around him. The eye patch and scars pushed the intimidation factor a little more. But she knew several of his secrets as he knew most of hers. Maybe because of their past together, she was a bit more comfortable around him than the others who work in the organization. Or most likely it was because she'd loved him for so long.

How could anyone not love a man like Ryker? When she was sold to Master at the age of twelve by her parents for drug money, they'd lied and claimed she was nine. She'd been such a lost little girl. Ryker had taken pity on her by becoming her only friend and warning her to keep quiet about her true age. Now at twenty-one, she wanted to be treated as an adult, but he still wanted to protect her.

"Are you all right? How do you feel?" he asked. His gaze dipped to her hips and quickly returned to her eyes.

Heat spread across her face, neck, and chest, one of the drawbacks of being a natural blonde with fair skin. She understood his message loud and clear. He worried about what harm their sexual marathon had done.

"I'm fine. Sore, but I'll be right as rain as soon as Doc lets me go home." She grinned. The corners of her mouth felt stiff.

Home was a one-bedroom apartment in The Circle's compound. Ryker had tried to set her up in the mansion with him when they first moved, but she'd refused. Seeing him a couple days from a distance or more during the week was bad enough. Living with him and not being able to touch would've been torture.

"What do you think you were doing, working retrieval?" he asked in a harsh voice.

She wanted to feel hurt that he felt a need to scold her like a child, but for some insane reason she liked knowing he worried. Even his anger was better than the usual emotionless attitude she got from him with the occasional polite interest and impatience mixed in. She lifted her gaze. Then again, after what they did last night, for him to treat her in the same way should be difficult, if not impossible.

"Marie, are you okay?" His voice filled with concern. Now that was more of what she wanted.

The dark smudge beneath his eye and the ridges at the corners of his mouth visibly told her that he was tired and stressed out. The scars on the side of his face appeared whiter than usual, as if stretched tight.

More memories came flying back to slap her in the face. One stood out that made her face hot. He hadn't climaxed one time. He hadn't worn a condom and she remembered how hard and big he'd been and how his stamina hadn't lagged throughout the night. How did he do it?

Oh, no. No! Her face felt as if on fire. Not only had she pleaded with him to have sex with her, she'd thrown herself at him, hung onto him, and even coerced him into taking her. No matter what she'd done, he hadn't been turned on enough to find release with her. Sure, any man could get hard at the sight of a halfway decent-looking naked woman, but having an orgasm when someone continued to beg—

Just thinking about it was torture. She covered her head with the sheet again. If only he would disappear and never look at or speak to her again.

"Go away." Shoot her and put her out of her misery.

"Listen. We have to talk about this." He sounded closer.

Why couldn't he understand? "Please go away. I'll talk to you later. I swear." As in, when she was old and gray and blind. Facing him was the last thing she wanted to do.

"I placed you in the IS department to protect you." Ryker's voice lowered. "What did the asshole do to you?"

"Bryan?" she asked.

"Not that asshole! The Wizard. The asshole who drugged you."

Of course. Her brain was still a little fuzzy. All she could think about was her and Ryker's surreal love . . . sex session? The way they'd behaved had nothing to do with love.

"No, he didn't," she answered.

"What the hell do you mean, he didn't?"

His angry tone had her explaining without catching her breath. "I mean, the guy wasn't the Wizard."

"Did he say he wasn't?"

She peeked out from under the covers. "He said the Wizard was a god and a genius. He wasn't talking about himself in the third person. I could tell he was talking about someone else." This was good. He would concentrate on the creep instead of the time they spent playing horizontal tongue badminton. "It was more like he enjoyed the Wizard's expertise in concocting the drug."

"Tell me everything that happened," he ordered. He wrinkled his forehead as he concentrated on what she had to say.

Across the room, Ryker folded his arms, leaning a shoulder against the wall, and listened to her story. When she hesitated and then told him of how the man cut off her clothes, fury gripped his chest. He pushed away and started to pace. Thanks to whatever providence was looking over her, he'd arrived before she'd been raped.

"What have you learned from this?" he asked.

He needed her to understand how dangerous field work could be for someone like her. Marie was a gentle soul and so helpless. Hell, at five-one, the top of her head didn't reach his shoulder.

"That Jack is right and I need to practice taekwondo." She bit her bottom lip.

The same lip he'd tasted last night. He turned his back to her. Hands on hips, he dropped his head and inhaled. A few seconds passed as he waited for his cock to soften and he regained his common sense. Time to get in control of his libido and not embarrass himself. "It's good to know a martial art, but you're not going out into the field again."

"Yes, I am," she said in a small but firm voice.

He twirled around. "No. You. Are. Not." What was wrong with her? Didn't she understand he wanted to keep her safe?

"Have you forgotten your promise to me?" She sat up and crossed her arms, one eyebrow raised.

The thin cotton hospital gown hid little. The pink circles beneath the cloth drew his gaze as her nipples jutted out, begging for him to tweak them. Damn! He shifted his hips, hoping to adjust the sudden tightness of his pants. Those moss-green eyes caught the movement. Double damn.

"Refresh my memory." The way her gaze stayed glued to his groin, he could barely remember his name.

"That I would never answer to another master again. Or have you decided to be mine?"

"Hell, no!" He strode to the bed and stood over her, his glare intended to intimidate. How could she accuse him of that? They'd spent too many years under that hammer. Master—hell! How many times did he have to remind himself he no longer had a master? *Theodore Palmer* was dead, and good riddance.

"Then quit telling me what I can and cannot do!" She kneeled in the bed and glared back, nearly nose to nose.

"Children, children." Jack strode into the room. "I could hear you two down the hallway."

"Jack, tell this moron I hate working in the Crypt and want to do field work." She poked Ryker in the chest. The Crypt was another name for the Information Systems Department located beneath Sector.

Ryker looked down as her finger jabbed him several more times. Where was the timid beauty who had a hard time meeting his gaze? He kind of liked her like this. Damn! He was so hard he ached. This was driving him insane as everything she said and did cause him to want her more. Was the drug contagious? Maybe he'd already lost his mind.

"You better be happy I don't tie you up in bubble wrap." Just the thought of tying her down brought a groan he covered with a cough.

"Ryker." Jack nodded toward the door.

Perfect timing. He needed to get away from her, even if for a few minutes. It was as if his body expected to sink into her whenever she was near. Once tasted, always desired. Besides, the things they did last night were nothing compared to what he really wanted to do to her.

"Behave," he warned her, shaking his finger. Before she could retort, he stepped out of the room with Jack. "What's going on?"

"They found another dead body. That's six so far. I have a feeling if we hadn't gotten Marie out, she'd have been number seven." Jack shook his head.

"What do the authorities know so far?" He walked away from the room. Last thing he needed was for her to overhear the real danger she'd been in.

"They're aware of four women. Of those, five have Club Rachael's stamp on their hand. The latest one has The Iron Rocket stamp. But the guys in the lab believe there may be another stamp beneath it."

"What about drugs?" Ryker asked. He turned off Sector's hallway and hit the release on the double doors. The strong wind pushed at him. He hesitated before walking out onto the long balcony running along a mountain cliff. Blue skies with a few wisps of white clouds spotted the sky. He lifted his chin and took a deep breath of the fresh air. The sensation of floating had him clasping the back rail against the stone wall. He hated heights but loved the view. It had taken him three months to work up the nerve to stand out there. Phobias were weaknesses, and he worked hard at ignoring or facing them. He treated his fear of heights as a small weakness easily dealt with over time. Larger weaknesses he couldn't fix were filed away and ignored. Thus another reason he'd placed Marie in the Crypt.

Below the balcony, a few miles away, movement of two trucks threading in and out of the trees caught his attention. They travelled the long, snaky road leading to the mansion and the less visible entrance into the underground facility. The vehicles looked no different than the maintenance or delivery trucks that visited a thriving estate. One of the benefits of living in the center of ten square miles of mountainous land was that Sector, The Circle's headquarters, could hide in plain sight.

So far, no one could trespass without being apprehended and then promptly disappearing.

Jack cleared his throat. Ryker returned his attention to what he expected would not be good news.

"Besides a couple with traces of cocaine, all of the girls had Blossom Flower in their system."

The same drug that freak shot into Marie. It made women more compliant in having sex. From what they'd learned through underground talk, the Wizard's plan was to get them on the drug, making them easier to handle. Then later he'd sell the women overseas to the highest bidder.

"Someone is screwing up royally. Marie said the man who drugged her wasn't the Wizard." He told Jack what Marie had said.

"They should call the bastard a ghost. We haven't tracked him down yet." Jack leaned against the railing along the edge and looked over the valley. "What are you going to do about Marie?"

Ryker swallowed. How could Jack lean over the rail like that without getting vertigo? "Send her back to IS when she's better."

"She's not going to like that. I suggest letting her help. She has a stake in this now. Being drugged and nearly raped, she'll want to see the guy put away." Jack turned and rested a thigh on the rail.

Ryker almost squirmed but caught himself. Did she feel that way about him? Did she think he raped her? Maybe he needed to talk with her, make sure she understood why he did what he did.

She'd put up with enough from Theo. Not only a pedophile and a sadist, the man's obsession with King Arthur had shifted into eliminating people who he believed to be a danger to his growing power. She'd seen the elite of The Circle's operatives flee Theo's madness and follow their new leader. Yeah. His brother, Collin, was a savvy strategist and under his guidance made the OS—Onyx Scepter—a powerful entity.

Yet while Collin was growing up, believing himself to be the only surviving member of his family, Ryker endured a hellish existence as he and Marie struggled to outlive Theo's unpredictable behavior. They clung to each other in comfort and encouragement. Yes. He understood her need to feel safe. Did she look at him and see another master? A monster cut from the same cloth due to Theo's mistreatment? The thought was enough to make him want to throw up.

All he knew was that he planned to shelter her from any more harm. Images of flushed soft skin and heated thighs caused his breath to catch. Who was he trying to convince that was the only reason?

He breathed deeply as his gaze turned outward.

And why the fuck was Jack leaning over the rail so far?

"That's just tough. I can't do what's needed if I'm worrying about her." He didn't like the look Jack gave him. His second-in-command saw too much. "We've got too much to do without showing her the ropes." Maybe the son of a bitch would fall off.

"That's a cop-out if I've ever heard one." Jack crossed his arms.

That did it. He wasn't about to stand there and listen to that shit or watch him fall. Ryker slapped open the doors and headed back to her room.

"What are you going to tell her?" Jack asked, following close on his heels.

Ryker continued walking.

"She deserves a chance to prove herself." Jack wouldn't let it go, like a freaking bulldog. "Let me or someone else train her, work with her. I don't get you and her, but I've stayed out of it until now. You placed her in the safest area in The Circle, and she still almost got herself killed. Do the right thing and teach her what she wants. That's the best way to keep her safe. Or do you really care about her?"

Before he realized what he'd done, Ryker slammed Jack to the wall, his arm across the man's throat. Nose to nose, he gritted his teeth. "Don't ever question me about her safety. I'll do what I believe is best for her. As you've been doing before, stay out of it." He shoved him to the side and walked away.

One of these days he was going to beat that smirk off Jack's face.

CHAPTER FOUR

"You know you're a male chauvinist, Doc." Marie wrapped the sheet tighter around her body. She'd convinced Jack to bring her oversized T-shirt with the neon-pink pajama pants, but after they x-rayed her, probed and poked at her, she still fought the chill bumps spreading across her arms and legs.

"Sorry. It's my generation's curse." Dr. Cooper shrugged as his small grin faded. "But the boss said he wanted to be here when I told you about my findings." He cleared his throat and pretended to read the chart in his hand.

"I really don't understand what business it is of his. This is my health." Why couldn't anyone understand? She needed to distance herself from Ryker. He was like an addiction to chocolate. She'd tasted him—well, kind of—and she wanted more. He was constantly in her thoughts. How could she look at him again, knowing he couldn't bring himself to climax while in her, no matter how much she begged? Yeah, Master had really done a number on them. She didn't want to be defined by her past but it continued to step out of the closet and slap her around.

"What did you find out?" Arms crossed, muscles bulging, Ryker stood near the door. It was hard to believe she'd been with him only hours earlier. The tingling in her body teased her. She wanted his hands on her again, the need building to a crescendo that was killing her.

Doc started on a long dialogue including long chemical names that had more consonants than a Russian phone book with several Latin dictionaries thrown in. She had no idea what they referred to or meant and could only hope to grasp the basics.

Ryker cleared his throat. "Doc, you're losing us. Can you keep it in layman's language?"

"Ah, sure." He inhaled and nodded as if he had decided on the best way to simplify a complicated drug. "As you know, the substance called Blossom Flower is a designer drug used to rev up the sex drive. In a female, it makes her extremely excitable and submissive to a sex partner. While a male becomes more aggressive to the point his baser instincts take over, and he loses control of his humanity." The doctor's face was a beet red as he focused his conversation on Ryker.

"We know that much. How long does it last? We heard it can stay in the blood stream for days." Ryker motioned to hurry up.

Jack walked into the room and leaned against the wall near the doctor.

"Actually, make that months."

"No!" Marie shook her head. "No way. It'll kill me."

"It's not fatal. But you may at times wish it was." Dr. Cooper's gloomy frown didn't comfort her.

"What do you mean?" Ryker asked.

"We don't know yet what triggers the flashbacks, as they're called. But overstimulation could cause it to flare up and, uh . . ." He cleared his throat again.

"Spit it out, Doc. We're all adults here." Jack needed to stay out of it. Though she knew he wanted to be there for her as a good friend, his presence only added to the tension in the room. Besides, at this point, nothing would comfort her as she waited for the rest of the diagnosis.

"The drug in her system will be difficult to control and she'll—" He paused and looked at the floor as if he searched for something. "She'll need to find relief until I can find something to tone down her reaction or it works its way out of her system. Thankfully the drug was slightly different than what was given to the other girls." As soon as the last word left the doctor's mouth, both Ryker and Jack made a move toward her. She didn't like their expressions. They looked upset, as if she'd been told she had terminal cancer. But she wanted answers before she fell apart.

One hand raised to hold them back, she asked, "Let me get this straight. The drug will cause me to have a driving need for sex at any time and any place. You've got to be kidding."

"No, I'm not." Doc's face flushed a bright pink. "You'll find it very uncomfortable to deny yourself relief. It can be through intercourse or some other way to relieve the pressure, you could say. That is, as long as you're releasing natural endorphins, helping your body to calm down until the drug works its way out of your system." His face was almost purple by the time he finished. Marie was beginning to worry about his health.

"What about a tranquilizer or something to keep her relaxed?" Ryker asked.

"We can administer a little more, but after the second dosage, the drug in her system morphs and stops it from working. The endorphins cannot be man-made or supplied by another—it must be the same body's. That's what we've learned so far. Whoever concocted this possesses a twisted, malicious intellect." Doc wiped his forehead with the corner of his white lab coat.

"Is this some kind of sick joke?" She looked at Ryker. He'd never been a prankster. From the alarm tightening his face, she doubted he planned to start now. She covered her mouth as tears threatened to spill over.

"Sorry. I wish it was." Doc cleared his throat. "That's the thing about the new synthetic drug. It's so sophisticated that it can manipulate a specific area of the body. In turn, it comes at a cost. The side effects can be numerous. With something this complicated and new, it will take us a lengthy time to solve and create an antidote without a sample of the drug itself."

"He pumped enough in me, you should be able to get some out." Hopeful wishing brought her voice to a high pitch on the last word. She blinked several times to hold back the tears.

"Sorry, Marie. We're having problems separating it from the bloodstream. We're unable to do a full scale analysis of the compounds." Doc looked over at Ryker.

Then she remembered something else the doctor had said. "What other girls?"

Ryker muttered, "Shit."

"What?" she asked. When Ryker refused to look her way,

she turned to Jack. "This is stupid. I'm the one affected. I need to know everything."

A silent communication passed between Ryker and Jack. Then Ryker nodded, ending with a jerk of his head toward the door.

"Come on, Doc. These two have a lot to talk about." Jack slapped the older man's back as he steered him out of the room.

She folded her arms. With raised eyebrows, she waited for his explanation.

"Are you okay?" Ryker brushed her cheek.

"You ask that a lot." Her gaze centered on his lips. The burn scars didn't reach that far. They appeared to be soft and it was the type of mouth designed for kissing. She remembered their one and only kiss. She wanted another one.

With a crooked finger beneath her chin, he lifted her gaze to his.

His tenderness scared the crap out of her. He'd been her knight in shining armor at one time. She'd been ignored by him for so long that she doubted she could handle his abandonment again when the drug left her system. Unable to resist for now, she grabbed his hand and held it against her cheek, closing her eyes, soaking in his warmth and touch.

"Marie?" The husky tone of his voice opened her eyes. She examined the face she loved so much and for so long. The scars and the patch blurred, and she remembered the sweet, humble young man. She remembered the horrible things the Master did to him in front of her, things they had to do to survive. "Stop it. Stop thinking about it," he said in his deep, gruff voice. He held her chin between his thumb and forefinger. "We'll figure out a way to survive this too."

He was right. Master was dead and could no longer punishment her. The scars from his knife and whip would slowly fade. Though Ryker had changed—becoming aloof and cold, after his death—he came to her rescue yesterday. So why was he being so attentive to her? Was it only for the sex? Only to help her in such an awkward and unusual situation?

She'd worked so hard to distance herself from him and their past as she guessed he'd wanted to do the same, she'd forgotten how he read her so well.

"I'm fine. Tell me about the other girls. How many were there? And what do they have to do with you and The Circle? I've never known you to get involved in the locals' concerns." When he got that mulish look, she added, "It's important for me to know." Without thinking it through, she kissed the center of his palm and released it.

He hissed as if she'd burned him.

She probably should be insulted by his reaction, but she understood. Displays of affection between them had been forbidden for so long. With the drug running through her system and the resulting outcome, she decided she had nothing more to lose at this point.

He nodded. "Yeah. You're right." He pulled a chair close to her bed and sat with his elbows on his knees as he leaned forward. "It started about a year and half ago. The first girl's body was found by some boaters near the Chickamauga Dam. About every other month another body has turned up somewhere in or near Chattanooga. Each one has had the drug in their system. Then a few months after finding the second body, two of my male operatives were arrested for nearly raping a woman. They had the drug in their system, and a week later another body was found. The newest victim had been drinking with the woman they'd attacked. Someone had placed the drug in their drinks."

"So all four, out drinking together, had been fed the same drug? Only one of the women lived a little longer? Where was she during that time? And what did they hope to accomplish by that? Was the drug killing them?" she asked. Her chest felt as if it was turning to stone. Had they hidden something from her?

Though he spoke calmly and rationally, frustration leaked between each word. "We believe the Wizard was experimenting first on the women and then to see how the men would react. Maybe find another way to use the drug. The women had twice the amount of Blossom Flower that you did per the lab report Doc received. We think the Wizard became careless, not warning his people that too much would kill them. While the men were large and the amounts affected them differently, they continued to have problems controlling their basic urges for several weeks." Sadness pulled at his face. She knew he never believed in harming someone weaker. He'd taken punishment from their master without complaint to protect her.

"Did they get better?"

From what the doctor had said, the drug was still in her system, and who knew when another attack—flashback, as he called it—would happen. All operatives working for The Circle should be in total control of their basic urges. She hated to think she would go months being aroused and seeking help with little hope of assuaging the cravings. Would she attack the nearest male when it happened? Like the men had the woman?

The way Ryker avoided her eyes, she knew. They didn't have an opportunity to get better. The Circle couldn't take a chance of their operatives being placed in prison and leaking information about a large, secretive mercenary organization inside a mountain in Tennessee. Even if the government possessed some knowledge of The Circle, they didn't know the whole extent. So the operatives had been eliminated. All loose ends tied up.

"What are you going to do about me?"

His eyebrows lifted. Was he so surprised by her question? Maybe that was a good thing. Maybe the thought of eliminating her never crossed his mind.

"As soon as Doc gives the signal, you're going back to IS."

"No. I'm an adult now. Whatever you believe, understand this. I'm not going back. There has to be more I can do, and entering data into the computer system isn't it. I want to help find the person responsible for making and distributing this drug. For killing those women. Those men didn't deserve what they got either. You got rid of one mad man and I want to help rid the world of another one." She wanted him to understand how important this was to her. And how could he expect her to pretend what happened to her and between them never . . . well, happened?

"Let me handle this." He scowled. Before, whenever she'd seen that look, she'd backed down. Not this time.

Almost nose to nose, she glared at him. "You can tell me to work in the IS department all you want, but I'm determined to find the little SOB who did this. I'll do it too. So if you want me to stay safe, you'll help me."

She may be crazy but she wasn't stupid. Her skills didn't include tracking down and apprehending criminals. His did. He was better than good. Few people in the world outmatched Arthur Ryker in the skills needed for his job. When a person had been trained since childhood on ways to kill and maim . . . a chill skittered down her back. He never took orders from anyone but Master and even then he'd taken those grudgingly.

His shoulders slumped and he shook his head. "The first time you don't follow my directions, you'll find yourself chained to a desk in the basement. Do you understand me?" He spoke between gritted teeth. A sure sign she'd pushed him as far as she could.

"Hey, you're the expert. I won't have a problem doing as you say, but I have some conditions." She straightened her shoulders. Her pride held her gaze to his. No way would she allow another person to bully her, including Ryker.

"Conditions?" He sat back in his chair and his gaze narrowed.

Too late, she remembered how their master would lay conditions on any pleasure received, nothing good given without a price being paid.

"Ryker, I didn't mean—"

"Give them," he bit off.

She shuddered and rubbed a spot over her heart. She'd always been that way. When he hurt, she did too. Pulling herself together, she took a deep breath. "I want to be involved in the plans; no leaving me in the dark. I won't be treated like a child. I want to be part of the operation. And just as important, I want you to teach me how to protect myself."

Ryker's back straightened. "If you'd stay put, you'd be safe and wouldn't need to learn anything." He resisted the urge to shake her. By being involved, she'd be in more danger. He couldn't risk her life. His attention would be divided between protecting her and stopping a psycho, which could cause problems. And teaching her how to hurt and maim those who would attack her—his gaze travelled down her petite, sexy body—he didn't expect to be successful. Besides, she was too softhearted.

"You can't be everywhere. We're not joined at the hip." Her eyes glazed over as if she remembered another time. "I don't want to feel helpless."

He stared at her for moment. People talking in the hallway blended with the humming of the instruments taking her blood pressure and heart rate. She remained still, waiting for his decision. She was right. No one deserved to feel defenseless.

"Okay. I'll accept your conditions. But I have some of my own," he said, anger tinting the edges.

He watched her blink several times. She hadn't expected him to accept her conditions so readily, much less place some of his own. That was good. He wanted to avoid letting her know how hard he found saying no to her. Angry from feeling helpless with her new stubbornness, he hid most of his feelings while he practiced controlling the rest.

"I'll show you how to handle a handgun and fire it, but nothing bigger than that." When she opened her mouth, most likely to protest, he raised his hand. "Give me some time and I'll think about it some more. As you know, for the last few years, we've had trouble with several of our operations going sour. I don't want you to place yourself in a position to get hurt. In the meanwhile, be forewarned: while you're still under the influence of that drug, you're my responsibility."

He guessed his look of surprise matched hers. He'd said the last before he thought it through. But he knew there was a reason. No other man would help her find relief from the side effects, because he refused to allow it. The thought of anyone else touching her made him want to go ape-shit on their ass.

"A gun is a good start." She tightened the sheet around her. "But what are you . . . uh . . . Doc said I could take care of it myself. This is crazy. I can't believe this is happening to me."

He fisted his hands as he watched the tears stream down her face. He could handle explosions by terrorists and being tortured for information, but seeing her cry killed him.

"No. I'll do whatever it takes," he said. What had she expected him to say? That he would hire a surrogate lover for her?

"Okay," she whispered.

The room felt too bright and too hot and too . . . too much. Ryker stood and took a deeper breath. "Let's get one thing straight. This is only until the drug is out of your system."

She slowly nodded, keeping her gaze on him. "Ryker?" she asked with a hesitation in her voice.

He crossed his arms, gripping his biceps. Her forlorn look almost pushed him into wrapping his arms around her. He had to remain detached, emotionally and mentally. She wasn't a young kid anymore, clinging to him after Theo ranted about how bad she was and how he would punish her when he found her hiding place. The place Ryker had hid with her.

"Yeah?"

"Are you sure you're okay with this? I hate to ask you. Maybe we'll be lucky and Doc will come across something that'll stop it."

When he saw her lift her chin, he knew she'd be okay. He'd always admired how gutsy she could be even when the odds lined up against her.

"Shh!" Unable to resist, he placed a clumsy finger over her mouth. "You would do the same for me."

Her face flushed scarlet, and she pulled the sheet tighter around her. "You're right."

"I'll have your things moved into the mansion."

"No!"

"There's no use arguing. If you should have an attack in the middle of the night, it could take too long to reach you. That can be dangerous."

"What? A total of ten minutes?"

"Either you move into the mansion where you have your pick of three bedrooms near my own, or I move into your apartment. I don't plan to sleep on the floor."

Her eyes widened. Then she looked down. "All right. As long as I can pick my bedroom."

"On the same floor."

"Yes. The same floor."

He almost sighed. She gave in faster than he expected. Between providing her relief and discouraging her aspiration to go out in the field—ah hell! He needed to find a way to survive the next few weeks and not make her hate him.

CHAPTER FIVE

Marie flopped backward onto the feather-soft bed. It sat in a room the size of her apartment's living room and kitchen combined. A small sitting area near French doors led out to a balcony and looked over a small valley near the Great Smoky Mountains National Park. Fine evening mists hung over the treetops, and farther out the numerous ridges tinted blue gave her a peaceful feeling. She knew the electric fence surrounding the house was hidden, allowing the occupants to believe they lived in a normal—but extremely large—home.

"Enjoying the bed?" Jack strolled across the room. Making himself at home, he dropped into a chair and thumped his heels onto the coffee table as he folded his hands across a flat stomach.

Shaved head and bulging muscles defined in a skintight faded blue T-shirt, he was gorgeous and exotic with his many piercings and tattoos. Marie had met him several years ago when he'd been promoted from the ranks, and she quickly realized his ferocious looks misled most. Though nearly as talented in dealing death as Ryker, he could recite poetry and loved cats. In fact, he had a sweet little snow-white feline named Kinky that he babied in his private suite.

"Yeah. I've never felt one so soft." She rolled over and sat up, arranging the pillows behind her. "This place is amazing."

"Wish you had taken Ryker up on his offer to live here the first time?" He raised his brows.

"No."

"Why?"

"We talked about this before. I want to be my own person and Ryker always felt responsible for me. I need to take care of myself." She blushed. How could anyone believe she was capable of that? She had screwed up enough on her first assignment to be captured. Maybe she was one of those people who needed a keeper.

"You had bad intel. Don't take it as your failure." His warm blue eyes shuttered and he looked away, picking white fur off his pants. "If you don't want to be here, just give me the word and I'll take you to a safe place until the drug wears off."

Considering what she required to survive the next few weeks, she wasn't sure how to respond to his offer. She opened and closed her mouth. No matter how gorgeous he was, she never felt that way toward him. There hadn't been room in her mind or heart for anyone but Ryker.

"No. I better stay here," she croaked.

"If you change your mind, I'll take you out of here in a flash."

"Over my dead body." Ryker slammed the door closed and glowered at his second-in-command.

"I wanted her to have a choice," Jack said in a calm, even tone. He remained seated as he stared at his boss.

"She made her choice when she begged me to fuck her last night." Ryker's arrogant smile stretched the scars on his face. The image gave his countenance a menacing cast.

"Ryker!" She covered her hot cheeks.

"Damn it, man, be a little sensitive." Jack came to his feet, fists clenched at his sides.

"You can sniff around all you want, but she's mine and I don't share." Ryker stalked across the room to stand between them. "Bryan said he needed to talk to you."

She'd never seen Ryker act this way before. He'd controlled his temper when others would lose their heads. To think of it, she'd heard he'd hit Bryan yesterday. What was going on with him?

He stepped toward Jack when the other man didn't move.

"Ryker," she said, frustrated with his chest-thumping. "Listen to me." She came to her feet while keeping her distance from the two men.

"What?" he snapped without taking his attention off Jack.

"He was only being polite. You could take lessons from him." She crossed her arms and dared him to say anything hateful again to his second-in-command.

Ryker glanced her way for a second and then said to Jack, "Go. She'll tell you her decision later."

Even Marie could tell Ryker believed there was no decision to be made, that he would see to her needs, and Jack could jump in a lake.

Jack hesitated but thankfully left without another word.

"Why do you treat him that way?" she asked. By the scowl on his face, he didn't like her question.

"Why? How can I trust that son of a bitch? He's one of Mas— Theo's creations."

Ryker stood with his feet braced apart, like a captain on his ship, unmoving as he waited for her to answer. Theo had taught him that stillness often brought the best solution to a problem.

Every time he talked with Jack he wanted to punch him out. He'd been promoted to second-in-command by their master a month before Ryker had taken over The Circle.

Since the man did his job well and followed orders without question—more often than not—Ryker ignored his connection to the former regime. No need to change something that worked. But he didn't trust him. For that matter he didn't trust anyone. Noticing the soft green eyes watching him with concern, he amended, he trusted only one person.

She shook her head. "We're all Master's creations. How can you blame him for that?"

Ignoring her question—no need to upset her with his answer—he looked her over. "How are you feeling?"

The blush spreading across her face showed she understood what he really asked. As she returned the once-over, her eyes flared with heated interest. Just knowing he would be touching her again hardened his whole body. Lust and fear roiled together.

"I'm tolerable." Her voice shook. "And quit askin' me."

He liked how her southern accent thickened whenever she

was turned on. Last night, she'd dropped her Gs on several of her requests and stretched several one-syllable words. Marie had a softness to her that hid the strong-willed woman she'd become. Even with the type of experiences she'd endured, she still radiated innocence.

"Tolerable, huh?" He moved closer.

Marie gasped as the back of her knees hit the bed. "Yeah." Oh, goodness, did he always smell so good?

"Are you hungry?" he asked in a rumbling voice. With only a good, deep breath away from touching her, his body heat warmed her.

She looked up as he towered over her, wrapping her in his spell. His tongue brushed his bottom lip. Had he even realized he'd done that?

"Yeah." She could only manage one-word answers. The emotions the drug produced were so much like what she normally felt, yet different. For some reason, she knew at this moment she experienced something purer and not driven by an artificial stimulate.

"Good. I asked the cook to send dinner to your room. I figured you'd enjoy something less formal for your first night here. We can talk without interruption." Neither his voice nor face betrayed what he was thinking.

Being alone with him could be good or bad. It depended on how her body reacted and how he responded. What was she thinking about? She was scared spit-less. Attacking a man, begging him for sex, was something she never imagined doing, even with the man she'd loved for most of her life.

She needed to keep her mind on food and not think of how his warm skin felt beneath her fingertips. Or how his hands gripped her thighs, dotting her with bruises he didn't mean to leave.

Stop, stop, stop!

A knock on the door broke their silent perusal of each other. Ryker let in the cook and the housekeeper. They laid out the dinner with silverware and crystal. A bottle of wine on ice was uncovered with a flourish and a brace of candles lit. As the couple left, one reached over and turned off the lights. The flames from the candles brought an immediate intimacy to the room. Marie wasn't sure what to make of the romantic dinner.

"Sit. Eat." He waited until she was seated and he began slicing his steak. "I told them to cook yours well done; I know how you hate to see it pink inside."

Following his lead, she cut a piece of the steak and bit into it. She closed her eyes for a few seconds as she chewed. The juicy, smoky flavor burst across her tongue. When she opened her eyes, Ryker looked down and expertly sliced a sliver and brought it to his lips without lifting his head. He'd been watching her eat.

Her gaze followed his hands as he worked the knife. Her breath shortened. She hungered for his touch more than food.

Instantly, she shut the thought down.

When he poured her some wine, she asked, "Do you have a soda? I'm not much for wine or any alcohol." With the drug in her system, she imagined it best not to take a chance.

"Sure." He called downstairs. Within minutes, a tall glass filled with ice and a bottle of cola sat next to her plate.

By the time they finished, the candles had burned to half their length. The dessert of strawberries and cream was a perfect final touch. Their conversation remained light throughout the meal. He'd touched on popular books and current events. Nothing too in-depth or controversial like a perfect gentleman on a date. Marie leaned back in her chair and looked at him. Was that his intention? Offer her a chance to experience what they had skipped over? She'd never imagined being with him in this way. Nor, for that matter, had she imagined yesterday ever happening.

She loved being here, having him sitting across from her. Another new memory for her to tuck away. No way would this last. Too many bad memories shared.

Yet, the way he watched her allowed her to return the favor. His white dress shirt and navy blue slacks brought out his dark good looks. Perfect with the eye patch and scars across his cheek and down his neck. His hair, a little longer than normal, hid and revealed the scars as he moved. He looked like a swashbuckler. He looked relaxed, maybe a little contented.

"You've got a little cream near your mouth." He grinned.

She wiped around her lips.

"You missed it. Let me." He came around the table and leaned down. She lifted her chin and waited, closing her eyes. She shivered. Instead of cloth, she felt his lips pressed the corner of her mouth and his tongue traced her bottom lip. "There. All better."

"Ryker?" She wasn't sure how she did it, but she placed her hand on his chest and pushed. "What are you up to?"

Guilt flitted across his face. He stepped back and looked out the French doors.

"Ryker, answer me please." She shivered again.

"I know the drug makes you . . ." He waved a finger toward her and then jammed his hands on his hips as he glared at the floor. After a heavy sigh, he added, "I wanted to make it easier for you to ask for my help."

"Quit pitying me." She squared her shoulders and glared back at him. So that was it. He thought he was helping by romancing her. She resented how it took her being drugged to get his attention and the reaction she'd always wanted from him.

"Damn it! I'm not," he said.

He turned toward her as someone rapped on the door.

"Fuck off," he snapped. Without pausing he reached for her.

"Ryker!" She crossed her arms, not caring for his attitude.

The door opened. He turned toward the intruder and growled, "I said—"

"We found the Wizard," Jack cut him off. Marie watched with amazement as the man calmly entered and sat in Ryker's vacant chair. Not many people would brave his temper.

"Where?" Ryker asked.

"In Gatlinburg. He's staying in a rented chalet with twenty of his closest friends," Jack said. "And he's put out a contract for the return of the woman who broke into his house. We believe they have two other women drugged and ready for the market."

Ice ran down her spine. Why would the guy want her? He obviously could get any woman he wanted. How could she say that? She didn't wish the drug on anyone.

But why go to the small town nestled next to the Great

Smoky Mountains? Maybe by being a well-loved tourist location, it was a perfect place to hide as thousands of strangers rent cabins of all sizes everywhere on the mountains. Anyone could easily blend in.

Ryker looked at Marie. She appeared slightly disturbed by the interruption and his display of temper. Then again, she knew him better than anyone. It amazed him how innocent she could still look after the years of neglect from her parents and the abuse by Theo. Even in her frustration with him, she allowed him to see how much she trusted him. A trust he hoped never to betray. If she ever grew to hate him, it would kill him. What little soul he had left would shrivel and evaporate.

He pulled his gaze from her and looked at his second-in-command. He didn't care for how Jack thought he could barge in whenever he wished. He needed to teach him some boundaries.

"He didn't go far," Ryker said.

"No. For an intelligent man who developed such a powerful drug, he's doing some stupid things," Jack said.

Ryker caught the man cutting his eyes over at Marie, examining her as if he expected to find her abused and defeated. Yep. It was time to teach him some hard lessons.

"Tell Bryan to send the details to Liam." He knew Jack hated Liam's guts as much as Liam did Jack's. No one knew the reason for their animosity. There were rumors of Liam's ex-wife being involved. Ryker couldn't help but wonder if Jack had a thing for unavailable women. From what he'd heard,

Jack had a hard-on for Olivia, Ryker's brother's wife, and rumor was he'd slept with his own brother's fiancé.

"Liam?" Jack said the name as if he had a bad taste in his mouth.

"He'll be working lead on this one." Ryker turned and faced Marie. Her confused expression said she understood what he'd done but not why. Just as well. He had a hard time explaining it to himself. His distrust of Jack played only a small part. That much he was certain.

Jack gripped the arm of the chair, his knuckles turned white as his lips pressed together. Ryker had to admire the man's control.

"What's my role in all of this?" Jack asked between clenched teeth.

"You're to stay here."

"So I'm to sit around here with my thumb up my ass?"

"That's all up to you. You're in charge here while I'm gone."

"What the hell?" Jack shot to his feet and kicked the chair, sliding it across the floor. "You're going to track down that bastard and leave me here?"

Ryker stepped up, nearly nose to nose. "Yeah. When you learn to stay out of *my* personal business, then we'll talk about your place in *my* organization." He waited to see if Jack dared to challenge him.

"I don't like it." Jack turned away.

"Get over it," Ryker bit off. He looked over at Marie. Her paleness revealed how much their arguing bothered her. "Jack, go. Now," he said without taking his attention off her. Time for them to talk. Plus she needed to rest.

Then he'd get with Liam to plan how they'd rescue the

women and get an antidote from the Wizard for Marie. His men better think up a good plan as they were headed for Gatlinburg in forty-eight hours.

Before he left, he'd make sure she was well taken care of. If successful, he would return from the mission before she realized he'd been gone. His absence should give her time to rest.

But he knew there was no way he would. Not after tasting her.

CHAPTER SIX

Marie moved to the sofa. The way Ryker's gaze tracked her every movement gave her the jitters. She needed to be as far away from the bed as possible in the suddenly small room. Sure, she wanted to touch him again. But the drug had already dirtied what she'd dreamed of having from him for so long—the closeness brought on by lovemaking. Yet, what they'd shared couldn't be considered lovemaking. Not when he hated every minute of it.

It was a given. If he'd enjoyed being with her, he'd have climaxed. Their past be damned. That was it. She knew how his mind worked. Having sex with her had been a duty. A way to protect her as he always had—no matter the cost to him personally. He'd helped her and nothing else. No different than he had when Theo had been alive and demanded payment for leaving Marie alone.

She had to quit harping on it. Just erase it from her memory. She could manage for the next few weeks on her own. She owned some battery-operated friends. They would do. They would have to.

"No matter how far you try to get away from me, I'm not letting you out of my sight tonight. Not until I know you have it under control." Ryker walked behind the sofa. She felt him lift a lock of her hair. "I'm the only one who can help you."

She twisted around. "I'll be okay without your help." He dropped her hair as if guilty of something. What had he been doing? Smelling her hair?

"I don't think you understand. Jack won't be helping you." Ryker leaned over the back of the sofa, cupped her face, and kissed her. His tongue stroked hers. The moist caress heated her blood. Her thighs clenched.

Was the drug amplifying her reaction to his touch?

The tingle of a million ants crawling over her skin gave her the first clue. She whimpered. Then her first flashback washed over her, building a need larger than any other.

She climbed the back of the sofa and wrapped her arms around his neck. He grunted when he lifted her and she squeezed. Without thought or care, she crossed her ankles at the small of his back. Using all her strength, she held on.

"I don't want Jack or you." The words came out of her mouth but they both knew one was a lie. Her fingers dug into his shoulder blades. She couldn't get close enough to Ryker. Her heartbeat sped up and felt like it would burst. "What are you waitin' for?" From the moment she understood what it meant to be with a man, she'd wanted Ryker and only Ryker.

He carried her to the bed and leaned over. Her arms and legs remained tight around him.

"Honey, you need to release me."

She hesitated for only a second. His hard, warm body

felt so good pressed against her hers, but she wanted more, wanted to show what she could do for him.

"Oh. Okay. You're the boss." In a smooth move, she dropped to the bed and slipped her hand behind his waistband as she unsnapped and unzipped his pants with the other. Using both hands, she double-fisted his cock and worked a few strokes. Then her mouth covered the moist tip and enveloped him in one long, strong draw.

"Christ, Marie." The long groan signaled his pleasure.

His fingers gripped her head as he pulled out of her mouth. Once he released his hold, she returned to lick her way to his balls and suck in one tight orb.

"No!"

He clasped two handfuls of hair next to her scalp and dragged her up his body without hurting her. Maybe the sensation of her body rubbing along his rock-hard one masked any pain, but she liked how his hands then cupped her ass and maneuvered her across the bed.

He pushed her jeans and panties to her ankles. His mouth covered her where she throbbed. His tongue showed a talent she never imagined. Each lick drew a moan from her. Electricity tingled and danced from his expert finesse and shot through the bundle of nerves he played with.

She lifted her knees to dig her heels into the mattress as she arched her back, rhythmically thrusting her groin against his mouth. Tiny shudders travelled up her torso and down her legs with each tug of his lips and teeth. Her hands gripped and released the covers beneath her.

He appeared to be enjoying every texture and taste he pulled from her. Long and short strokes built higher flames until he jammed two fingers into her wet heat. She screamed as she shook the bed with her release.

Her hands stilled. When she reached for him again, he stopped her by clasping her wrists in one hand.

"Don't." His voice sounded strained as he wiped his chin on his sleeve. "Do you feel better?"

To call her confused would be an understatement. He refused her touch. She wanted to help him find release too. What was he trying to prove?

Ryker wanted to sink into her again. His body shook from the need to climax. He couldn't resist looking at her. Her flushed face and wanton position with legs spread wide and the apex moist from his attention tempted him to return. If not for the feeling he was using her for his own perverted reasons, he'd sink back into her. He never wanted to take advantage of her.

Instead, he pushed away and stood as he tossed the comforter over her. After a deep breath and with as much dignity as he could muster, he shoved his stiff cock back into his pants and tenderly zipped up.

"If you need me again tonight, dial one on the phone next to the bed—it'll ring in my room."

He reached the door and stopped when she said, "I remember my first night at Main Sector. I saw what Master made you do in front of him and the thing he made you do to him. What we just did tonight and the other night has nothing to do with him. Nothing to do with the past. It's time we moved on, Ryker."

She needed to forget that part of their lives. He sure as hell wanted to forget. So why couldn't he? That young man no longer existed. He looked over his shoulder, unable to resist drinking in every beautiful inch of her one more time. Too bad. She'd wrapped the comforter around her and sat up.

"You don't know what you're talking about," he said.

"Keep telling yourself that. I know you better than anyone. Maybe even yourself. Drug or no drug, I still want you." The material dropped, and he caught a flash of the soft flesh he already wanted to run his tongue across again as she moved underneath the sheets. "I'll accept your help in keeping the drug under control, but I won't accept you treating me as if I'm part of a job." She turned over, giving him her delicate, scarred back.

His eyes stung. She'd been so helpless against Theo's sick games. At twenty-three, he'd been confused by the strong emotions of hate and by a perverse desire to receive his childhood idol's approval. He didn't deserve her trust. Protecting her from Theo at the time had been his intent, but he'd wondered often if there had been another way. Had there been a well of dark, bubbling evil waiting for the opportunity to return to Theo's *good graces*, and he'd only used Marie to return there? He wanted to scream at her that she was wrong. Instead, he eased open the door and shut it behind him.

He never thought of himself as a coward.

Ryker hated to sleep. Even in his dreams, he was always aware of what was happening, but he still couldn't stop it. No matter how he exercised or worked, the damn nightmare returned.

Each minute of it moved vivid and clear behind his closed eyelids. He relived every aspect of *that* night though it played out like any crazy dream. That same night his life changed into a living hell. Over the years, his dream, his nightmare, became twisted and transformed into a marathon of allegories. The type he refused to dwell on. The nightmare remained the same.

Eyes forward and heart pounding, Ryker lifted his knees higher and pumped his arms, running full force in the middle of the deserted Atlanta street. The echo of his bare feet smacking the wet pavement bounced off the dark buildings and cut through the silence.

Would he be late again? Even without a wristwatch he knew time was about to bite him in the ass. He swallowed and grimaced. A sour taste filled his mouth. Fear. God, he hated it.

Humidity covered every inch of his bare skin, giving him no relief from the heat even moments before the sun rose. He inhaled the damp air and took three more strides before releasing a long breath, hollowing his stomach. Sweat dripped into his eyes as he continued his fast pace. He blinked several times and rubbed at the sting, and then shook his head to clear his vision.

The street lamps glowed like white dandelion balls. The traffic lights swayed in a nonexistent wind. A rumble of thunder caused him to falter. He knew that sound, lived with it every moment of his life. The ground trembled but a split second after the explosion. Dread weighed him down, pulling at his need to stop and give up.

He shook his head again. Moisture sprinkled his shoulders.

Doubt ate at him as he propelled his body into another burst of speed. His heart pulsated in double time. He leaned into the run and the calves of his legs tightened, threatening to cramp. Every inch of his body tensed. He struggled for a little more speed. With each teeth-jarring step, his cock slapped his inner thighs.

This time he would find a way to save them.

The oily smell of burning rubber mixed with the pungent bitterness of scorched skin and hair warned him he was almost there. His subconscious warned him to stop. Yet he refused to give up.

This time they could be alive.

The glow like the rising sun drew him closer. First, he felt the heat.

Engulfed in flames, the limo showed no signs of life. The bomb had done its job. Two bodies in the back and one behind the steering wheel were nearly unrecognizable as humans in the midst of fire and smoke and twisted metal. People stood near the buildings, fear and shock frozen on their faces.

Then he heard the screaming.

"Someone's alive!" he shouted as he scrambled for the passenger door handle. "Help them!"

The metal burned into his hand but he didn't let go. Pain shot up his arm, numbing his fingers, as every muscle stiffened from the shock of the red-hot handle. Blood flowed from his fingers and sizzled on the metal. The windows shattered.

He flung up his arm, protecting his eyes. Glass stung his skin. Then he screamed as flames sucked him into the car. Fire surrounded him, and he opened his mouth to scream again but no sound came out. All of the air in his lungs evaporated.

He couldn't breathe but the screaming in his head continued.

Ryker shot out of bed, his hands in the chunbi stance, standing at attention, hand holding fist. He shivered. Wide-eyed, he looked at his surroundings. A stark room and bare walls so much like his life.

The chill from sweat pouring off his body felt ten times better than the lick of flames. He no longer wondered when he would forget that night or when the mad caricature of it would stop. After the burns healed, he had small stretches of the day when he believed it was possible not to think about the explosion. That was, until he caught his reflection in a stray mirror or darkened window. The scars never lied.

Because of him, his parents died in that fiery explosion.

"Yo, boss."

Ryker stepped away from the large screen he and Jack had been staring at for over three hours. He took a long sip of his coffee. Last night, the dream had been harder on him than usual. He forced himself to pay attention. His eyes stung as he examined the map of Gatlinburg and several other towns nearby.

The map, broken down by areas of Blossom Flower activity reported by the authorities, showed splatters of bright colors. Each color indicated where they suspected the Wizard's people played a part. The vicinity of the large cabin had the heavier shades. They intended to block every route to ensure no one escaped this time while they saved the women held inside.

Sal shifted on stick-thin legs encased in black jeans, his

hands stuffed beneath his arms. He looked nervous and guilty.

"What's going on?" Ryker wondered if the guy had ever put an eye out with his foot-high mohawk.

"Liam said to tell you that an OS operative is asking for you." He swallowed, causing his Adam's apple to bob along with his hair. "He claims your brother sent him. I placed him in conference room two."

So Collin had heard about their trouble. Ryker glanced over at Jack.

His second-in-command gave him a blank look before moving his attention to Sal and then back to the map.

Ryker had suspected for a while that Jack spied for The Circle. Yet how he felt about the Onyx Scepter's operative showing up at this time wasn't enough evidence to question Jack's loyalty to The Circle. But each day Ryker waited for him to screw up. Then he would take great pleasure in returning the man to his brother, piece by piece.

"Okay. Go back to your station."

Once Sal rounded the corner, Ryker stepped over to the screen. The OS operative could wait until hell froze over. He didn't like the idea of his brother sticking his nose in The Circle's business.

"What did he want?" Jack asked without taking his gaze off the screen.

"Some jibber-jabber computer stuff." Ryker ignored the sideways look he received. He hoped the man dared to question him further. Any excuse to send him packing would relieve some of the tension mounting with this mission.

Instead Jack nodded and pointed at a location on the map.
A couple hours later, they had a plan.

Marie would hate it.

"No fucking way!"

Marie's eyebrow rose at Ryker's outburst. She wanted to laugh at the mixture of anger and surprise on his face but she preferred choking him. He truly thought he could leave her at Sector while he gallivanted off to save the day.

The room became quiet. Jack and Bryan turned away and stared at the computer screen, pretending to give them some privacy.

Ryker crossed his arms and looked down at her. No matter what he planned, she owed the Wizard a little lesson on how to treat women.

Sure, the Wizard hadn't been there when the young geek tied her up and stripped her, but his drug was the reason she fought the need to tear off Ryker's clothes every second. Was the Wizard's girlfriend a cold bitch that forced him to such extremes? Or was he so ugly he had to drug a woman to have sex with him? That had to be it. No self-respecting man had to drug a woman for any reason.

She finally said, "Yes, way. I'm going with or without you. This is my fight too. You want him for what he did to the women and your operatives. I do too. No woman deserves to be forced into that type of slavery. Plus I have a more personal reason to take him down."

"You're wrong," he said in his raspy voice.

She placed her hands on her hips. Both eyebrows rose this time; she waited for him to understand he wouldn't win this time. His amber glare softened.

He sighed and relaxed his stance, his arms dropped. "That's only part of the reason. We do need to stop him from hurting more people, but I'm ramping up this operation because he dared to let one of his men touch you."

The heat of anger shone from behind his amber eye. She wanted to soothe him, trace his scars and tell him not to worry, but he needed to listen to what she was telling him first.

"You're right. But I wasn't really hurt." She raised her hand, stopping him from interrupting. "Even so, I was the one he shot up with the drug. That gives me the right to be the one who captures him and forces him to hand over the antidote."

"What if the plan fails? Chances are he'll sell or kill you." His voice deepened. He glanced over at Jack and Bryan as if he didn't want them to hear.

"I'm willing to take that chance. If the circumstances were reversed, would you feel any differently?"

He opened his mouth and then shut it. The scars on his face became lighter as he shifted his jaw.

Bless the baby's heart.

He wanted to argue. She was confident he would think of something else to hold over her. In the meanwhile, he was so cute, looking at her as if he wanted some cotton to wrap her in.

"Meet me downstairs in the shooting range. I want you to work on handling a gun." His hand pressed into her back. Was he trying to get rid of her? What else was he planning?

"Jack's been teaching me taekwondo." She sidestepped from his touch. Her nipples had hardened from that simple contact. Being so close, she could smell the soap he'd used that morning. Her chest tightened. He smelled good.

"He's a lousy teacher then."

"What?" Her hands fisted. "Don't take your foul mood out on Jack. I've been taking lessons from him for only a year. It's not like I can practice every hour of every day."

What was it about him and Jack? She'd never understand men.

"If you're coming—"

"No if. I'm coming with you." She jabbed his chest.

He sighed again and looked at the ceiling for a second. "When you come with us, you need a way to protect yourself that doesn't involve years of training. A gun. That'll do it. You'll only need the basics. Plus, I'll make sure you know enough not to shoot yourself or anyone else in The Circle."

"I know how to shoot a gun." No one could live with a bunch of assassins and mercenaries without learning a little about guns and how to shoot them.

"You're not letting her go," Jack said, his forehead wrinkling as he looked their way.

"This is between me and Marie. So stay the fuck out."

"Don't talk to him like that," she stepped in.

"Jesus H. Christ, woman. He's not on your side." Ryker growled in his frustration.

"You're not ready to go on missions yet." Jack shook his head.

She glared at her so-called friend. Whose side was he on? Obviously not hers.

"You know, Ryker is right. Stay the fuck out of this."

Jack's eyebrows rose but he kept quiet.

Someone please save her from crazy testosterone-filled men. "I'm going to the armament room to pick out a gun." She turned away and headed toward the door.

"I'll be down there in a few minutes." Ryker waved over Liam. "Go with her to the basement shooting range and pick out a gun for her to use. Something that'll fit into her small hand."

She gritted her teeth. He was determined not to listen to her. She would figure out a way to make him. For now, she'd give in and let him *teach* her how to shoot.

"Okay, boss." Liam walked toward the door. His vivid blue eyes and ebony hair touched with silver at the temples gave him a Pierce Brosnan look. He'd joined The Circle, as he liked to say, "when he was a wee lad," playing up his beautiful accent. If ever asked about returning home to Ireland, he would shake his head and change the subject. The man was a genius at *finding* any kind of equipment or supplies The Circle could need. Plus he was a dangerous man to cross. The gossip was he never met a weapon he didn't like. Since the previous security officer defected to the OS, he handled security and logistics for The Circle.

She'd just stepped out into the hallway when someone shouted.

At the other end, two guards had the arms of a man with neon-blue hair pulled back into a long braid. He used their hold to jump up and twist his body, taking the men down with him. Before they could recover, the man was running toward her.

"**M**ove!" Ryker shoved her behind him. "Stop, asshole." He pointed his gun toward the threat.

The man slid to a stop. He slowly raised his hands and focused his dark almond-shaped eyes on Ryker.

"Collin Ryker sent me." Instead of the expected Asian accent, he spoke English with a slight drawl. "The Wizard has something of mine. So you can let me go with you to find him or I'll follow."

"How's it going, Ice?" Jack moved to the side and nodded toward the man. "My brother's still having problems with his ex-fiancé since she's working with him now?"

"A. J.?" Ice Takahashi cocked his head. "I stay out of Rex's business. Safer that way."

Ryker knew of Ice, that he'd acquired his name from what ran through his veins. Of all the stories bandied about, one was that he'd tracked down and killed his own father.

If a man didn't protect his family, he was a man not to be trusted. In Ryker's way of thinking, a good reason for him to leave.

"I don't give a damn what he has of yours." Ryker lifted his chin. "Go back to Collin and tell him to keep his nose out of my business."

"He said you would say that. He told me to tell you that you owe him."

Ryker straightened his shoulders and stepped closer to the man. "I don't owe him jack-shit."

"He said you took his kill." Those cold dark eyes stared back.

Ryker knew most would agree he had the greater right to the kill if they knew all of the facts.

"Boss, you want me to throw him out?" Liam shouldered his way through the crowd surrounding Ice.

Ryker had to give his little brother credit. Collin was a smart man. He had to be to escape Theo's perverted clutches all those years ago. If only Ryker had known too. The years of pain and depravity the man had forced on him. The way he made him beg. Now wasn't the time to think of that.

His brother was known for being a master strategist. Whatever reason he sent Ice would most likely be revealed in its own good time.

Ryker nodded. "Okay. Jack'll get you up to speed on our plan."

CHAPTER SEVEN

Ryker pressed the gas a little harder after rounding the curve. The roads in and near Gatlinburg were narrow and curvy. He heard Marie moving around, probably trying to get comfortable. A few miles back he'd stopped to tie her up and place her in the trunk. They'd padded the trunk the best they could without it being obvious. Before leaving Sector, they made sure she had plenty of air, and confirmed that there were no holes in the mufflers. He didn't want to arrive and find her sick or worse.

Before leaving, he'd argued with her again. The mission was dangerous enough and could easily change into a fiasco. So he'd worked on the plan for two days before they left Sector—every scenario covered—but anything could happen.

Only one problem he hadn't counted on popping up. *Up* being the significant word. His cock was hard as the stainless steel knife taped under his biceps. Tying her up was an erotic task better done during a different time and place. The way the rope pressed into her delicate skin and the surprised moans she made behind the gag.

Damn! He better get his mind on the job. He lifted a leg and shifted his cock to a more comfortable position. No doubt about it, he was one sick fuck.

A good enough reason to stay in control and not let Marie know how she affected his concentration. So far they'd been lucky: no flashbacks to contend with during the mission. But the thought of dominating such a vibrant woman heated his blood, just as the thought of her fighting back made his whole body throb. If he hadn't known better, he would swear he'd been dosed with the drug.

"Hey, boss. You're coming up on the first checkpoint," Liam said through the miniature communication device in his ear.

Once he travelled along another hairpin curve, he spotted the two guards ahead. A large black SUV blocked the way. On top of the vehicle spotlights lit up the road. He dropped the Mustang Shelby GT500 to a crawl, signaling to the submachine gun-toting guards he wasn't planning to ram them. He stopped in the middle of the brightest area.

The shorter of two guards came up to his window as Ryker rolled it down.

"You need to turn around. This is a private road." Red-headed with freckles across his nose, he looked like a grown-up Opie.

"I've got a present for the Wizard." Ryker made sure the guard's flashlight hit him in the face. Most people knew if a man had scars like his, a submachine wouldn't scare him. In fact, they usually scared the one looking on.

"Shit!" The guard stepped back. "Uh, what kind of present?"

He opened the door. The guard lifted his gun and the other one came to attention, pointing his at Ryker too.

"Whoa! Take it easy, fellas. I'm getting out to show you. She's in the trunk." He towered over the short man. The guard moved back a little more, but kept his gun on him.

"She?"

"Yea, dickwad. The Wizard sent out word he's looking for her and willing to pay." Ryker pressed the remote button, and the trunk lid popped open.

Marie's wide-eyed look had his heart pumping. If they hadn't practiced that expression, he would've given away the game by scooping her out of the trunk and apologizing for putting her in harm's way.

The guard blasted the light into Marie's eyes. She squinted and turned away.

"She fits the description." The guard's flashlight travelled down her body. "What's your name?"

Ryker said, "Ty Roman." Most of the underworld knew of the infamous bounty hunter and psycho assassin. What the underworld didn't know was that Ty had been taken prisoner a few years ago by The Circle and then disappeared. He'd stuck his nose in the wrong person's business.

The guard's loud gulp confirmed he'd heard of Ty.

"Hal, call headquarters and tell them Ty Roman's bringing in the girl for the money." The guard kept his gun trained on Ryker as he backed up. "Close the trunk and go on up the road for about a mile. They'll be waiting for you. Go slow. They'll need time to open the gate."

Then the world went dark with a slam. She could hear a few more muffled words exchanged. Then the car rocked when Ryker slipped into the driver side and closed the door. He cranked up the engine, and they started moving again.

A couple minutes later, she heard Ryker talking with someone, though she couldn't make out the words. He'd been careful tying her up, but the trunk wasn't all that big and she was getting a cramp in her right leg. Most people probably thought the trunk would be comfortable situated over the shocks. No. She felt every bump and dip, and her legs cramping didn't help matters. Of all the bad things Master had done to her, thankfully closets and rope didn't factor into it.

Stretching, she kicked, thumping against the side, hoping to get the feeling back. Then she heard laughter. They probably thought she was trying to escape.

The car rocked to a stop. Ryker would open the trunk any minute with the Wizard's men looking on. Or the Wizard himself could show up. Whoever opened the trunk, she hoped they hurried. The gag pinched the corners of her mouth, and her skin burned from where the rope rubbed her wrist. Deep inside, she knew the irritation stemmed from the nervousness twisting her stomach into knots. Time to prove to Ryker that she had the stuff to work undercover and be an operative instead of an IS geek.

Being involved in such covert jobs should be a snap. She'd been surrounded by operatives for over eight years and often had to lie and pretend to be someone else to survive.

The trunk popped open.

Showtime!

Marie liked how effortlessly Ryker scooped her out of the trunk after he knocked one of the guards out of the way. He acted proprietorial and all, but she had to remind herself his actions were all a sham for the Wizard's people. All a part he played as a bounty hunter bringing in his meal ticket.

"I got her. No one touches her until I get my money." Ryker held her close to his chest, one arm around her back and the other at the bend of her knees. Without a free hand, he gambled with his and Marie's lives, but he suspected their interest in reclaiming her would protect them long enough to do what was needed.

"Like we can't take her from you." One guard smirked and aimed his Uzi at Ryker.

"Stupid, that's Ty Roman," another guard warned.

"So what! He looks like Freddy Krueger. Scars don't mean shit. 'Sides, who says he's really Ty? No one alive knows what he looks like."

"He's got the girl. That's all that matters. So shut the fuck up!" a voice said from the shadows.

She stiffened. The guy who had shot her up with the drug stepped into the light. Skinny with greasy hair sticking up in every direction, he wore a T-shirt that read, "Stud Muffin." Talk about an oxymoron.

"Yeah. That's her." He glanced over to Ryker. "Did you get to enjoy some of the merchandise?"

The glint in his eye worried Marie. How would he react to the truth?

"Some man was giving it to her when I interrupted. So you would need to talk with him. If he's awake yet." Ryker shifted her in his hold. "She's heavy. Let's talk inside after I sit her down."

Hey, she didn't appreciate that. She glared at Ryker.

"Yes." The guy nodded but he didn't move. His stare remained on her. Something was wrong.

Afraid that he noticed her lack of fear, she wiggled as if she struggled to get down. Ryker lost his grip and her feet hit the ground. Without hesitation, he picked her by the waist and tossed her over his shoulder. She grunted as all the air left her lungs.

"Come on in. We have a room fixed up perfect for her." The guy strode up a long sidewalk that came to a side door to the house.

From what she could see upside down with blood rushing to her face, the building was huge. The full moon lit it up enough for her to see three stories with two of them hanging over what might be a ravine as she heard water rushing over rocks nearby.

The room they walked into appeared to have wall-to-wall electronic equipment: computers, monitors, large screens with different channels playing at the same time. The large treadmill in the center of the room threw off the geek vibe. Obviously, Mr. Stud Muffin worried about his body.

They continued to the farthest wall where one plain door separated large game and movie posters. The fellow shoved opened the door and stood to the side. He smirked as Ryker walked into the other room. After being in such a big space crammed with noisy equipment, the tiny bedroom came as a bit of a shock to the system. A light blue blanket covered the double bed and a long dresser and mirror covered one wall, and that was all. No decorations, windows, or closet doors broke up the blandness.

"You can leave her there." He pointed to the bed. Her stomach sunk. What was he planning?

Ryker threw her on the bed. She bounced, landing on her back and tied hands. The mattress almost enveloped her with its softness.

"Come back in here and we'll have a drink while you count your money." The geek walked out.

Ryker bent over to pull off the tape from her mouth.

"Better leave that on for now. She'll be fine." Without seeing if Ryker followed his orders, he turned and headed toward the bank of screens.

The look Ryker gave her could only be called a warning. They didn't have much time. Finding the girls was top priority, along with the antidote for the drug. The Wizard was the likely candidate to possess that.

Well, crap! The tingling sensation racing across her torso warned her that the drug was kicking in. Now wasn't the time. She closed her eyes and thought about being in the snow and ice during the winter—anything to take her mind off having hot sex with Ryker, his strong fingers touching her. His warm body against hers. His mouth covering the place that ached. *Double crap!*

Ryker needed to hurry.

"Mr. Roman, what's your poison?"

Poison? Ryker shook his head. What did the bastard think he was? Some super-villain from a James Bond movie?

Ryker noticed a guard closing the door into the bedroom. Two guards stood near their boss at the far end of the bar. Another stood near the exit, although all continued watching some action movie on the screens. If they had been his men, he'd fire them. For now, their inattention would come in handy.

"I don't drink while I'm working." Ryker crossed his arms and glanced at his watch. In four more minutes, Liam and his men would attack. And during the noise and excitement, he'd release Marie, and they would get the hell out of this crazy house while his men found the other women and maybe the Wizard.

The nerd pressed a series of buttons on a wall, and a bank of monitors lifted as a long bar slid out of the wall, complete with mirrors and shelves of glasses and booze, revealing another door.

"Single-minded in purpose. I admire that in a person." The nerd picked up a tumbler and poured a generous portion of Jim Beam. "Relax. The job is over. You appear to be the type who appreciates good whiskey."

With a shove, he slid the glass down the bar to Ryker.

Two minutes left. Ryker anticipated they'd drag by.

"Oh, I forgot to introduce myself." The nerd poured another tumbler full of whiskey and raised the glass. Ryker ignored his and stared at the man. "The name is Malcolm Reynolds." He held out his hand.

"How's Zoe and Kaylee?" Ryker tilted his head and raised one eyebrow. A buzzing sounded in his ear. His men were breaking into different rooms of the house, preparing to take out more of the nerd's men.

The look on the man's face almost caused Ryker to chuckle. The asshole thought he was so smart using a defunct sci-fi television series' character name.

"You surprise me, Mr. Roman. I would never guess you to be a fan of *Firefly*."

"It's not good to pigeonhole people by their professions." Ryker leaned against the bar. He forced himself not to look at the bedroom with Marie inside. "Take you, for example. Some people might think a fellow who loves video games and computers must be super smart. But you and I know that's not absolutely true." The nerd's smile faded with each word.

"Do tell me more?" The nerd poured four fingers' worth of whiskey and took a big swallow.

"I prefer knowing who I'm talking to." He needed a name. At the least, a better fake one than he'd been given before.

"Bill Henderson."

Yeah. That sounded real.

"Let's see, Billy—"

"Bill." The nerd slammed down the glass, sloshing good bourbon onto his hand and the bar.

Ryker grinned. His scars prevented him from giving a nice, even smile. Instead, it was most apt to resemble a smirk.

"It's like this, Billy." Something about the kid irritated the hell out of Ryker—besides his being the one who shot that crap into Marie. Maybe he enjoyed taunting him because he thought he was so much smarter. "During the time your men let me through and brought me inside—and you kept me close to your side because I make you nervous—my men have been searching through your house for the women you kidnapped." The panicked look Ryker received brought a deep satisfaction in knowing the fellow wasn't as smart as he thought. "I'm just curious. How will the Wizard feel about you losing his income?"

"You son of a bitch!" Billy threw his glass and ducked behind the bar.

Ryker leaned to the side. The glass shattered on the floor behind him. He jumped over the bar and then backed up. Billy pulled a gun. Before he could fire, Ryker kicked out, sending it flying through the air. Billy disappeared through the doorway behind the bar, and three of the guards followed. Before Ryker gave chase, the last guard in the room shouted and fired. Shots zinged by his head as it rained glass around him, and another guard ran into the room.

Ryker dove for the floor. Then he spotted the sawed-off shotgun on another shelf. Without thinking, he pulled it out and peeked over the bar, firing at the nearest guard. The scream shook up the other guard. Without thinking, he turned toward his buddy. Ryker pumped the shotgun as he stood and fired again.

The guard dropped his weapon and cried out, grabbing his side. Overhead, gunfire and shouting from Ryker's men echoed downstairs as running footsteps punctuated each burst. The occasional thump and scream warned that people were being hit.

Shit, he'd better check on Marie. Several holes in the sheetrock and broken monitors warned that bullets may have pierced the wall. The possibility of one hitting her had him heading toward the bedroom when a crash stopped him. A quick pump and he pointed the shotgun at the door leading outside. It hung lopsided on its hinges.

Liam crouched inside with two guns at ready, looking around for Billy's men.

"The asshole slipped out the door behind the bar with some of his men. Go after him. I'll get Marie." Ryker reached the bedroom door and glanced back. Liam hadn't moved. "What are you waiting for? An engraved invitation? Get your ass moving!"

"Yes, sir!" Liam jumped over the bar and paused, looked for immediate danger before running into the darkness.

Ryker turned the knob and pushed open the door. The room was dark. A flash of light warned him. He twisted and fell to the floor, grabbing Marie by the ankles, tripping her. She landed on top. Marie dropped the piece of broken mirror on the way down.

"It's me!"

"The guns shots, the screaming and running—I was scared." She wrapped her arms around him.

He hugged her to his chest. "Shh. It's okay now."

She punched his arm. "Don't you ever tie me up and leave me like that. I don't care how loose you make the knots. That plan stunk!"

"Ouch! Okay. Let's go see if they found the women." Relief lightened the tight feeling in his chest. Her body trembled. She felt a little warm. "Are you sure you're not hurt?"

"I'm fine."

She didn't sound fine. He helped her to her feet. She pulled away and walked into the other room, hugging herself.

She gasped. He took her by the shoulders, blocking her view of the bodies, and pushed her toward the other door behind the bar. "I have a feeling this will lead into the rest of the house."

It opened into a foyer. A Circle operative, guarding the front door, lifted his chin toward the next floor. Ryker, with Marie one step behind, carefully moved up the stairs.

"Hey, boss. We got them." Another one of his men stood at the opposite end of a long hallway.

In the room, Ice sat on a bed, holding a woman in his arms, rocking back and forth. She was beautiful with long black hair and exotic eyes. Another woman stood nearby, talking and making wild hand gestures to a Circle operative.

"Just let me go. I have people looking for me, and you don't want to cross them." Her blondish brown hair fell around her shoulders. The little turned-up nose and sprinkle of freckles gave her a girl-next-door look.

"Take her to Sector," Ryker told the young operative.

"Who are you? Are you the boss of these apes?" The woman with the turned-up nose frowned.

Marie clearly didn't care for the woman's attitude. "These apes saved your butt. You need to be thankful."

The woman's eyes widened. "Okay, okay. But I need to get home." She obviously hadn't expected another woman to remind her of her manners.

"What did I tell you?" Ryker glared at the man and jerked a thumb at the doorway.

The operative grabbed for the woman, but she twisted and brought her knee up. He squealed and fell to the ground in a fetal position.

Ryker hollered at Marie, telling her to move away as she knelt by the operative's side. The operative screamed obscenities at his attacker.

The woman backed away from Ryker. "Don't touch me!

You have no right. I've had enough of all of this bullshit and no one's going to force me to do what I don't want to."

Marie scrambled out of the way. At the same time, Ice kissed the woman in his arms on the forehead and let her go. Before anyone could react, he gave the woman with blondish hair a chop near her neck. She fell like a piano from a ten-story building.

"She won't give you any trouble now," Ice said to Ryker.

Gingerly, the young operative regained his footing and not too gently tossed the woman over his shoulder and limped out of the room. Ice placed an arm around the other woman and walked out.

Ryker grabbed Marie's wrist and started down the hallway. A few of his men came out of the rooms they passed, their search for the Wizard unsuccessful. Everywhere they looked Circle men were tearing the massive cabin apart, looking for information on the Wizard's whereabouts. They understood the importance of finding the man and the antidote.

Suddenly the lights went out. More shots reverberated through the hallway as flashes pinpointed the locations of the shooters.

Ryker pulled Marie off to the side and pushed their way into a small bend near rooms already searched. His body pressed into hers, covering her from any stray bullets.

"Stay here until I tell you the way is clear." Ryker shifted and looked back to where the shots had been fired. Marie groaned.

Ryker turned back to her. "You're hit. Damn it! I knew you should've stayed back at Sector. Tell me where it is." His hands slid over her body, searching for dampness from a wound.

Well aware of how crazy she sounded, Marie didn't care. "If you don't get me off now, I'll scream, and we'll see how many you can fight at one time." Logic told her this wasn't the time or place, but if he didn't do something quick her body would explode into a million pieces and not in the good way.

"No blood."

"No shit, Sherlock."

"The drug?" His hands stopped their movements.

"What do you think?" She hated being short-tempered but patience and the drug's flashback didn't mix well.

He stared at her. She had no idea if he really saw her in the dark, but she imagined that amber eye flaring with as much need as she had for him.

His mouth covered hers, and his hand jammed into her jeans under her barely-there panties. She caught her breath, and his tongue dipped further as his fingers rubbed the hard bundle lubed with moistness.

Someone yelled in the distance. He tilted his head back. Marie pressed her body hard against fingers. "I waited too long. This won't be enough. I need more."

"Christ, Marie." His lips brushed her ear as his hand hesitated for a second as if he couldn't decide what to do next. Then he moved his hand away. "This is fucking crazy," he whispered.

"Shut up your complaining and get to work." Her heart pounded so hard she was afraid it would burst. The sound of a zipper going down broke the silence. It was hers.

"Sorry, darling, but this will have to do." He lifted her and pressed her to the wall.

Before she could ask what he was doing, he jerked up her blouse and popped out a breast from her bra. His mouth pulled at the nipple as his fingers returned to the moistness between her legs. In the same rhythm, he sucked and thrust hard. She groaned and he covered her mouth with his free hand. When she bit his thumb, he moved his hand to her other nipple and pinched. She hooked a leg around his hip and met his thrusts.

To stop herself from screaming she stuffed her fist into her mouth. The delicious waves washed over her and grew limp but he continued to suckle and fuck her with his fingers. Another wave hit her and tears streamed down her face as she moaned against her fist. The need and Ryker finally stopped.

Her heart pounded so hard. The world spun, fading in and out. She leaned back against the wall and moved her bloody hand, taking in gulps of air.

In careful movements, he pulled up her pants and zipped them closed. He cupped her breast, lifting it with care to place back into her bra. She gasped when his thumb grazed the sore tip. He paused a second before straightening her blouse.

"Let's go," he whispered as he smoothed the tears from her face. Then he released her.

Her hip slid against his swollen groin. He hissed. She stroked her hand over the hard ridge.

"Let me help you," she offered.

"No." He grabbed her fingers and pulled her behind him as he headed downstairs and out the door.

She shook her head. The man wasn't human.

CHAPTER EIGHT

Marie glanced over to Ryker as he maneuvered the Mustang around the numerous black Circle Humvees and vans parked every which way in front of the large cabin and along the drive. Several of the operatives would stay to analyze what they found in the hope it would pinpoint the Wizard's hideout.

Ryker looked angry. Most people thought he looked that way all the time. She knew differently.

"Why can't you come when you're with me?" She could sit around and feel sorry for herself or bring out in the open the problem of him not having an orgasm with her. Choosing the latter made sense.

"You're not making sense. We're together right now."

He understood what she was saying. Did he really think he could avoid talking about it?

"Do you feel sorry for me—is that it? I've heard men can get it hard for any woman. But I've never heard if they can come without being truly turned on."

"Jesus H. Christ, Marie. The shit women come up with amazes me."

"We come up with that crap because, one, we're not men. Two, men won't actually talk with women about their feelings!"

"Can we talk about this after we get back to Sector?" He looked into the rearview mirror for the tenth time.

Marie turned as far as the seatbelt would let her. Bright headlights were narrowing the space between them fast. Then she checked the clock on the dash; it was two in the morning. The rate of speed and no blue lights on top warned of trouble.

"Is it a local unmarked car?" Last thing they needed was to have the police pull them over. Ryker never inspired confidence in the locals. He looked too deadly.

"Nope."

"A drunk?" One of the dangers of being on the road so early in the morning was a person often met drunks going home after bars closed or parties ended. Her fingers gripped the door armrest.

"Nope."

The car whipped around and eased up beside them on the narrow, curvy two- lane road.

"Who would—" She snapped her mouth shut as the window lowered on the passenger side of the black Charger. The nerd grinned and then lifted his middle finger.

She screamed when the other car's tires cut in front of them. Ryker's quick reflexes saved them from being pushed off the road into the dark crevasse. Metal grinding against metal and tires screeching were all she heard for the next lifetime.

The Charger shot past them. The bar of red taillights became smaller by the minute.

Scared and panting like she'd kept the Mustang on the road by will alone, she looked at Ryker, her mouth opened to speak, but she snapped it shut. From the way his jaw popped from grinding his teeth so hard, she doubted he would listen to her.

Her body tingled. Crap! The drug was kicking in again. Her fingers dug into the leather upholstery.

"Uh, Ryker?"

He shifted the gears and stomped the gas. The force pushed her shoulders into the seat. She closed her eyes. Her breasts ached and ripples radiated from her groin. Thoughts of Ryker kissing and sucking on her nipples took her breath away. She groaned. Her eyes popped opened. Closing them wasn't a good idea after all.

From the corner of her eye, she caught Ryker checking on her as he jerked the steering wheel, bringing the car back from the edge of the road.

"Don't tell me it's happening again." His raspy voice caressed her senses. Heat rose across her neck and her face. She'd kill the Wizard at the first opportunity if she didn't die from embarrassment before this was over.

"You act as if I have a choice in the matter."

"I'm a little busy right now. You'll have to take care of it yourself."

"Fine! But we know it obviously won't last." She unzipped her jeans and stuck her hand between her legs.

Ryker jerked on the steering wheel again. Shit! Fuck! Seeing her working at getting herself off was about to send him to an early grave. With each little whimper and moan he struggled to keep his gaze on the road. He released the gearshift long enough to adjust his cock. He hurt so bad he wanted to groan along with her. Hell. He was in hell. When had his life turned into a porn version of a James Bond movie?

His cell phone rang. He pressed a button on the steering wheel.

"Yeah!" Happy that someone interrupted his torment, he almost shouted hallelujah.

"Where are you?" Jack asked.

"Chasing down that son of a bitch who drugged Marie."

"I got you on the GPS. We'll see what we can do to intercept."

At that moment, the Charger braked and turned onto a small one-lane road.

"He's turned onto a road so narrow we could hit another car head-on." Ryker swerved to miss a low-hanging branch, and his driver-side tires shot gravel into the trees. "He knows these roads too well. Too many places he can stop and ambush us. The road we're on, does it show up on the map?"

"Yeah."

"Does it come out onto another main road?"

"It branches off in about ten miles. One way to a dead end. The other leads into Pigeon Forge."

"I'll find a spot to pull over until you can send some help. Block the exit into Pigeon Forge."

"They should be there in less than fifteen minutes. We'll have the road block up in ten. Is Marie okay?"

Ryker looked over at her. The scene was out of every teenage boy's dream—for that matter, every red-blooded man's.

She had her jeans to her knees, and blouse and bra up to her neck. One hand rubbed and thrust at her pussy while the other tugged at a turgid nipple.

"Damn." He released a shaky breath.

"What?" The worry in Jack's voice added fuel to Ryker's jealousy.

"Don't worry about Marie. I'll take care of her real good."

He pressed the off button and started looking for a flat area he could park on the one-lane road. Off in the distance, the red taillights of the Charger disappeared around a corner. After a mile, a place opened up; gravel lit up white by his headlights covered a small area on the side. Ryker pulled the Mustang over to the edge of the road and shut the engine and lights off. He hit the switch that controlled the interior lights, making sure they wouldn't turn on if a door opened and give their location away too soon.

He opened the door and moved around to Marie's side. She looked up, her eyes drooping from the hungry need to climax. In a barely restrained move, he pulled her out of the car, leaving behind her jeans. He sat her on the warm engine hood and spread her legs. Then his mouth covered her. Licking and sucking, filling his need to taste her. Nothing was sweeter. Her legs wrapped around his neck and her hips lifted each time his tongue swiped at the hard nub.

When he plunged two fingers into her moistness, she fell backward and arched into his touch. He nipped at her and set a rhythm, thrusting harder, wishing he could fill her with the hardness pressing against his zipper. A quiver he felt deep inside of her warned she was about to come.

He kissed her thigh and took a couple deep breaths. "Cover your mouth, love."

She pressed her arm against her lips.

He nuzzled her softness and dove in again. His mouth sucked the nub hard. The scream muffled by her arm came out as a groan into the darkness. Once the contractions slowed, he rested his head against her thigh and removed his fingers. Unable to resist, he licked his fingers.

"That is the sexiest thing I've ever seen." On her elbows, she lounged on the hood with her eyes glittering in the moonlight.

"When I get you back to Sector, we'll see what we can do about this." He patted her swollen nether lips as if it was a good pet. Inhaling her scent had him wanting more, but any movement caused his cock to ache and he needed a second to recoup.

"As in, take me to bed and do it right?"

His head rocked back and forth on her thigh. It felt right being this near her. Touching her without thought of what would happen to them next.

"No. As in seeing Doc and making you stop needing me like this," he said above a whisper.

Her gasp said he better move away before she took revenge on what was still hard beneath his jeans.

"Wait a minute and I'll get your pants and shoes." He'd just noticed her bare feet.

A few careful steps brought him to the car door and her clothes. One shoe was in the car and the other outside on the ground. As he started to help her pull up the jeans, she pushed him away with her foot.

"I can do it myself. I don't need your help. At this moment, I rather you didn't touch me."

He stood by helpless as she got dressed. Her hands shook so bad, he finally gave in and jerked her sneakers from her hands and slipped them on cold feet and tied the laces. Her lips stretched tight as she remained quiet for a few seconds more.

She sniffed and rubbed her arms. "I'm sorry that I'm such a pain to deal with."

"Don't say—"

At that moment, they heard a car's engine rev as it came around a far corner and down the straightway. Liam pulled up beside them. "Everything okay?"

Relieved he could skip explaining how he really felt, Ryker leaned into the window.

"Yeah." He pointed down the narrow road. "I have a feeling he's setting a trap. He probably hopes I'd follow him on down the way. If he doesn't come this way or out at the road block, you better wait until daylight and let the helicopter go in and see."

"Sounds good."

"I'm taking Marie back to Sector. Call me as soon as you find out something. I want that asshole." He slapped the top of the car as Liam took off a little further down the road.

Marie sat in the car with her head back and eyes closed when he slipped behind the steering wheel. During the ride back, she didn't say a word. He then understood the meaning of cutting tension with a knife. It was so thick that he had to crack the window to breathe.

He pulled into the underground garage and parked near

the elevator. Without wasting time, she jumped out of the car and slammed the door, rocking the car. He opened his mouth to say something and decided she had a right to be angry. She hadn't asked to be drugged, and she didn't really want him pawing her. The drug made her want him, no matter what she'd said.

Maybe after a good night's rest she'd feel better. Only he doubted it would help him.

"He's the most infuriating man I've ever met. Did I tell you that he hasn't once climaxed? Oh, he gets all hard and such, but I don't get his rocks off. I don't have what it takes." She kicked at a pillow that had the misfortune to be on the floor. "Obviously, he thinks I'm a big bother—"

"Mercy, woman! That's a little more information than Ryker would want me to know." Jack poured a cup of coffee and sat at the small table in the corner of her suite.

Marie stopped in front of the small buffet that had been set up on her return. She pushed back her wet hair. The shower had helped her feel human again. Considering she'd been up for twenty-four hours, she probably needed a little nourishment, though rest would do her more good at this point.

Jack was probably right. He looked so out of place with the feminine furniture, holding a delicate cup in his large hand. Desert camos and boots didn't go well with china and Queen Anne.

"Sorry. My nerves are about shot and I'm so woozy from lack of sleep that I don't know what I'm saying." Her face reddened as she thought of what had come out of her mouth. She settled in the chair opposite him.

Jack knew almost everything about her as they'd been friends for years.

Before Master had died, Jack had lived the summers at the former Main Sector in Atlanta, but the other seasons at the Northern Sector. She'd been lonesome as Ryker had been exiled to the Northern Sector by Master. At first, her friendship with Jack started out with her asking about Ryker and how he was faring. Jack kindly filled in her spare time with stories of a courageous Ryker training and fighting bad guys. On rare occasions over the years, she'd gotten to see Ryker, but Master always found an excuse to send him away until he was ordered back to confront his brother. The meeting hadn't gone exactly like Master had expected. Ryker killed him instead. Though violence sickened her, she'd wished many times she'd been there. Maybe seeing the ringleader of her nightmares dead would help her see the future a little clearer.

"Go. Get some rest before Doc shows up in the morning." Jack sat his cup down and stood. "I'll see you when you're ready to practice again. We can go over some new moves."

She frowned. Ryker had insisted the doctor examine her. If not for something about Ice and the woman he'd brought to Sector, Ryker would've marched her to Doc's suite in the mansion and woken him at the crack of dawn.

"Any moves she practices will be with me." Ryker strode across the room and leaned over and kissed her cheek.

She blinked up at him. How much of their conversation had he heard? Why was he being on his best behavior? And the biggie: did he actually kiss her cheek like a husband arriving home from work?

Jack lifted one pierced eyebrow and walked out.

"Why are you so rude to him all the time?"

"You need some rest. Go brush your teeth and get in bed."

Her spine straightened. "Go away. I don't feel like dealing with you right now." *Go and boss someone else.*

He crossed his arms and stared.

"Okay. Whatever." She threw up a hand and rolled her eyes as she stepped into the bathroom. Admitting to herself how much she enjoyed him being there, bossy or not, brought a smile to her lips.

Despite that, she took her time brushing her teeth, drying her hair, and doing everything else she could think of to delay returning to the other room. When she opened the door, Ryker was under the covers, on his side with his eye closed and black patch in place.

"You're not asleep. So don't even pretend." She fought back her grin.

What sane woman would not be excited by having a real live pirate in her bed? Especially, one who looked like Ryker. A lean build with muscled arms to hold her, and dark, thick hair to sink her fingers into as his mouth did wicked things to her body.

He raised his head and looked at her.

"I decided it would be best if I stay here with you."

"I'm not in the middle of having a flashback." She stopped next to the bed and almost pinched herself. He looked better than any battery-operated gizmo.

"Come on." He lifted the sheet. His boxer briefs were navy blue. "Quit staring. Just because I'm hard doesn't mean I expect anything."

Her gaze darted away. What was wrong with her? She never stared at a man like that before the drug screwed up her system.

Too tired to argue, she crawled in bed. Her body felt as heavy as an armor tank. Even with a foot between them, his heat warmed her back.

"Do you remember when you first came to Main Sector, you used to crawl into my bed at night? You claimed monsters were under yours." Ryker smoothed the sheet over her arm.

"Yeah. I hadn't lived with Master but a month before I found out you were a pushover for wet eyes."

"I did what I could to protect you."

"You were barely an adult. Master had all the power. He sent you away to New York not long after that."

"It was my fault. I should've fought harder for you."

Without turning, she reached behind her back and caught his hand, pulling it over her waist.

"It was my drug-addicted parents' fault for selling me to a pedophile for money to feed their habit."

"I should've stopped him." His rough voice was deep with regret.

She kissed his hand and closed her eyes. Regrets never had a place in her life. If she allowed them in, they would swallow her whole.

CHAPTER NINE

Marie woke when Ryker eased out of the bed. She looked at the red numbers on the clock. They'd slept for five hours. She could do with ten more. Her eyelids were heavy with needed sleep; she forced them to stay open.

"Go back to sleep. I'll wake you before Doc arrives." Ryker quietly pulled on his clothes and then glanced back at the bed. He tucked in his shirt and adjusted himself. His cock looked to be semi-hard.

She remembered waking earlier from a nightmare and Ryker pulling her close, holding her tight. All he'd done was kiss her shoulder and whisper, "Shh, you're okay. I'll keep you safe."

For a man to crawl in bed with a female and not—well, it felt good to be held and nothing more. She turned her back, trying to relax and gain a couple more hours of rest, even without his warmth.

Her mind refused to cooperate and shut down. His reminder about those first few months of living at the compound in Atlanta brought back memories of his kindness in soothing away her nightmares. Maybe that was when she first fell in love with him. What good would it do in admitting she still was? They were both damaged and really didn't know how to have a normal relationship.

Having sex while a synthetic drug upped her sex drive didn't make a relationship. She needed to concentrate on stopping the Wizard, obtaining an antidote, and then maybe rethink her role at The Circle.

"Would you like for me to leave?"

Ryker moved his gaze from the window to Jack. He gritted his teeth to hold back from saying how much he would like that. If only the man offered to leave Sector forever and not just the room.

"You can return to the OS anytime you want." So much for holding back.

"Maybe one day I will, but for now you need me here. Your concentration has been shit all day."

After flipping the blinds closed, Ryker pushed away from the window and turned toward the computer screen. "I have a lot on my mind. Tell me again what you've learned."

"Not much. Liam's in there now. We're hoping the two women will be more forthcoming. At first, Ice wasn't going to let us talk to the woman he hovered over, but we convinced him it was for his own good."

"Where is he now?"

"In cell three."

"Was that really necessary? You did tell him we only wanted info?"

Jack leaned his back against the office wall and crossed his arms. "Yeah. He wouldn't listen. It took ten guys to bring him down and three of them are with Doc now. One of them will be out of commission for a few weeks. His wrist and three ribs are broken."

Ryker grunted and nodded. "From what I've heard, Ice was being gentle."

"I'd hate to see him being rough."

"What about the other woman?"

"You're not going to believe this. She's Mikolas Savalas's kid."

"Damn, that's all we need is trouble from him and his brood." Ryker headed toward the door.

"Actually, this should help us. We've saved his daughter. He'll owe us."

Jack was right. Mikolas had connections all through the criminal community in the Southeast. Though Ryker didn't have much to do with pickpockets and thieves, they always had information he could use. Information often was more valuable than gold.

"As soon as we've finished questioning her, make arrangements to drop her off with Mikolas. Be sure he understands we'll expect repayment at a later date."

"She claims she's not going back home."

Ryker glanced over to Jack as they walked down the stairway to the interrogation rooms. "There's no choice. Make sure you hand her over to her father, not one of his men. I don't care if you have to tie her up and put a bow on her."

He opened the observation room's door and stopped. Marie stood inside listening to Liam question Katerina Savalas. Instead of concentrating on what the young woman was saying, Ryker couldn't take his gaze off Marie. She wore a simple green top and blue jeans. With her hair pulled back at the nape of her neck, she looked wholesome and beautiful and way too young to be involved with The Circle. Nothing on the exterior betrayed what her life had been like or what they had done hours ago.

Even reminding himself she was twenty-one, he still felt like a pervert as he wanted to shove her against the wall and sink into her. Would he ever have enough of her now that he knew what she felt like? That she tasted of sunshine and smelled like spring flowers?

Shouting and banging pulled his attention from Marie. He noticed Liam and Katerina looking at the door. Ice stood in the doorway of the interrogation room, his neon-blue hair in his face, his chest heaving, and a panicked look on his face.

"Where's Mai?"

"She's eating lunch." Liam slowly rose to his feet. "Is she your girlfriend?"

Ice shook his head. "No. *Imouto*."

"Ee— What?" Liam asked.

Ryker pressed the speaker button. "Liam, take Ice to his sister and check on his guards. They'll probably need Doc." He then turned to Jack, who had rushed in during all the shouting. "Don't you have an interrogation to do? Don't forget to take her back to her family. Make sure the old bastard knows he owes us. I'll have Liam listen to the recordings and give me a report."

"I haven't forgotten." Jack shot him a frown and left the room.

"What about Ice's sister?" Marie asked. She shifted her weight and crossed her arms.

The circles beneath her eyes confirmed she needed more rest, but Ryker sensed she would resent any suggestions concerning her in a bed.

After Doc had examined her that morning, he told them what they'd already suspected. The drug was weakening but would continue to cause her to act "irrationally" for some time. How much longer was anyone's guess. She needed the antidote. In the meanwhile, they were still working on something to help her body cope.

Damn, he needed answers on the Wizard's whereabouts. Someone had to know where he set up shop.

"We've finished questioning her. Ice can take her home." He watched as Jack sat across from the Savalas girl. She scooted back in the chair and wrinkled her nose as if she'd smelled rotten garbage.

"Were they shot up with the drug?" Marie's question was filled with concern.

"No. From what they said, and after Doc's examination, they hadn't been injected or dosed with anything. Ice's sister gave us a couple good leads though. But the other woman had a little more information, and we're hoping to confirm what she said." He nodded toward Katerina.

"Well, I need to see Charlie and now is as a good of a time as any. Let me know what you find out." Marie stepped around him toward the door. Charlotte Sweet, called Charlie in the garage she managed for The Circle, was her only female friend.

Ryker grabbed her arm and breathed in deeply her light

scent. No other woman smelled like her, like summer breezes. "You need some rest."

"I'm okay. Charlie called, worried about me. It'll do me some good to talk with her and relax."

"You know how I feel about—"

"That's your problem, not mine." She pulled her arm away from him and strode out the door.

Marie knocked on the apartment door marked C13 and waited for an answer. Ryker hated it when she spent time with Charlie. Who did he think he was? Charlie wouldn't get her in any more trouble than anyone else in the organization.

A woman with soft brown curls around her face peeked through the crack in the door as she opened it as far as the chain allowed. There was no crime in The Circle facility—who in their right mind would dare?—but Charlie had grown up in the slums of Atlanta and refused to leave her safety up to chance.

"Fuck, Marie. You have some crazy timing." Charlie, known as a wild woman, went through men as fast as gas through a 454 engine in a muscle car. Marie knew for sure that she had a heart of gold and was the *best* of friends.

"I can come back later."

"Shit, no. I forgot the time. Give me a second." She slammed the door.

Marie grinned. Not offended by her friend's behavior or language, she patiently waited. The deserted hallway was unusual. On most days the underground barracks for single Circle operatives were jam-packed with people coming from or going to their shifts. The same barracks she'd lived in until Ryker decided she needed to sleep near him. With that thought her skin prickled. She leaned against the wall and pressed a hot cheek to the cool sheetrock.

Then she heard voices inside Charlie's room. One voice was much deeper than the other.

The door opened and a half-clothed male stumbled into the hallway.

"Ah, damn, Charlie. I hoped to have another round of fun." The man dropped his shoes and jabbed his arms into the sleeves of his shirt. With his tousled chestnut hair in his eyes and well-defined abs, Marie remembered seeing him working out in the gym. He was one of the pilots for The Circle's helicopters.

"Yeah, yeah, yeah. Later, Tom. I'll make it up to ya." Charlie slid her hand down the man's bare chest and grabbed the waistband of his jeans and jerked. "You better be ready to keep up."

The man hissed. "Be careful. I'll keep up all night, baby. You tell me when."

She kissed him hard and then shoved him in the chest toward the stairwell.

Charlie turned toward Marie. "You look like crap. Come in and I'll fix you a margarita."

Marie watched Tom stagger away. Then she followed Charlie into her rooms.

Each set of rooms in this part of Sector consisted of a large living room–kitchen combination along with a bedroom and bath connected to it. Plenty of room for The Circle operatives as more time was spent on the job than off. If an operative wanted a little more room to stretch, the facility included exercise and game rooms with areas to relax and watch large screen televisions.

Marie made herself at home and sank into the sofa. Worn but in good repair, the leather sofa cupped her aching body. Charlie handed her a tumbler filled with her favorite drink before sinking into her own leather recliner. Before pushing her feet up, the mechanic lifted her butt and pulled a man's tighty-whities from under her, tossing them to the side.

"I told him grown men don't wear those ugly things." She grinned as she took a long swallow of her drink.

Thankfully, Marie didn't have a mouthful of drink when Charlie said that. They burst out laughing and then took several sips, letting a few quiet moments pass, grinning big at their own private thoughts. Marie liked Charlie for that reason. She didn't have to talk all the time. No driving need to fill in silence. They became friends two years ago when Jack brought her into the fold. Charlie had been beaten up pretty bad by some guys. What little Marie was told, they had claimed Charlie was unnatural in her talent for fixing anything mechanical. That was it. The men felt threatened by a woman's ability to do a better job than they did.

"How's it going, living in the mansion?" If not for Charlie's eyes sparkling with curiosity, Marie could write it down as interest in an old building. But knowing Charlie and her sex drive, she wanted to know about Ryker and his bedroom antics.

"I have my own bedroom and it's twice the size of your whole apartment." Marie said it more to pick on a friend than to do anything resembling bragging.

"You know what I meant. He's no Liam Kelly but with those scars, the man would have many layers worth pulling back."

Marie shook her head. Most times, Charlie acted carefree and relaxed with her sexuality, but bring Liam into the room and she became tongue-tied and bashful. She would look anywhere but at him.

"You've never told me why you won't look Liam in the face." If not for the drink, Marie doubted she would've ever asked her friend that question.

With a dreamy look in her eyes, she said, "It's stupid, really. He's so fucking beautiful. I feel so guilty for looking at him. Like I'm going to dirty him." Charlie looked at her axle-greased nails. "How would he feel being touched by a woman like me?" She ruffled her short curls. "I heard his ex-wife was beautiful. How could he look at a woman who dressed and looked like a boy?"

"Well, you don't look like one now." Marie referred to the short white T-shirt Charlie wore that outlined her perky breasts and showed off her flat stomach, and the skinny jeans that made her legs look longer than they were already. A pair of zipped- up work overalls covered her trimmed body most of the time. "You need to find a way for Liam to see you in your off-duty clothes. That would get his attention."

"I'm not Liam's type. Enough of me. Does the big hunk like it slow or fast? Rough or gentle? I bet he can pick you up and—" Marie blushed. "Hot shit. He did, didn't he? You're so lucky to be the height you are. Do you have any idea how few men can pick up a woman like me? It sucks being five feet and thirteen inches."

Marie choked on her drink. Charlie slapped her back. The help was almost as bad as choking.

"Stop. You're killing me."

"Sorry. I forget my own strength."

Marie chuckled, forgiving her. In an effort to change the subject back to Charlie's crush, she said, "I don't understand what you see in Liam anyway. He's such a player, going from one woman to another . . ." She covered her mouth, her face hot with embarrassment. Charlie's habit of going from one guy to another was as bad as Liam's womanizing. Only Marie guessed Charlie hoped to find a substitute for the man she really loved. Liam.

"Stuck your foot in it, didn't ya?" Charlie started laughing as hard as Marie.

"But you leave them happy. I don't know how you do it, but you're still friends with every one of them."

"It's a talent." She wiggled her long fingers. "These are not only talented in fixing any mechanical contraption made, but they can make a man want to slap his mama for not warning him about me."

Marie laughed so hard she rolled off the sofa. This was what she needed, a few minutes of hanging out with a friend. One who knew everything there was about protecting herself. No one messed with Charlie.

CHAPTER TEN

Marie leaned over the book and sighed.

"What are you reading?" Jack closed the door behind him.

She slammed it shut and shoved it between the sofa cushions.

"You shouldn't be reading something you're ashamed of." Jack teased.

"I'm not. Ashamed, that is. What are you doing here? It's not time for my taekwondo lessons."

"Actually, it is."

She looked at the clock and sure enough, it was a quarter past one. Time had slipped away while she read. Even before being sold to Theo, her parents were too involved in partying and getting high to remember to send her to school often. Then Theo preferred she stay ignorant. He'd said education was wasted on women, but thankfully she had a knack for picking up the nuances of reading. Marie always wanted to read the romances she'd seen in magazines. She'd worked hard and now was a voracious reader, though certain words slowed her down.

She ordered them online and had them delivered to a local mailbox service. The beautiful women looked so exotic and happy in the arms of such muscular men. Ryker could easily pose for one of the book covers. Maybe a pirate story.

Luckily, not being a great reader didn't hurt her job. Keying information into the computer in the Crypt was easy. She guessed Bryan suspected she had difficulty, as he always gave her the easier tasks. Her handwriting did look like a child's.

"It won't take me but a minute to change." Flustered by her tardiness, she tripped and caught herself as she was heading for her bedroom.

When she returned, Jack's head was bent over the book. What did he think of the notes she'd written on the side? There were so many words she didn't quite understand until she looked them up. She liked to write a short explanation in the margin.

"A romance novel. I'm surprised, Marie." One pierced eyebrow rose as he silently read.

"There's nothing wrong with romances. They have happy endings. The world doesn't have enough of those." Hands on her hips, she dared him to make fun of her.

"With the life you had, I'm glad to know you haven't given up on happy endings." He closed the book and sat it cover-up on the end table. "Don't ever be ashamed of believing in love. Nothing's wrong with it at all."

"I rather you didn't say anything to Ryker. You know, about the reason I write in the books."

He looked at her for a few tense seconds. "It's yours to tell." In the usual Jack style, he ruffled her hair. "Come on. Let's go and practice."

She closed her mouth with a snap and followed. She'd never realized until now how much of a softy Jack was despite his gruff exterior.

"Your patterns have improved a lot." Jack referred to the series of taekwondo moves used for practice.

Marie fought her grin as she moved her hands down into double fists at belt level, the chunbi position of readiness. Jack had told her many times, it was best to look solemn during her lessons. Otherwise, when it came time to use her moves for defense and she smiled, the bad guys would attack, thinking her to be an easy target. Crazy, but it made sense.

Jack followed along, occasionally slapping her arm or leg to correct an error, or grunting as a sign of approval. Then she stopped with one fist enclosed by the other hand at waist level, and gave Jack a quick bow.

"You're getting better every day." He tossed her a towel and took one for himself. "Have you practiced with the Sig Ryker gave you?"

"This morning." Marie wanted to ask where Ryker was yesterday and last night. He hadn't checked on her. She'd slept alone and missed his warmth. Chances were he wasn't far. He'd promised enough times to be nearby if the drug kicked in again.

"Good. Ryker was right. Until you master this, a gun will come in handy." Jack nodded, leaving the room and heading toward the showers.

"Maybe I've misjudged him."

Marie squealed and turned around. "You scared me."

Ryker stood on the other side of the mats. Arms crossed over his chest and a scowl on his face, his usual expression along with his standard jeans and dark T-shirt.

"Go. Clean up and change. They brought in the nerd. I want you listening in."

No doubt in her mind who he meant. She had some questions of her own to ask the asshole who gave her the drug that was making her life crazy.

In less than thirty minutes, she exited her suite to find Ryker waiting for her in the hallway. First he'd disappeared for a day and night and then he returned with a prisoner and immediately sought her out, demanding she listen to the interrogation. His hot and cold attitude shouldn't bother her. He'd used the same one for years. But it still drove her nuts.

Although they had shared an intimacy beyond the sex, a closeness they'd never experienced with anyone else, he constantly worked to keep her at arm's length. They had a shared past. She swallowed to erase the tightness in her throat. Well, he could tough it out. He needed her in ways he didn't realize. He needed a woman who understood where he was from and how he deserved to be loved. And besides, she needed him too.

They walked side by side to the end of the hall. He pulled on a lamp jutting from the wall. A section slid to the side, revealing an elevator. Marie loved the old mansion and all its hidden passageways. She'd been told that at one time the mansion belonged to a bootlegger. She stepped to the side and held on to the rail. They rode in silence down to the cell area.

The door slid open. In front of them a narrow passageway

stretched out to what appeared to be infinity under the dim lighting. Only the occasional buzzing from fluorescent lights broke the quietness. The burning sensation of a cleanser assaulted her nose instead of the expected musky scent of dampness of an underground detention facility. By the time they walked several yards, Marie regretted going along with his newest demand. An eerie feeling trickled down her back. Creepy didn't quite describe the atmosphere.

They turned into another passageway and all hell broke loose. They heard shouting and smoke billowed from an open doorway.

"Get behind me," Ryker said, pushing her to the side. He bent down and pulled out a gun from his ankle holster. They moved to the side, waiting for whoever was inside to come out.

What happened to those inside?

More shouting and three shots echoed from the room. Someone screamed in pain. Then the walls shook and darker billows of smoke rolled into the passageway. Rocks and pebbles pinged against the opposite wall.

Marie fell against the wall with Ryker covering her. A few seconds passed and someone groaned in the other room.

"Are you okay?" He brushed at her hair and sprinkles of white dust made her sneeze.

"Yeah." She sneezed again. "You okay too?"

He nodded and looked into her eyes as if he wanted assurance she was telling him the truth. Then he turned his attention to the room where the explosion had come from, his gun aimed at any potential attackers.

"Jack! Liam! Are you all right?" Ryker edged a little closer to the door. He glanced at Marie and jerked his head for her to stay against the wall.

Then a shadow emerged from the smoke.

"It's Jack." Marie grabbed Ryker's arm.

"Damn it!" Ryker clasped her hand. "Don't ever do that. It could get us killed."

"I thought you were going to shoot him." Red-faced, Marie kicked him in the shin. "I'll do that instead."

"This isn't the time to act like a child." Ryker's aim remained steady.

"I know. You just make me so mad sometimes," she stated. He had to understand, she needed to express her feelings or she might as well call him Master.

Ryker shook his head and returned his attention to Jack. "What the hell's going on in there?"

Jack dabbed at the cut on his lip with a dust-covered sleeve and winced. His left eye was nearly swollen shut. He swayed and steadied himself by placing a hand on the wall.

"Billy's dead. I have no idea where those guys came from, but they must've broken into the air shaft because they popped out of the vents. They hit Liam in the head and beat the shit out of me until I couldn't stand. They surrounded Billy and yelled, 'This is for Katerina.' Then they shot a full round into him." He stopped talking long enough to spit blood out of his mouth. "Then they blew up the shaft after they climbed back into it." In the time Jack explained what had happened, his left cheek purpled and grew twice its size. A gash on his forehead had painted the right side of his face red.

At that moment, five guards came running down the passageway toward the cell.

"What the fuck took you so long to get here?" The artery in Ryker's neck bulged.

Marie had never seen him so angry. She gingerly stepped around fist-sized rocks littering the floor and looked into the cell. What was left of the skinny nerd was covered by powder from the falling walls. She moved to check on Liam. He still had a pulse. About that time, Doc came running in with an EMT behind him. She moved out of the way.

Strangely, air still flowed from the shaft they blew up. She guessed it was outside air being sucked through the destroyed vent by the open door.

"Some fucking top-secret compound we're running here when any-damn-one can come in and kill a fucking prisoner of ours and get the fuck away!" Hands on hips, Ryker continued to curse as Doc helped the men load Liam up on a gurney and take him out of the demolished cell.

"You handed her off to Mikolas, not her brothers?"

"Except for a couple gun-toting thugs who looked nothing like her or her dad, he was alone. She was pissed when I threw her at her dad's feet."

"At his feet?"

Jack waved off the nurse, refusing to have the cut on his forehead cleaned and bandaged.

"I had to tie her up and gag that infuriating, smartass mouth of hers."

"You what?"

"She refused to go and I had no other choice."

"I'm surprised they didn't shoot you too."

"What makes you think that?"

"Her brothers are mean as hell, but smart. No one treats their sister like that and lives."

"Shit. I'd hate to be the guy to date her."

"If you want to keep your dick between your legs, you'll stay away from her." Ryker kicked a rock out of the way. "I've heard if her brothers don't cut it off, she will, and then pickle it."

"Be still my beating heart. Danger in a woman is the best aphrodisiac."

"You're as dumb as you look." Ryker shook his head.

Marie jabbed Ryker in the shoulder. "Quit acting ugly."

His amber eye widened. When she continued to glare at him for his rudeness, Ryker briefly grinned before moving away to chew out someone else.

Her heart thumped. Even during a setback with all that anger inside, he could smile at her. The man surprised her at every turn.

"You're good for him," Jack whispered.

"How's that?" Considering how Ryker half the time acted like he thought she was in the way and the rest of the time like she was an obligation to endure, she disagreed.

"I've seen him smile more in the last week than the whole time I've known him."

"That's hard to believe," she said.

"You know all those stories I used to tell you?"

She nodded. "Yeah. I remember."

"You know how Master punished those who didn't follow orders by sending them to the Northern Sector?"

"Yes." What was he trying to get at?

"While there, we were expected to train and work from sunup to sundown. In upstate New York, I can tell you the winters were a frozen hell. If we didn't do as we were told, we often found ourselves locked in a cold cell without food for a few days. It wasn't fun."

"I knew Master was angry and wanted to punish him, but I had no idea. He was with me one day and then the next gone. You were the only one I could get to tell me anything." She hated thinking back to that time. She'd been so lonely and afraid. Jack had tried to be her friend, but Master rarely let her out of his sight as she grew older.

"Ryker never told you?"

"Told me what?" Like Ryker talked to her since taking over The Circle. More like ordered her around and mostly argued with her.

Jack rubbed his hand over his shaved head. "I probably shouldn't tell you this, but Master was upset when he caught you in Ryker's bed."

"It wasn't like that. He never touched me. He treated me like a little sister. For goodness' sake, he slept on top of the covers. He was nice. I was scared. The things Master made me do . . . well, I had nightmares a lot back then. Still do."

Jack stared at her for a second and then said, "Don't we all."

CHAPTER ELEVEN

Marie shut her bedroom door. A single light next to the bed gave off a soft glow. She didn't remember leaving it on. She and Charlie had forgotten the time and stayed out later than usual for a weeknight. Starting her shift at six in the morning placed a crimp in her social activities, and most of those were with Charlie.

She hadn't seen Ryker in days. Between the breach in security and the ongoing search for the Wizard, he'd been too busy to boss her around. And thankfully, the few flashbacks she had were handled easily by herself. Doc claimed they could vary and could possibly fade away with time. He just wasn't sure how much longer.

Needing something other than sex and Ryker on her mind, she worked at improving her aim and practiced her taekwondo patterns with Jack, whenever he could get away from his boss.

She glanced at the light again. Shaking off the odd feeling, she tossed her purse on a chair. Maybe the maid left it on.

As she walked further into the suite, she realized someone was in her shower. The running water stopped. Unable to move, she stared at the bathroom door until seconds passed and it opened. Ryker stood in front of her with only a towel wrapped around his hips and the patch over his eye. Did he shower with it on? To think of it, the times he'd been in her bed, he'd worn it.

"Is your shower broke?" She bit her bottom lip. The scars along his ribs didn't take away from the beauty of his well-toned body. Her gaze roamed over his broad chest and followed the slight sprinkling of hair to the towel's edge. She'd heard it called a happy trail. She totally understood now.

"How are you feeling?" he asked.

Crossing her arms, she moved over to the seating area—anywhere away from the bed—and she sat on the edge of the sofa.

"I'm fine."

"Marie."

She looked up. Half of his face was in the shadows. She'd heard the story. He'd been only eleven when Theo had taken him away from his parents' burning car. Being young probably saved him, but it had scarred him inside and out so badly. Only a person with a strong will at that age could survive losing loved ones and the sight from one eye.

"You confuse the crap out of me." Had those words come out of her mouth?

She'd wanted to act cool. Had he been avoiding her again? It had been nearly three weeks after the explosion since she talked directly to him. The chicken-hearted turkey had ordered Jack to pass on his messages and demands. Mainly, he told her to let him know if she needed his "services." Services! She wasn't a car in need of a tune-up.

"How's that?"

She huffed and shook her head. "You can't even take the time out to talk to me yourself but then you show up like . . . like that!" She waved her hand toward his towel doing a poor job of hiding his arousal. "I haven't called you. I don't need your services." The last she almost spit at him.

"I had my reasons." His hand dropped to the towel.

Well aware of how crazy she sounded, she couldn't help it. His nonchalant attitude bothered her. "I don't care to hear it. So keep that on and pick up your clothes and leave."

She wanted him out. Living in the mansion with him was concession enough. She didn't need any more of his sympathy. At least that was what she repeated to the mirror each night.

One end of the towel slipped, hanging onto his cock before he swept it to the side, letting the cloth fall to the floor. Oh, my, he was beautiful. Every delicious inch. There wasn't anything God created more wonderful than a man who took good care of himself. Muscles shifting with each movement as skin rippled across defined abs.

Unable to move, she felt hypnotized by the sway of his cock as he slowly walked across the room. She remembered well how long he could remain hard and what he could do with it. Her fascination was natural. And Dr. Freud was only half right about every woman wanting one. She just wanted hers attached to a man. Preferably Ryker.

That hard part of him touched her first and before she knew it, she had a beautifully naked man holding her. She inhaled the scent of soap and clean virile man. Was there a better smell in this world?

With her cheek pressed to his chest, she heard the rumble of his voice. "I'm trying to find that bastard. You need the antidote. We have no idea what else the drug will do to you."

Familiar warmth travelled up from her groin over her torso. She brushed her lips across one male nipple. He hissed. Her tongue swiped at the beaded tip.

"Is that the only reason you're here?" She lifted her eyes to his, her cheek remaining on his chest.

His amber eye looked down at her, his face softened.

"I'm here to help you. You're being stubborn. You know I can satisfy you better than any toy you own. I never could resist a damsel in distress."

She closed her eyes and inhaled his scent one last time. Palms pressed to his heated skin, she pushed off him and moved away. He released her without a struggle.

"Why? Why now? Did you find out something new?"

Everything inside her was screaming at him. She wanted him to come to her for the same reason any man came to a woman. He wanted her. Yet Ryker only felt sorry for her, wanted to help her relieve herself. She straightened her shoulders and faced him. "Whatever is planned, I'm a part of it."

"I thought you wanted to continue your lessons with Jack."

"Don't be that way. You know I need to keep busy. I've been working wherever you let me here, but I want to do more. You disappeared. I had no idea when you'd be back."

"You only had to call."

"Quit!" He was driving her crazy with his one-path mind.

"You know why I didn't. Until you're willing to be more than a cock to me, I think we should concentrate on finding the Wizard and nothing more."

He crossed his arms. Why was he even sexier angry? She glanced down. And her rejection of his offer hadn't lessened his excitement.

"You're not trained for this," he said.

"What kind of training do I need? I'll get it. What are you planning?"

"Jack and Liam are going in as potential buyers of Club Rachael."

"Then I'll go with them"

"Hell, no."

She crossed her arms. "Why are they going in pretending to buy the club? I take it something suspicious came up about the place." He was crazy if he thought she'd given up on this.

"Turns out, the guy, Mike Mulcahy, who owns the club where most of the girls were last seen, also owns the house in Gatlinburg through his company, Lone Pavilion Industries. The company is based in New York City. Lone Pavilion is involved with the local Japanese *yakuza*."

"But this is Tennessee."

"That's part of what we can't figure out. Why is he here? What's his connection to the Wizard?" Ryker stepped into her closet. "Why did he buy two nightclubs so far from home base and in the same small city? And how in the hell did an Irishman get involved with a *yakuza*?"

"Two?"

"Yep. He also owns the Rocket. The paperwork shows a

man named John Smith but when we looked closer, it was Lone Pavilion Industries. Again, Mulcahy."

"John Smith? Not very original." Marie craned her neck to see what he was doing in her closet. "Why would he hide the fact he owns the other club?"

"That's why I don't want you anywhere near him. He's an unknown threat."

She moved to the side and looked inside. One section of the closet that had been empty before now held several dark T-shirts and pressed jeans on hangers. The see-through shelves were filled with underwear and socks. He'd moved in without asking her permission.

"I have the largest stake in this," she said in her huffiest tone.

Unsure of how she should feel about his invasion, she turned away, refusing to watch him dress. She heard a drawer open and close. Before she realized it, she peeked. Except for more scars, he was beautiful even from the back. Buttocks tight and shoulders wide, he bent over to step into his boxers. She swallowed a gasp. She'd never seen a man's cock from this angle. Erotic, to say the least.

"Marie, if you don't stop staring, I'll give you an up-close and personal tour."

Face flaming red, she marched into the bathroom and slammed the door.

Ryker chuckled. He'd started to feel like a fool, bending over until she turned around. She thought she didn't need him, but he knew better. He wanted to make sure she had a mental picture of what she was missing out on.

Hell, what was he thinking? For that matter, what was he doing? Theo had always thought he knew what was best for everyone else. Ryker stared at his trembling hand. Just the thought of turning out like that maniac scared the shit out of him. A normal hand brushed over the scars running from his pinky to his shoulder. If he wanted, a few more surgeries could disguise some of the worse ones. But what was the use? They matched the scars he had inside.

He snapped the waistband of his boxers and jerked a shirt off a hanger.

Time for him to give in to Marie. He hated admitting defeat, but he suspected she would do what she wanted. She'd handled herself rather well at the cabin and didn't panic. At least this way he could plan the operation and protect her, better than letting her go all willy-nilly.

Willy-nilly? A favorite word of his mom's. He shut his eyes for a few seconds. In his mind's eye, he saw her in the sunshine, opening the curtains, telling him it was time for school. "Good morning, this morning! No more lollygagging around. Upsy daisy!" He rubbed the ache in the middle of his chest. She had so many funny sayings. Some days his childhood felt like a fantasy. Collin had been a great playmate. They never felt a need to compete against each other like other brothers. Not until his parents died and Theo separated them, telling Collin he was dead, while telling Ryker that Collin was trying to take everything away from him, that he resented his older brother. He shook his head and pulled up his jeans.

Theo and all his lies.

Maybe he needed to give his brother the benefit of doubt, a chance to prove he could be trusted.

He didn't have time for regrets. The operation needed his full attention. By allowing Marie to participate, he could keep a close eye on her and be there if she needed him. Never would he allow her to suffer because of his inattention or mistakes.

He twisted the bathroom door handle. "Marie, open up." Any thought of using his shoulder to bust down the door was shoved to the side. The old home had thick oak doors in every room and unless he wanted a dislocated shoulder, he'd be patient. "If you still want to be part of the operation, you need to be ready to go over the plans at 0600 hours. Conference room two." He waited for a few seconds.

"Okay. Now go away." She sniffed.

Damn. He didn't mean to make her cry. Undecided, he stood staring at the pattern of the wood.

"Go away, Ryker. I hear your breathing."

He pressed his hand to the door and bowed his head and nodded. Then he walked away.

CHAPTER TWELVE

Marie's body hummed the same beat as the music in Club Rachael. The underlying tingle worried her. She recognized the feeling. Now wasn't the time for the drug to kick in. The last time it had hit, she'd struggled for over an hour to find her release with the help of her plastic-encased boyfriend. Besides, it wasn't like she could excuse herself to go to the bathroom and take care of the problem.

"Liam, you're supposed to be acting like a professional businessman. So keep your fucking hands off Marie's butt." Ryker's voice pounded into her skull.

The small two-way receivers inserted in their ears gave Ryker's raspy drawl an unearthly sound. And hearing his voice was enough to make her thighs clench. Liam's attempt to piss off Ryker had nothing to do with the drug ramping up her body's needs.

"Hey, boss, I need to look the part. If I'm a high roller with a rep for walking on the edge, I would be all over my young lady." Liam winked at her.

"Don't make me come in there and wipe the floor with your

*ass. Pay attention. Mulcahy's pulled up and is heading toward
the service door.*"

They'd been told he had an emergency and would return
before midnight. Then he'd see them. He'd turned down
Liam's offer for the club but accepted his proposal to talk
about it. Less than fifteen minutes later, a refrigerator-sized
man stopped near them.

"Mr. Mulcahy will see you now."

Marie stood with Liam.

"The woman stays here," the big man said.

"Considering he's getting his funds from me, that wouldn't
be such a good idea." Marie fluttered her eyelashes at the big
guy.

"That's my girl. She doesn't back down." Liam kissed her
hard and loud.

"*Damn it, Marie. That's not what we rehearsed. I knew I
shouldn't have let you go with him. Liam, get your mouth off her
and find a way to salvage this. Both of you, get back to the fucking
plan.*"

"For Christ's sake, take a chill pill," Marie whispered.

"What did you say?" The big guy stepped closer.

"I was telling my lover that it's a little chilly in here." Marie
gave him a wide-eyed look of innocence.

When the big guy looked her over, his gaze lingered over
her chest. The dress they insisted she wear was no bigger than
a handkerchief. With her breasts nearly hanging out, her hard
nipples stood at attention from the increased tingling. Once
they left, she could take care of her problem, but in the meanwhile, she'd be in hell controlling what her body screamed it
wanted. It was as if her nerves—or whatever it was that had

gone haywire—knew he wasn't Ryker and that helped a little.

"Go through the door on the left. You'll be shown to the boss's office."

Liam placed an arm over her shoulders. She struggled with her smile, trying to maintain the air of a couple immersed in each other. He opened the door and looked inside. At the other end of the hall stood a man as wide as the door he guarded. He looked almost identical to the other one. The door behind them slammed shut and silence weighed heavy.

"Mr. Mulcahy is waiting for you." The man towered even over Liam and eyed her with a mixture of interest and distrust.

He opened the door and they entered a room that would look perfect in an Englishman's cottage. Leather-bound books lined a couple walls. A small sofa and matching overstuffed chairs arranged in front of an unlit fireplace invited guests to make themselves at home. The dim lighting cast shadows in the corner where a large desk sat facing the door.

The squeak of metal on metal alerted them that someone sat in the desk chair. A light snapped on over the desk. Mulcahy wore a black-on-black suit with a red tie. His coal-black hair cut short showed off almond-shaped eyes. Half Irish and half Japanese? That was the possible answer to how an Irishman could be involved with the Japanese mafia.

Another movement behind the desk chair caused Liam to straighten up and step in front of her. No one possessed such blue hair. Ice Takahashi stood near Mulcahy with his arms crossed and his eyes unreadable. Was he working undercover for Ryker's brother or had he turned traitor?

"Ah, Mr. Kelly, now what can I do for you and The Circle

this dreary evening?" The Irish lilt sounded strange coming out of a man with such exotic features. Mulcahy leaned forward and folded his hands on the desk. The smirk on his handsome face revealed how much he enjoyed Liam's discomfort.

"The Circle? I'm not sure of what you mean." Liam said with a bit of his own Irish lilt, betraying his concern as he ignored the man's use of his actual last name.

Marie eased to the side. She appreciated Liam's protective gesture, but she was determined not to cower. Something flickered in Ice's dark eyes. In the years of treading on the edge of life and death while she lived with Master, she'd learned to read subtle movements and between the lines. He appeared irritated with seeing her. When he turned his attention away from her, he glared at Liam as if he blamed her companion for her presence. Was she reading everything wrong?

"No need to play coy with me, Liam Kelly. Indeed logistics and security are your specialties for your new master." Mulcahy's cold black eyes watched her show of bravado. "Hello, my pretty. Where did you pop from?"

She lifted her chin. If he knew Liam was a Circle operative, she doubted he would believe anything she said.

"You've trained her quite well. I hate it when women believe their opinion is worth listening to." He tilted his head. "Are you a new recruit?"

"Leave her alone. She has nothing to do with this."

"Ah, it's like that now, is it? You want to protect her." He stood and walked around the desk. "It's not love but something else. Is it only because you're a gentleman and believe in protecting the wee woman? Maybe more." He rubbed his chin and tilted his head the other way. "Are you fucking her? No? She appears the type who must be in love for an old brute like you to get between her lily-white thighs. Such a tiny bit. I like them small and energetic. So what could it be? I love puzzles, and I'm very good at figuring them out."

"We need information." Liam moved in front of Mulcahy, blocking his view of Marie.

"What in the hell are you doing, Liam?" Ryker's voice caused Marie to jump. Thankfully Mulcahy didn't notice, but Ice lifted one eyebrow. She'd completely forgotten the receiver in her ear. Her face heated.

"Isn't that easy," Mulcahy said. "I'm guessing your new master is nearby and listening to this conversation!" His voice rose with each word.

"I have no master." Liam balled his hands into fists. They'd been patted down minutes before Mulcahy had shown up. So their guns and knives had been left at Sector.

Liam cursed but didn't move.

She'd never seen Liam lose his temper.

"You're not second-in-command. So does Jack Drago tell you what to do? I heard your wife was good at taking orders from him. In fact, that she begged to suck his cock on a regular basis until he kicked her out of his bed."

A deep, ache-filled yell emerged from Liam as he reached for Mulcahy. At the same time, Ice dove over the desk and shoved Liam, sending him against the far wall. Mulcahy leaned back, arms crossed, watching the two men fight.

Ryker screamed orders over the receiver as Liam jumped up and knocked Ice off his feet. Ice attacked full force, his hands and feet moving in a blur. Liam kicked out but his foot slammed into a piece of furniture on the way up. His height was at a disadvantage. The solid thud of flesh hitting flesh filled the small space, turning her stomach. Afraid one of the men would swing too wide and hit her, she moved back and searched for a weapon to help.

Then meaty hands grabbed her shoulders. She looked up into beady eyes belonging to one of Mulcahy's gargantuan guards. Before a scream could escape, his ham-like fist crashed into the side of her face. Stars flashed in front of her. As darkness pulled her under, she heard Ryker shouting in her ear, *"I'm on my way, Marie."*

She mumbled, "Too late."

Marie rolled to her side. Shooting pain travelled from her temple and down to her jaw. What happened? Sure wasn't a hangover. Except for a few beers or a margarita with Charlie, she never drank enough to cause her head to ache as if it would fall off. She peeked between her eyelashes to check her clock.

Deep red silk curtains covered a large window. An enormous mirror against one wall and a round one above reflected the bed. Red satin sheets covered the mattress with a darker red comforter thrown at the bottom. The ebony furniture had an oriental design that somehow made the red darker and more sinister. The abundance of red felt like sitting in a blood-covered room. Not a good sign at all.

She sat up and dug her fingers into the mattress. Dizzy and feeling sick, she rubbed her eyes and smoothed down her hair. A cool breeze brushed her skin. What in the world? She looked down. Where had the red nightgown come from? Her nipples appeared to be a dark red beneath the material. Her stomach churned. Who'd dressed her? Or even more horrifying, who'd undressed her?

When a huge man opened the door and moved to the side for a smaller man to enter, everything came back to her. She brushed at her right ear. The receiver was gone.

"Good morning, Ms. Beltane. It took a wee bit of research to find information about you." Michael Mulcahy wore a red polo shirt and black slacks. Christ, did the man know no other colors?

He did look good with his tanned skin and toned muscles. The words "lean" and "mean" came to mind.

His eyes, so dark and bottomless, gave her chills. She rubbed the bumps off her arms. The movement felt wonderful. Her palms slid toward her breasts. Oh, crap! The drug decided to go to the second stage while she was knocked out. She grabbed the sheet and curled her fingers into it. Raising the cloth above her breasts, she covered what he'd probably already seen.

Without hesitation, he rested a hip on the edge of the bed.

"Why are you interested in me?" She hoped The Circle had done a better job of hiding info on her than they had Liam.

Mulcahy skimmed a finger down her bare arm. She leaned toward him. Horrified, she jerked away and scooted toward the headboard, as far from him as possible. Her body started to shake like a junkie needing a fix. Tears welled in her eyes.

"I recognized the symptoms. Dilated eyes, light glistening on your skin, sensitivity to touch, and"—he sniffed—"and the delightful musty smell of sex is the key. Who shot you up with Blossom Flower? Is that how The Circle controls their female operatives nowadays?"

Disgusted with him and her own reactions, she slid out of the bed, taking the sheet and wrapping it around her to face Mulcahy.

He'd risen too and his grin changed to a full smile. She imagined a shark would show as many teeth before clamping down.

"You better let me go."

"Is this where the damsel in distress claims I'll regret it?"

"That's right."

"Who will save you, Ms. Beltane?"

"I don't need a man to save me." She began easing toward the door as she kept him in sight.

"Brave words for a woman alone with a man in his bedroom. A woman who is under the influence of a powerful aphrodisiac drug." He lowered his chin and voice. "Who will save you?"

His exotic eyes and lilting accent were intoxicating, but she sensed underestimating him could get her killed.

"You sure do act as if you know a lot about the subject. Are you the one they call the Wizard? Did you develop it?"

He chuckled and began tracking her around the bedroom. "If only I was a genius. No. I merely supply the Wizard with the means and—ah, you knew it wasn't me. You only wanted information and I just provided you with that. You're a clever woman." His deadly stare warned her that he didn't care for clever women. "Maybe I should test the drug's control and see if I can make you hungry for my touch."

From the way his gaze ran over her, it wouldn't take much to encourage him. Regardless of how much her body hummed, the thought of letting him touch her made her want to gag. Though tempted, she knew throwing a fit wouldn't solve anything.

Marie jumped when someone knocked on the door.

"What?" he shouted. His long fingers rubbed his chest as he watched her.

Ice opened the door. He glanced her way and then centered his attention on Mulcahy. "The operatives from the OS are here."

The OS. Ryker's brother, Collin, led the organization. In fact, for years, the two organizations fought until Theo was killed. Since then the brothers worked at keeping the peace. Collin owed her. She'd saved his and his wife's lives at one time. Which of his operatives had business with Mulcahy?

Maybe if she could alert them, they'd help. Then again, whatever the OS was up to could spell more trouble for The Circle, and she would be in the middle of it. Though the brothers tried to get along with each other, it was a thin layer of gentility.

Ice had been with the OS. Was he still? She looked pleadingly toward the stone-faced man.

"Good. Be sure our guests are served coffee and the honey buns that Cook baked this morning." As soon as the door closed, Mulcahy pressed her to the wall. "If I had the time . . ." He leaned down and kissed her throat as his long fingers cupped a breast.

A rush of pleasure surged through her and she arched her back. Oh, God, no! She couldn't let this happen. Remembering her lessons, she pushed her whole body toward him. The unexpected movement propelled him backward and his foot caught on the edge of a rug. He landed on the floor.

Without wasting time, she jerked open the door and ran into the hallway.

CHAPTER THIRTEEN

"How's that nose coming along?"

Ryker hands squeezed Bryan's tensed shoulders. The man turned his head. Green and blue streaks underlined his eyes. After having his nose broken by Ryker and set the next day by Doc, his recovery was slow moving.

"Fine. I can breathe out of the right side now." The wary tone caused Ryker to hold his chuckle. He'd learned some smartasses like Bryan needed a lesson in fear before they understood he meant what he said. The man would in no way endanger Marie's life again.

Ryker looked around at all of the men and women working in the bullpen toward one goal, finding Marie. He wanted to know what was taking so long to find her. They had the capability to locate a rogue camel carrying explosives in the middle of the Sahara desert; why couldn't they find one small woman?

"What have you found so far?" Ryker gritted his teeth as he slapped the man on the back. Even though they had four men outside the club while Liam and Marie were inside, they hadn't seen her leave. Mulcahy's car had been parked outside. Ryker had completed their interrogation moments ago. He was certain the men would be looking for another organization to work for before long if he allowed them to live.

Bryan coughed and then said, "We still have no idea where she could be."

Without realizing he'd done so, Ryker lifted Bryan by the collar. "That's not the answer I want. It's been over twenty-four hours, and the longer it takes, odds drop steeply on any chance of finding her."

"Boss, maybe you need to let Bryan go. Otherwise, if you put him in a coma, he can't trace this locator." Jack slid a sheet of paper across the desk next to the keyboard Bryan's fingers trembled over.

"Locator? Marie has a locator?" Ryker released the man. Truthfully, he was ashamed of his actions toward the poor man, but knowing Marie needed him and he couldn't get to her drove him crazy. Everything about her drove him to extremes.

"Just like you and me and even poor old Bryan here." Jack slapped his back. Bryan flinched and turned pale.

"She wasn't an operative. Why would the old . . . yeah. He was an old paranoid asshole. I could see him doing that to her." Ryker guessed Theo had done it not long before he died. An ex-mistress of Theo's had worked with the OS to bring him down. If Theo had tagged all of his women with a locator, she'd been dead long before going to the other side.

"He had a good reason for being paranoid." His second-in-command raised one pierced eyebrow.

Ryker ignored his jab. No need to go over his reasons for

killing Theo. It had to be done and everyone had expected it to happen eventually. The old asshole hadn't suffered enough. A sword between the ribcage and into his heart was too quick. Pedophiles deserved to die more painfully and slowly, sliced up piece by piece, starting with their cocks.

"Get the coordinates now or I'll be pulling my foot from your sphincter in ten seconds!" Ryker stood over Bryan as the man pounded on his keyboard so fast his fingers blurred.

Fear loosened its grip in Ryker's chest for a moment. He knew it would tighten again as he moved closer to her location. What would he find? Mulcahy obviously took her for a reason. From what Liam could tell before he was taken in for surgery, Mulcahy had no idea she was a Circle operative. Liam made sure to confirm he'd picked her up off the street as a cover. His gamble of expecting Mulcahy would let her go had failed.

"Is it true what Liam said about Ice?"

Ryker cut his gaze over to Jack. "Yeah. But I believe there has to be more. Collin wouldn't break the peace over drug money." He didn't go into how Liam was acting strange.

"I agree. It's because of Mulcahy's backing that this drug is out there. Ice's sister was almost pulled into it." Jack shook his head. "No way would he side with Mulcahy. Ice was working undercover. I can contact Rex and see what's happening."

"No. We don't need his help." Ryker crossed his arms.

"But—"

"No. This is Circle business."

"Boss! I got it!" Bryan clicked on the keyboard some more. "I've fed the info into your cell phone and aboard the Spirit."

"Jack, call the helipad and tell them we're leaving in five."

Ryker knew it would be more like ten minutes before they left but everyone would work faster. "Have Tom pull a team and be ready in three."

He heard people scrambling behind him as they pulled equipment vouchers to hand out weapons.

"I've already pulled one and they're waiting on the pad."

Ryker squinted at Jack. "You're not going. Tom will be satisfied with whoever you have waiting."

"I'm going, with the team or not." Jack's mulish expression said it would take a fight to change his mind.

A few seconds passed as they glared at each other. Ryker wanted to mash the man's face in. Had Jack betrayed Liam and Marie to Mulcahy? Or was it an OS ploy and was Jack a part of it?

"No." Ryker reached for the Uzi handed to him and threaded its sling onto his shoulder.

"I know you don't trust me, but I'd never hurt Marie. I don't like knowing someone might," Jack said.

"I don't give a fuck what you like or don't; you're staying here." He adjusted the Uzi underneath his arm and then slipped on a bulky jacket.

"Please." With his arms stiff by his sides and hands fisted, Jack waited for his answer. One of the employees held out an Uzi, waiting for the two men to come to an agreement before handing it over to Jack.

Damn. Jack obviously meant what he'd said about Marie. That was part of the reason he didn't trust him.

Ryker inhaled and rubbed his eyes. Maybe that explained part of his animosity toward the man. He'd never allowed personal feelings to interfere with his goals. Then again, the goal of saving Marie was very personal no matter what he told himself.

"Then get your ass moving. We're losing daylight and I want Marie safe in Sector by nightfall." Ryker nodded.

"Thanks, boss." Jack grabbed the machine gun and sprinted out of the bullpen toward the exit to the helipad.

Ryker followed behind his second-in-command. He hoped like hell he hadn't screwed up.

Marie had no idea how she got away. Maybe Mulcahy's guard thought he could handle her. She pulled at the stiff, itchy clothes, trying not to think about how she was sans underwear.

When she had darted out of the bedroom, she'd found herself in a loft overlooking a large city. The Bank of America Plaza with its gold leaf spire gave away where Mulcahy had taken her. Atlanta. Though she'd grown up in the area, Master rarely allowed her out of Main Sector without an escort. She and Charlie had visited the city last month, and if she remembered correctly, they had stayed at a hotel only a few blocks away. The Circle owned the property, and the manager reported to Ryker.

She'd found a way down three flights without being stopped until she reached an area being renovated where workmen had thrown their work overalls into a corner while they left for lunch. Without thinking twice of what was on it besides paint, she picked the smallest and pulled it on.

She was so happy to have clothes to cover the gown. While keeping an eye out for painters, refrigerator-sized thugs, and Mulcahy, she rolled up the sleeves and legs. When she reached the outside, she'd almost skipped barefoot down the sidewalk. Tickled by how people gave her a wide berth, she ignored them. Let them believe her crazy. Maybe there was a safety factor in looking like a kid wearing grown-up clothes. She was proud that she'd escaped on her own. Except for stopping every few feet to clean off the occasional pebble or wad of gum, she made good time reaching the street where she remembered the hotel stood.

Eyes wide, she gritted her teeth. Nothing but a parking deck with a deli and a dry cleaner on either side. No hotel. She stood staring at the levels filled with cars. Charlie had warned her how the city streets often looked alike and how many were called Peach-something. What to do next? Where should she go?

The shadows lengthened as the sun sank behind the tall buildings. She needed to find a phone. One of the drawbacks to everyone having cell phones was a person rarely ever saw telephone booths. Another was that she hadn't memorized any of the numbers she'd saved in her Blackberry. How would she let Ryker and Jack know where to find her? Even if a miracle happened and she found a public phone, it wasn't like The Circle's number could be found in a phone book or on the Internet.

Biting the side of her mouth, she stepped to the side as her gaze searched the area. Several of the storefronts had "Out of Business" or "Closed" signs. Nevertheless, she felt like she was in control for the first time in a long time.

Then it hit her. The humming in her body had died down to a manageable level. Her chest had loosened up too. She looked around. A need to touch and be touched wasn't driving her crazy anymore. Was the drug finally wearing down? Doc had said it could take months.

To think of it, every time she was calm or relaxed, the symptoms were mild to non-existent. Whenever the flashbacks knocked her on her butt, her adrenaline was pumping like crazy. She needed to get to Doc and see if he knew what it meant.

Well, she was back where she was a minute ago. How was she to get to The Circle without money or a car?

Her only hope of help was to go to a rescue center in the area. Mulcahy would never guess she would try something so simple. If she begged for a couple bucks, she could ride the MARTA to the Georgia Dome. She remembered that a center was near there—one of many painful memories from when she was twelve. Tears welled in her eyes. Her parents had met Master there and sold her, claiming she was nine, and left her without a thought. Later she'd heard they died from a drug overdose. They'd never had that much money and restraint was missing from their vocabulary. Obviously.

He'd bragged of how he loved shopping for kids at places like that. Like they were a commodity to be bought and sold.

After taking a deep breath she turned to look for the nearest MARTA entrance and there, about a half block from her, was Mulcahy with several of his thugs. She sprinted across the street and down an alley, not caring what she stepped on. They shouted at her and the scraping of their hard-soled shoes echoed behind her. The alley came out to a busier street and sidewalk. Without thinking, she ducked into a shop. Thankfully it was full of customers and jammed packed with

T-shirts, airbrushed car tags, and big chunky costume jewelry. She stood behind a tall display near the front door and watched as Mulcahy and his guys hustled by.

"Can I help you?" The saleswoman eyed her with one bushy brow lifted.

"I was just looking." Marie hurried out and turned toward the opposite direction. Afraid that Mulcahy would backtrack, she continued to look over her shoulder. Her feet ached from the cuts and bumps she'd received escaping, and glancing back only slowed her down further. She pressed a hand to her chest, feeling the thumping as if her heart wanted out. Was this what they meant about being scared to death? Surely her heart was about to explode. One more look back and she smiled in relief. Time for her to find a way to contact The Circle and Ryker.

Then hands grabbed her shoulders, but quickly released her when she squeaked and came to a halt. She covered her mouth and turned to face the person. All she saw was a faded blue T-shirt. She lifted her gaze what felt like several feet. An oversized—vertically and horizontally—shaved-head Uncle Fester stood in her way, checking her out in a way that gave her the creeps.

"Hello, pretty little thing." He smiled. His teeth, brown and rotten, announced his crack habit.

"Sorry." She stepped to the side.

He did too. "Don't be running off. You need to pay a toll."

"I don't have any money." She stepped back and he followed.

"Unzip that getup and show me your tits. That'll get you a free pass." His sunken eyes glittered.

No way would she do that. She noticed a couple of muscle-bound guys step out of a bar and laugh, elbowing each other on seeing what must be their friend giving her trouble. He'd obviously charged the same "toll" to other unfortunate women using the same sidewalk.

"I'd rather not." She turned to run, and his hand clasped her arm and squeezed.

"You ain't going anywhere." He jerked her against his sweaty, damp body.

Without a thought as her body slammed into his, she brought her knee up, hard. He howled and dropped to his knees. She hadn't been certain it would work. Thankfully the momentum was enough to reach through his drugged mind. She'd remembered how her parents could open up gashes on their heads and not even realize it until they saw the blood flowing down the side of their faces.

His friends shouted and Uncle Fester tried to stumble to his feet.

She ran.

CHAPTER FOURTEEN

For two hours they'd been searching for Marie. Ryker squeezed the steering wheel, trying to refrain from breaking it. Another road was shut down due to maintenance. How in the hell did Atlanta expect people to get around? Where in the world did they get their money during the bad economy?

A ringing filled the SUV. "Answer," he ordered the voice-activated phone.

"Boss, she's moving. Considering where you're at, she should be coming in range and heading toward you." Jack was at the van, keeping an eye on the tracer equipment. Not exactly what his second-in-command wanted, but Ryker had laid out the terms, and he should consider himself lucky to be that close.

About that time, Ryker caught a glimpse in the crowd of a woman with long blonde hair streaming behind her as she came around the corner, running full tilt. The traffic surrounding his SUV came to a standstill, again. A couple seconds later two stringy-headed men ran a few steps behind her. Then a big bald-headed man, huffing and limping, followed.

Ryker hit the wheel with his fist. He couldn't wait any longer. The traffic could be stalled for hours. He jumped out and stalked down the sidewalk, heading straight for Marie.

"Ryker! Oh, gawd, watch out!" She clutched his arm. "Run. They're crazy."

The men came barreling toward them. As Ryker tripped one and brought his double fist down on his back, Marie kicked the other one in the groin. Several people standing out of the way groaned.

The large man with the bald head hobbled to a stop. Marie took a step toward him. He threw up his hands. "No, don't!" Then he scrambled away with the other men clambering behind him.

Ryker quickly hid his gun as she turned.

"Did you see that? He was scared of me. What a pussy!" Marie looked so cute in the zipped-up overalls and dirty bare feet, her chin thrust out in defiance. With her hair all mussed, she looked like the scrappy little girl he remembered.

"Let's get out of here." No time to reminisce. Ryker wrapped an arm around Marie's shoulders and headed back to the SUV parked in the middle of the road. Horns blowing behind him, he cranked it up and made his way out of the traffic. "Are you okay?" He glanced over. She grinned so big, her beautiful eyes twinkling with news. "What?"

"For a while last night, I thought I would go crazy if I couldn't get back to you and let you . . . you know. But this morning I was able to control it and it got weaker by the hour. Then as soon as I touch you, danger all around us, all I can think of is this." She unbuckled her seat belt and slid her hand up his thigh and cupped him.

He jerked the steering wheel. "Bloody hell! Give me a warning next time."

"Ryker?"

"Yeah?" He swallowed and looked at her again. In a split second, he returned his attention to the road. The expression on her face burned in his brain. Such hunger revealed in her sweet face, her white teeth biting her bottom lip while she stared at his groin as her hand massaged him.

"Don't wreck us," she whispered. Then she unhooked and unzipped his pants. Her hand dipped behind the cloth and slipped out his hard cock. "Move your seat back a little bit."

How he found the strength, he wasn't sure. He shook his head. "No. We don't have time—"

"Do it now," she said in a tone as firm as his cock. Her small hand stroked from tip to balls.

What man in his right mind would turn her down?

"Mercy, Mother Mary," he muttered, and then pushed the button on the side of the seat.

Her hand slid up. She had a firm grip, not unlike his on the steering wheel. Just thinking about her mouth, his testicles tightened.

Then her mouth engulfed the sensitive, moist head. She sucked and licked her way down, and returned to the tip in a spine-tingling slide of her tongue. His eyes watered from fighting the urge to close them and immerse himself in the moment. The woman had talent.

She swallowed his cock. Her throat squeezed, and he felt her muscles flutter.

Damn, damn, damn. His stomach and buttocks clenched in an effort to hold back.

When his eyes started to roll, he shook his head and stared hard at the road ahead. Damn, he wanted to cry.

Humming? She was humming. Did she want to kill him? He wasn't sure how much more he could take. Finally, he saw what he needed. With a sharp turn, his tires squealed into the parking deck. Four levels later he found the perfect spot. A light was out and no one was parked nearby. The vehicle's tinted windows would protect them somewhat.

He grabbed her shoulders and carefully pulled her away. "No!"

"Don't fucking argue with me. Get in the back. Now!"

She looked around. Then a big smile lightened her face. Without another word, she scrambled between the front seats. He wedged his way into the back with her. She was already unzipping the overalls. The red gown took his breath. He forced the thoughts of how she came to be wearing it out of his mind when she dropped the straps. Her breasts were beautiful, soft, full. He cupped them and then tugged the tips. She moaned, arching her back. Unable to resist, he sucked one nipple into his mouth as he rolled the other.

"Please," she pleaded.

He understood. They needed more. At first he tried to take off the gown but he was clumsy and frustration made him hesitate. So he ripped the gown down the middle.

She gasped but then reached for him. He plunged into her and continued to thrust over and over again. The SUV rocked and he didn't care.

"Oh, you feel so good," she said between moans.

Sweat trickled down his face and back. He wanted to let go, but he couldn't, his body refused. Her hips met his with equal force. Flesh slapping flesh filled the SUV. The air became thick with their heat.

Marie screamed. He slapped his hand over her mouth and ground his groin into hers as he bit the side of his mouth, holding back his own shout. When her body stopped shaking, he wrapped her in his arms and pressed his forehead to hers.

"Are you okay?" he asked, his voice raspier than usual.

Tears welled in her eyes.

Damn! He'd hurt her. His throat constricted.

She burst out laughing. "Every time you and I have the best sex in my life—really, how can it get better each time?—you ask me that question."

He smoothed the tears from her face and shook his head. "You're amazing."

"You're the one who keeps it real—"

A hard knock on the glass caused them to jump. "Hey, you two need to get a room. Someone was complaining to the attendant on the main level about the couple getting it on in the SUV." Jack stood next to the automobile, facing where oncoming traffic would emerge.

Ryker stared down into Marie's face. Her eyes were wide with panic. The drug's flashback had obviously run its course for now.

Marie reached over the seat for her torn gown. No matter how she twisted or turned the material, she found little that would cover her properly. Embarrassment burned her cheeks as tears fell.

"I can't take this anymore." She buried her face into the material and hunched over.

"Here. Put this on." His voice was low as Ryker handed her the overalls.

Sickened by the thought of wearing them again with nothing between her and the filthy cloth, she shook her head.

"I can't stand the thought of it touching my skin."

He pulled off his shirt and handed it to her. "Maybe this will help."

The T-shirt was soft from being worn and washed so many times. As she dragged it over her head, the sexy scent of Ryker surrounded her—even the warmth of his body remained in the thin cotton. A tingle fluttered down her torso. She didn't worry it was a flashback. The feeling was similar to the one she had always gotten around him since she'd realized how much he meant to her.

It had been the day he'd returned to Main Sector the last time. His banishment ended without notice. Why would Master tell her anything? After using the house phone in the study to give final instructions about the dinner planned that evening, she'd been returning to Master. One moment, head down, walking slowly down the hallway, she replayed through her mind what else she needed to do that evening. The next she sensed someone nearby. He stood next to the doors leading to Master's private office. Ryker had grown and matured from the sad, lean young man to the larger, powerful one with pain and secrets etched in his face.

"Marie?"

The way he said her name always sent shivers through her. Feeling as if her body floated toward him, she picked up her speed and jumped into his arms as she had when she'd been younger. The few times she'd seen her friend, her hero since his exile, made the intervening years drag by.

"Arthur, when did you get back?"

He allowed only her to call him by his first name. She reveled being in his strong arms. Her grin grew bigger as she leaned back to look into his face. His hold tightened as if he didn't want to let her go.

"Today. Master said he needed me here. That Collin is giving him problems." His broad hand rubbed her back. She remembered how he would do that after Master hurt her.

His hand stopped. It was as if he read her mind and remembered the last time he'd held her. Such innocent comfort. Only Master had made the innocence dirty.

He released her. She stepped back and soaked in the feeling of having him near once again.

"How long do you get to stay this time?" She rubbed her arms. The hallway was cool.

"I don't—" His forehead wrinkled and his gaze narrowed as he glowered. "What are you wearing?"

She crossed her arms over her chest. The see-through material alternately revealed and hid every inch of her body. Her nipples ached. His stare had her craving his touch.

Yet he'd always treated her like a little sister, protecting her, comforting her. Only now she was grown, though Master believed her to be seventeen. She wanted to forget the horrible things done to them when they were younger. Arthur had suffered more than she had. Each time he'd defied Master, he'd been sent away and punished daily, from what she heard.

"The girls who attend him are only allowed to wear these."
Her cheeks warmed. Nothing was allowed underneath.

He jerked his gaze from her breasts and cleared his throat.
His Adam's apple dipped as he looked into her eyes.

"You better get inside then. It's warmer in there," he said.

"How long are you staying?" she asked again. Seeing him
made her realize how lonely she'd been without him nearby.
Every empty day felt like a lifetime ago.

"As long as it takes." Then he walked away.

She'd wanted to know what he meant but days passed
without a word. When she heard the news—Master was
dead—she understood what he'd meant. Long live the new
Master.

"What are you thinking about?" Ryker pulled the SUV
into traffic, heading back to Tennessee and The Circle.

Jack and the other operatives had left ahead of them,
giving Ryker a little time alone with Marie. She'd never been
a talkative person, but in the last hour, she'd been absolutely
mute. The moments leading up to Jack's interruption had
been so intense for both of them. Ryker had been unprepared
for her tears. All he'd ever wanted for her was to be happy
and safe.

He noticed the chill bumps on her arms despite the late
evening sun coming through the windshield. He stretched in
front of her and flipped the tab on the air vent to blow away
from her.

She blinked and shook her head. "About the last time you
returned to The Circle." Before leaving Atlanta, he'd sent one

of his people to purchase her some clothes. She looked beautiful in the vivid blue top and matching snug pants that ended above her ankles.

Just on hearing her voice, his shoulders relaxed. At least she wasn't thinking of leaving. For the last four months, he'd expected her to pack up and walk away, and there wouldn't be anything he could do to stop it. Unlike Theo, he refused to kill operatives when they wanted to leave.

"I'd heard about what you went through. I'm really sorry," she said softly.

No way would he talk about that. "I tried to return more often, but Theo blocked me at every turn. There wasn't a day I didn't worry about you." Hell, at least he held back from saying he loved her.

"Thank you." She placed her hand on top of his where he held the gearshift between the seats.

They sighed at the same time and fell quiet. This time the silence comforted. The sun dropped below the tree line and a feeling of isolation from the world filled the vehicle.

Ryker relaxed for the first time since she'd been injected with the drug. The dark interstate stretched in front of them, broken by the occasional red taillights. He felt as if they could work things out. They had a lot in common, both damaged by the same man. Maybe if he explained a few of his hang-ups to Marie she would understand and not condemn him.

"Marie—"

An identical black SUV sideswiped their rear quarter panel. Ryker fought with the steering wheel, trying to keep them on the road and not doing a three-sixty off the side and rolling down the bank.

"Oh, no, not again!" Marie screamed.

"Hold on." He pressed the gas pedal to the floor and watched the headlights become smaller in the rearview mirror. "Damn! I wish I could see who was in it."

"Mulcahy?"

"No. He would never do his own dirty work." He glanced into the mirror. The headlights started growing bigger. "Here they come again!" The big SUV slammed into their rear.

Ryker and Marie jerked forward and their seat belts snapped them back.

His foot pushed the pedal the half inch he'd let up. Nothing. He could only see the glow of headlights reflecting off his bumper. If the SUV pushed any harder, they would go into a spin and tumble down the side of the road.

"Put your seat back and lie on your side and dig in for a rough ride." Once she did it, he shoved the brake as hard as he could.

Tires squealed and the smell of rubber filled the interior. The high screeching sound of metal tearing metal hurt his ears. The SUV behind him travelled up the back and from what Ryker could see as he glanced through the sunroof, the automobile flipped in midair. Cars were hitting their brakes and the other SUV landed on the side of the road about twenty yards away, rolling down the side of the interstate.

Before they could recover, a pop reverberated inside their SUV as the window behind Ryker shattered. Someone shot at them. No way could anyone recover fast enough in the rolled SUV. The gunfire had to have come from another car.

Not wanting to give them an opportunity to release another round, he punched the gas again. This time the headlights in the mirror appeared to belong to a late-model sedan.

"For goodness' sake, how many are there?" Marie's voice had a touch of panic, but she remained where he'd ordered her.

"Hell, I wish I knew."

Their chances had dropped drastically. He wasn't sure how much damage their SUV had sustained. He only knew they needed help.

"Get my cell phone out of my right pocket."

He lifted his hip a little to help her put her hand inside. As he navigated through the light evening traffic, the sensation of Marie's hand tunneling into his pocket caused his cock to stand up and pay attention. He stared hard at the highway ahead. When did he lose control of his own body? Yeah. Sick fuck.

She pulled the phone out and the interior of the SUV lit up as she flipped it open.

"Hit speed-dial two. That's Jack's number. Tell him we're being chased and under fire near Cartersville. We'll get off there, exit 288." He waited until the last minute before jerking the steering wheel and exiting I-75.

He hoped by going down smaller roads, he could find a way to lose the car. His wheels sprayed gravel into the other lane as he headed through a signal light. The four-lane road made it too easy for the sedan to keep up. Pushing the gear into off-road, he hit the median and shot across to a dirt road.

He glanced at Marie. She'd pulled the seat upright and was squinting at the phone's screen in frustration.

Returning his attention to the rearview mirror for a

second, he hoped with no road lights and the rough terrain, the sedan would bottom out. It did but continued moving, minus the muffler rolling in the grass.

The maintenance road or whatever it was continued smoothly for over a mile. Then they started bouncing around, unable to avoid the potholes and deep ruts. Slowly, the headlights in the dust behind him became smaller.

"Did you get him?" Ryker glanced over to Marie. Tree limbs and bushes scraped the sides of the SUV as the road narrowed to something slightly wider than a dirt trail.

"About the time he answered, we lost connection. This must be no-man's-land—it keeps reading no signal."

Her calm voice made him proud. The woman handled the insanity and danger with the mere lift of an eyebrow.

"Are you—" He closed his mouth and glanced at her again.

"I'm okay." She smiled. In the dim light he couldn't tell much more.

"Good." He returned his gaze to the windshield just as the road, path, whatever disappeared.

She cried out as the SUV slammed into the water. The hood popped opened and bent backward, cracking the windshield. The airbags exploded about the same time. White powder floated thick in the air. His nose slammed into the nylon bag.   Unsure of how deep they would sink, he didn't waste time unbuckling the seatbelt and shoving the door open.

"Ryker! Oh, my God! The water—"

Her panic reminded him of her mind-numbing fear of drowning.

"Everything will be fine. Unbuckle and take my hand." A

light coating of white on her cheek told him she'd been looking his way when they hit the water. "Keep your eyes on me. We'll be okay."

Muddy water rushed over the floorboard and their feet. He wrapped her legs around his waist and pressed her face to his neck. Her whole body shook but she held on tight. By the time they reached the water's edge, the sunroof was the only part of the SUV they could see. The interior lights flickered and blinked off.

"Let me go. The water is no higher than my knees." With a show of bravery, she released him and reached out for the embankment. Panting as they climbed hand over fist through the weeds and shrubbery, they wrestled with the slippery leaves and mud. The moonlight helped a little to guide them up the slope.

Ryker reached the top and turned to help Marie. Soaked from head to foot she probably looked the same as he did. Like a mud wrestler.

"Now what do I have here?" A huge man with a V-shaped scar on his face stepped out of the shadows, his MP5 pointing straight at them.

CHAPTER FIFTEEN

Marie froze. Water and mud dripped off her hair and nose. The crickets chirped louder, as if they protested the disturbance. Unsure of what to do, her gaze remained frozen on the huge man.

Ryker stepped in front of her, facing the new danger.

"I'll be. If it ain't the brain-damaged brother." Though the man's voice sounded friendly, he kept the submachine gun pointed at them. "What are you doing in our neck of the woods, asshole?"

"Put that gun down before you get someone killed, Drago." Ryker looked behind the man and asked, "Who's with you?"

"Just me." The man lifted his chin toward her. "Who's she?"

"I'm Marie Beltane," she said before Ryker could respond. Then she reached around to shake his hand. "Are you Rex Drago?"

"Yeah." He tilted his head and squinted at her from the corner of his eyes. "And?"

"I know your brother, Jack."

The big guy hesitated for a second but finally lowered his gun and clasped her hand. His engulfed hers, his touch gentle. Unlike Jack, Rex wore his dark hair long, down to the collar of his shirt, and had no visible piercings. He looked to be taller too.

"Speaking of assholes, how's he doing?" He released her.

"Last time I saw him, pretty good." She wrapped her arms around herself as she began to shiver. The early-summer evening was warm, but the breeze off the water—or shock—caused chills to run up and down her spine. Considering she'd endured a high-speed chase that ended with them flying off the road and crashing into the lake—and then almost drowning—any of the three could easily send a person into shock.

"Come on. I'll turn on the heat in the truck and you can wear my jacket while you warm up." Rex held out his hand, palm open, indicating a path between two sweet gum trees.

Marie eased between the trees, avoiding the prickly seed balls as she'd lost her sandals in the suction of the mud. Two strong arms lifted and pressed her to a warm chest. Except for a sharp intake of breath, she accepted the unexpected help as she knew who held her.

She grinned up at Ryker. His boots squished with each step. She bit the side of her mouth. If she burst out of laughing, would he dump her on the side of the trail? He didn't look happy at all. Maybe she'd better keep quiet. They would make better time if he carried her.

A black oversized pickup truck with chrome glistening in the moonlight stood idling a few yards away. Thankfully Ryker helped her into the cab; otherwise, she would've needed a rope to climb inside.

With Rex driving and Marie squeezed between the two men, they drove down another dirt road. About three minutes later, they bounced onto a paved drive. Roughly a hundred yards away stood a ten-foot-high brick wall. The full moon glinted off what appeared to be glass on top. Every four feet or so, a little globe broke up the length and prevented the wall from looking too prison-like. Most likely the small globes housed cameras keeping an eye out for intruders.

Rex lowered the window. Next to the truck, about a foot lower, was a decorative stand. A button and a two-way immersed into the design hid its utilitarian purpose.

"Hey, it's me. I have guests." Double doors opened up and Rex drove into a small tunnel.

"What is this? OS?" Marie's eyes widened as they emerged into a large grassy area. Nothing like what she'd imagined. Landscape lighting lit the large pool in the middle and the multi-level patio that ran the length of the one-level house. In one corner, a simple wooden swing hung from a large frame. A man stood silhouetted in the middle of several French doors leading to the patio.

"No." Rex snorted and looked at Ryker. "This is Collin and Olivia's country home."

What kind of country home had an enclosure like a castle?

She caught shadows moving along the interior wall and at the corners of the house.

And guards standing every so many yards apart?

Ryker lifted her from the truck. Marie placed her arms around his neck, pressing a little closer to whisper in his ear. "Will we be safe here?"

"Don't worry. I'll make sure you are." His attention centered on the man who hadn't moved from the shadows.

She hated feeling helpless. On realizing that Ryker would be at a disadvantage by holding her, she pushed at his shoulders.

"Let me down. The grass looks like carpet. I doubt if any sweet gum balls would dare land here."

She wiggled until he released her legs. He dropped his arm from her back as they reached the patio. Ryker stopped.

She'd met Collin only once. He'd been dressed in all black. Better to blend in the shadows as at that time he'd broken into The Circle. Tonight, he wore a simple light-blue polo shirt and khaki slacks. Lean with wide shoulders and not quite as tall as Ryker, he held himself in a way she recognized, a man with a self-confidence in his ability to kill. His amber eyes watched Ryker with suspicion.

"What are you doing in Georgia?"

"Like I have to tell you. Was that your sedan following us?" Ryker crossed his arms, his feet planted apart as if he stood on the bow of a ship.

A small grin lightened Collin's face.

"No. But he's a guest of ours now. Would you like to talk with him?"

"Yeah." His tone betrayed a little of his impatience.

Out of the corner of Marie's eye, she noted movement. She smiled at Olivia. Collin's wife had always been kind to her.

"Sorry we barged in on your time off." Marie waited to see how she would react. Of the two dangerous people standing in front of her, Olivia was the most deadly. She'd been The Circle's lead assassin before she'd fallen in love with Collin.

Dressed in jeans and a buttoned-up white shirt that looked as if it belonged to her husband, Olivia glanced over to Ryker and lifted an eyebrow. In a blasé movement, she flipped her hair over her shoulders. Her auburn hair swayed and brushed above the small of her back.

"What is this?" She slinked over to her husband and hooked her arm with his. "A family reunion?" Her tone wasn't exactly friendly.

With the high wall, the evening breeze barely moved the air, but Marie shivered.

"Bring Marie a blanket," Olivia ordered one of the guards. Then her gaze drifted down Ryker's damp clothes and returned to look him in the eye. "Do you need one?"

"I'm almost dry," Ryker said.

Olivia released a simple humph. "What brought you here?"

"We stumbled across Rex," Ryker said, and then explained his concern about the new drug and deaths in his territory.

Marie was happy he'd left out her drug flashback problem, although he told more than she had expected. Ryker appeared to respect their opinion of the situation even with trust being an issue.

While Ryker talked, a guard handed her a blanket. She wrapped it around her shoulders, and her shivers instantly started to ease.

"Maybe we can encourage the fellow into talking," Collin said to Ryker.

Ryker grunted and nodded.

Collin leaned down and whispered into his wife's ear. Then he kissed her cheek and walked into the house.

Without a glance toward Marie, Ryker followed.

Olivia remained on the patio, watching her.

Marie tightened the blanket around her shoulders and tried to act unworried about having Ryker out of her sight. He obviously felt she was safe. But she wasn't concerned so much about her safety than about his. Collin was a master strategist. Ryker preferred dealing with people head-on.

"Does he treat you well?"

The question startled Marie.

"Ryker?" She caught the concern in Olivia's eyes.

"Yes. Is he like Theo?"

"Oh, goodness, no. He doesn't keep a harem of young kids." Marie shivered this time more from bad memories than her wet clothes.

"Let's go inside and get you changed into some dry clothes." Olivia closed the French doors behind them and led the way down a wide hallway. Every room Marie passed reflected Olivia's class and style. Sleek furniture and classic designs filled the home. When she walked into the bedroom, she almost blushed on seeing the huge bed with rumpled sheets. Knowing how Ryker hated to be interrupted during times like that, she was glad Collin and Olivia didn't hold it against them.

Olivia pulled out a wispy-looking sleeveless peach-colored dress and a thin white sweater. Just right for an early summer evening.

"You can take a hot shower and dress in there." Olivia pointed to a door on the opposite wall. "There's a drawer next to the tub with extra brushes and anything you might need."

She turned back to where they'd entered. "I'll go and fix us a cup of hot cocoa. So much better than coffee to warm you up. When you're ready, walk down the hallway; one of the guards will point you to the kitchen."

Marie flipped on the light in the black-slate-and-glass bathroom. A large white shag rug covered the center of the room. The light above was a modern-style crystal chandelier. A mirror covered one wall, reflecting the claw-foot tub and separate huge glass shower and her.

"Oh, hell." She covered her mouth with one hand.

Hair plastered to her head and eye makeup running down her mud-streaked cheeks, she looked like a zombie in one of the books Charlie loved to read. Not wasting any more time, she started the shower and checked the drawer. Several travel-sized bottles of shampoo and conditioner and little tubes of makeup were nestled in the front with brushes and combs wrapped in sleeves in the back. Did they have unexpected guests to use their bathroom often?

She picked one of each and then stepped into the shower. Twenty minutes later, her hair still damp even after blow-drying it, she emerged from the bathroom wearing the dress Olivia had given her. She also wore hand-washed underwear dried by the same blow-dryer. The dress made her feel so feminine, and she lifted the thin material, swishing it back and forth. When she lifted her head, she stopped and stared at her visitor.

"Hi, Marie." A. J., The Circle's former security officer, sat on a cushioned chair near an old-fashioned vanity. She looked good. The premature winkles around her mouth and eyes— Marie remembered—probably caused by stress from Theo's demands, had faded. But her eyes still showed sadness buried deep inside.

"I thought I was using Olivia's bathroom." During the shower, Marie had realized the bedroom and bath were actually for guests. The rumpled bed obviously belonged to A. J. Had she gotten back with Rex? Marie had heard they'd been lovers long ago.

A. J. nodded. "I couldn't believe this was a guest room and bath either. Olivia has never believed in doing anything halfway."

"You're staying here?" Marie had heard A. J. and Olivia were big pals.

"Yeah." The woman continued to stare at her.

"Thanks for letting me use your shower. Ryker and I had a little run-in with a lake. It won." Marie picked up the sweater off the bed and slipped it over the chill bumps on her arms. Had the room become cooler?

"Rex had your SUV towed out. It looked like you had a little more trouble than that."

Marie remembered why she never felt comfortable around the woman. She always doubted every word that came out of Marie's mouth. Plus, she'd heard how dangerous she was, especially when Theo had ordered her to punish some of the more disorderly operatives. Did she enjoy giving pain?

"What's the real reason you and Ryker showed up? If your new master does anything to Olivia and Collin, I'll make sure you live long enough to regret it." A. J. stood, towering over her.

At five-foot-one, having a person tower over her wasn't unusual. So she ignored the attempt at intimidation.

"Olivia knows it was a coincidence."

"There's no such thing as a coincidence—"

"Abby, leave the poor girl alone. She's been through enough today." Rex blocked the doorway, his hands grasping each side of the doorframe. "Brain Damaged is looking for you."

Was he talking to Abby? No. He was looking her way.

"Brain Damaged?" Then she remembered Rex calling Ryker that at the lake. "Why do you call him that?"

"I guess that was before your time. I'm not surprised he doesn't tell anyone." Rex shifted and leaned against the wall. "When his parents' car exploded, Ryker ran out of the house and tried to open a passenger door to get them out. Another explosion threw him several yards away. Shrapnel and gasoline burned part of his face, arm, and back, but when he landed, his head bounced off the asphalt. They had to open part of his skull to relieve the swelling. The doctors were never sure if he suffered damage or not."

Once again the thought of such a terrifying scene for a child to witness and then survive saddened her.

"Then you have no reason to call him that." Marie refused to let anyone belittle the horrible trauma he must've gone through. His mom and dad had loved him and taken care of him and then they were gone in a fiery explosion.

She pushed her way past Rex as she heard A. J.—Abby, whatever she was called—laughing behind her. No, she never liked that woman.

Voices drifted down the hallway. She reached the room with the view of the pool and noticed a light from a nearby archway. No guards in sight. So she leaned to the side and peered inside. Brass cookware hung from the vaulted ceiling over a massive cabinet island. Near the stove, Olivia poured hot cocoa into black ceramic mugs.

On the opposite end of the huge country kitchen, arms crossed and head bent to listen intently, Ryker stood next to Collin. The brothers were almost the same build, though Ryker's arms and chest gave away his preference for weight training. Collin's hair was lighter—possibly from swimming in their pool—and Ryker's longer, most likely to cover scars and the band that held his patch.

She never really looked at the scars as more than being part of Ryker. The pain and suffering he'd endured as boy, she couldn't imagine and would rather not. He'd obviously gone through months of skin grafts on top of losing the vision in his eye—without his family nearby to comfort him. She hurt for that young boy. Then Master had lied and told Ryker his brother was dead. Surely he'd felt lost and alone.

Tears threatened to spill over. She blinked several times. She didn't want to embarrass him or herself.

Ryker looked up. His gaze travelled down the borrowed dress. The gleam in his amber eye assured her he approved. When that all-seeing eye reached her face, he excused himself and walked toward her.

"What's the matter?"

"I'm ready to leave."

He brushed her damp hair from her cheek. "They're having a car brought for us. It will be another hour. If you want, you can go and rest until it arrives. Collin and I have to question the prisoner again."

"I want to leave now." Not until he said it would be another hour did she realize she couldn't stand being around those who would harm or condemn him. How could she explain without sounding emotional?

A concerned look crossed his face. Then his attention moved to a point above her head.

"What did you say, you fucking T-Rex?"

Ryker headed toward Rex. Marie grabbed at his arm and missed.

"I didn't say anything to upset her. It's not her fault she's mixed up with an irrational bonehead like you." The big guy raised his fists up, ready to protect himself.

"My brother needs to teach his watch dog how to respect his betters."

"What? You think—"

A. J. stepped in front of Rex and held up her palms. "Enough! You both have the biggest balls and the longest cocks. So get in your corners and behave!"

Marie let out her breath when Ryker stopped a few steps away. He pointed at Rex. "You stay away from Marie. Don't even look her way."

The implied threat hung in the air until Collin cleared his throat.

"They should be ready." Collin walked over to a plain white door. "Rex, check with the guards and let me know if they spot anyone else trespassing."

Even Marie knew Rex was being given an assignment to keep him out of Ryker's hair. The big guy grunted and left the kitchen.

Ryker's gaze narrowed. Then he looked over to Marie. He threw her a crooked grin and turned to follow Collin.

"Here." Olivia handed her one of the mugs. "This is the real stuff. No premix. You'll love it." As if she wanted to prove it, she sipped, and closed her eyes with a hum. "Delicious. Summer or winter, I love it."

Marie lifted the mug. "Oh, this is good. Just enough vanilla and cinnamon."

"Yeah." Olivia grinned. After a few sips and small chitchat about the design of the house, especially the kitchen, she said, "Let's go with the boys to the basement for a little entertainment."

With a glance at the door, Marie was unsure if she wanted to see what they had done to the man—or planned to do now. Not her type of entertainment by far. She might not trust A. J., but Olivia had never been anything but straight with her. For her to suggest it meant it was important for them to witness a portion of the interrogation.

The steps wound down easily twenty feet with well-placed lights every five steps or so. Processed air blew out of narrow vents near the bottom of the stairwell. Marie expected a long hallway with rooms sectioned off by barred doors, not a brightly lit room the size of a football field.

Ryker and Collin stood near a desk with a black-clad security guard punching keys on a laptop. In the middle of the room was a ten-by-ten glass box. That was the best way to describe it. Inside all of that glass, a slumped naked figure tied to a metal chair warned Marie that the box actually served as a cell. A cell without a door.

The man's chin rested on his chest and his shaved head appeared to glow as if his scalp had only recently been sheared. Then she remembered they removed prisoners' hair to humiliate them further after stripping away their clothes. And it was always the last step before they terminated them, hoping the totally naked feeling would make them tell all of their secrets before dying.

Marie moved closer and stopped. The prisoner lifted his head.

Hands to her mouth, she gasped. "Liam?"

CHAPTER SIXTEEN

Ryker strode over to Marie and turned her by the shoulders. "What are you doing down here?"

"You didn't tell me it was Liam. Why would he try to kill us? He's one of us. He's been an operative longer than anyone I know in The Circle." She sounded lost, as if she'd found out there wasn't a Santa Claus.

He shot a furious look at Olivia. The woman merely lifted an eyebrow. What had she hoped to accomplish by involving Marie in this sordidness? Didn't she understand Marie needed to be protected? That she was too gentle to understand such betrayal?

"We're trying to find out his motives. And who all's involved," he said.

Her meadow-green eyes stared up at him. "Then we need to find out any way possible. Either he knows something about the Wizard or has a good reason to want us dead or out of the way."

Surprised by her easy acceptance of the necessity to interrogate Liam, Ryker nodded and walked back to the cell. On the way, he passed Olivia and ignored her smirk. The woman was way too sure of herself. Good thing she was Collin's problem, not his.

He motioned to the guard to lift the glass. A humming filled the room as an overhead crane lifted the heavy box. His brother had an inventive mind to develop such an escape-proof cell. The thick acrylic had several air holes no larger than a man's wrist at the top with the thin air vents above it. The prisoner had plenty of air, though was unable to go anywhere. With the feeling of being watched at all angles, compounded by the humiliation of being on display, a person would crack rather quickly. Ryker merely waited to see if his brother was right.

"Liam, are you ready to talk now?"

"I've been talking, you fuckin' tool." Liam lifted his head. His left eye was swollen shut from a couple blows the guards got in before pulling him into the holding box.

"You claim you were following to protect us," Ryker said.

Liam nodded and then grimaced.

"You remember the directive." Ryker waited until Liam grunted. "My orders trump all other commands and desires. You desired to follow us without permission. That's considered treason."

"No." Liam's head bobbed. "I'm loyal."

"Who sent you?"

Even with one eye closed, Liam's fierce look illustrated his feelings about the question.

Ryker jerked his head. A guard stepped up to Liam and jabbed a stun gun onto his thigh. For less than two seconds, forty thousand volts of electricity shot through Liam's nervous system. Ryker waved off the man. He didn't want the prisoner comatose. They needed answers. Quick.

"Liam." He slapped him.

The man's eyes were rolling around beneath his lids.

"Liam." With the thought of Liam's betrayal and how he could've caused Marie's death, he decided the guards had it right and Liam needed a stronger encouragement besides electricity and slaps. As he balled his fist to slam into his ribs, someone grabbed his arm. Ryker spun around and stopped, his knuckles inches away from Marie's nose. "What the hell do you think you were doing? I could've killed you." Fear heightened his anger, causing his tone to be a rougher than usual.

"If you kill him, you'll never get your answers," explained Marie. "Let me try."

Her eyes held such determination Ryker had never seen before. The drug. Enduring the effects of Blossom Flower had changed her. Made her tougher. Maybe even more focused. He'd always worried about others taking advantage of her. She never had a chance to stand up for herself until the drug gave her the courage to fight back.

"Okay. I'll give you three minutes with him. Don't get too close."

She nodded while her gaze remained on the prisoner.

Ryker backed away, giving her a little privacy. He walked over to the desk, where Collin sat in the guard's vacated chair. Olivia was nowhere in sight.

"Where's Olivia?"

Collin kept his eyes on the monitor. "Interrogations bring back bad memories for her."

Knowing how paranoid Theo Palmer had been, he understood. "Theo never trusted a soul."

"Until you, and he paid for that. But it's not Theo's interrogations that she'd like to forget. It's mine." He pressed a button on the laptop and a chart popped up.

Collin's confession surprised Ryker. Letting the subject drop, he leaned forward to read the information on the screen.

"I wonder how our parents would've handled all the new age equipment we possess now?" He was unsure of why he brought up a subject he normally ignored. Would Collin recognize it to be the peace offering he meant it to be? No other person would understand the pain it caused to talk about them.

With a slow slide, Collin turned and looked up at him. "I believe Dad would've hated it. He'd always been the old-fashioned type."

"Probably." He nodded in deep thought. "What would he have thought of us? Running parts of a whole?"

"He would've hated that too." Collin stood and placed a hand on his shoulder. "Listen. I had planned to wait to tell you this another time, but . . ."

For Collin to struggle with the words warned Ryker he might not like whatever he was about to say.

"I plan to step down from the OS. Olivia and I have enough put away in overseas accounts to live a good life away from all of this." Collin lifted his chin.

Talk about unpredictable. His brother continued to surprise him. "Rex taking over for you?" Ryker dreaded another war with the OS.

"Yeah. But with the understanding he'll report to you,"

Collin said, as if he was discussing the price of corn instead of handing over a billion-dollar organization.

Surely his brother didn't mean what Ryker thought he heard. When Collin lifted his eyebrows waiting for a reaction, Ryker found his voice.

"Hell, man, you got me there. I never expected that. Why?" Was it some type of ploy to overtake The Circle?

"Like I said, Dad was an old-fashioned fellow. He'd never approve of the OS being away from The Circle. Especially now that Theo's out of the way. Olivia wants to help some orphans in Russia or some Godforsaken former Eastern Bloc country that she read about."

The offer would solve many problems. Too often The Circle and the OS competed for the same jobs.

Ryker looked hard at the little brother he'd loved as a kid. On his matured face, he could see the same boy who tagged along on all the adventures they had together. They were only ten months apart and had been close friends until the death of their parents. He'd mourned his family but it had been his brother that he'd missed the most. Now a lot of suffering and a cruel past separated them. And Collin's wife was in the middle of it all.

"You know she's a fucking crazy bitch." He wasn't sure how Collin would take his insult, but it had spilled out of his mouth before he could stop it. He had to claim the revelation that Collin had just dumped in his lap unsettled him.

Collin chuckled. "Yeah. But she's my fucking crazy bitch."

Relieved that he wouldn't have to kick his brother's ass, another question came to mind. "Will T-Rex take my orders? You know I'll have to kill him if he doesn't."

There was no question to it. The type of organization he ran demanded everyone to be a little afraid of dying by his hands or he would face a mutiny whenever he had to make a hard decision.

"He might not like it all the time, but he'll follow orders. He knows how you've handled The Circle. You had a few rough patches in the beginning, but I believe you've got everyone under control now." Collin held out his hand.

Ryker looked down at it. With the exception of The Circle operative being questioned by Marie, his brother was right. His people usually toed the line. But was this offer some elaborate scheme? He couldn't think of how it could be a trap. Inside it felt right. Why not give it a shot? He clasped his brother's hand and shook. "I can't promise that I'm convinced with Rex leading the OS, but I'll give it good consideration. When do we start the process?"

Collin paused and looked into Ryker's face. Whatever he saw must have satisfied him.

"How about six months? That will give you and Rex time to come to terms."

"Ryker?" Marie's voice sounded concerned.

He couldn't believe it. With the astounding decision Collin had just revealed to him, he'd let his mind drift from Marie.

Liam remained in the chair with his chin to chest, drool running down his chest to groin. Marie had one hand on his shoulder. Her sweet, solemn face hinted it wasn't good news.

She had his undivided attention. He hated to see her so upset by her failure to get any information from him. They had been rough on Liam earlier with no results. What had she expected she could do?

"Don't worry. I'll get the info out of him," he said. Liam had been trained by The Circle to withstand interrogations, and they'd known that going in. So he wasn't surprised the man could resist Marie's questions.

"You misunderstood. I already did." She stepped away from the unconscious man. "I got the info."

"What?"

"He told me that the Wizard has a hideout somewhere on an island in the Florida Keys." She straightened her back and lifted her chin.

Why had he expected her to fail? She'd already proven she was a fighter and because of her size, she had to learn to use her brain to win.

"It does narrow it down somewhat, but that's several hundred islands of all sizes. The ones just large enough to build on are private, and finding information on them will be hard." He'd send several men down there. Hell, he'd even go and help search. She may tell him she was handling it and the drug's control had weakened, but they still needed the antidote. How many hours had passed since she . . . damn, what should they call it? Had a fix?

"Are you okay?" he asked before he remembered how frustrated the question made her, as he asked too often.

She rolled her eyes and answered. "I'm fine. Please, I'm ready to go back to Sector."

Ryker nodded. "Go on upstairs. I need a couple minutes with Collin. The car should be here." He cupped her cheek.

The dark circles beneath her eyes shouldn't have been there. All the chasing and shooting was wearing her down.

Instead of leaning into his touch as she'd been doing the last few weeks, she stepped away. He wanted to grab her and pull her back. Her reaction was for the best. The last few days, he'd decided they needed a little distance to reassess their situation. With the information Liam had provided so far and with what they could extract in the next few hours, Ryker would be away for a few weeks investigating. If she had a strong flashback, he could be with her within a few hours.

His gaze remained on her as she headed for the stairs.

"You know she's your weakness," Collin whispered.

"Yeah. That's a problem I have to work on." He turned away and walked back to Liam.

Ryker wanted more information, and he was certain Liam was holding something back. What could it be? For some reason, he felt it was something in front of his face that he wasn't focusing on. Others would say he looked for ghosts where there were none. He knew his concentration had been shot ever since he felt the first contraction around his cock while inside Marie. Nothing else had felt as important as feeling it again. But for now, he needed to concentrate on ending the Wizard's reign in the drug world.

Marie breathed deeply when she stepped into the room next to the pool. She hated the sterility and feeling of menace downstairs. How could Olivia live above such horror? Marie shook her head. What difference did it make from her living at Sector? Maybe the difference was the knowing, and in this case, in the seeing. There was a difference between insisting on answers and beating them out of a person. She understood Ryker possessed layers she was unfamiliar with but she refused to be hard like Olivia, who accepted the more brutal ones. Not all of The Circle's operatives killed to achieve results, and she wouldn't either.

She dropped into a big overstuffed chair, leaving the floor lamp off, and stared out at the blue water of the pool. Her thinly stretched nerves loosened up a little. The scene was so serene. Just what she needed, a moment of quietness. A separation from the violence below.

"Stay the hell away from me." A. J. came into view, stopping to turn to whomever she fussed at.

"But, Abby, I want to work it out." Rex moved in close, towering over her. Was he even aware he intimidated people by standing so close?

"Do I have to kill you to get you to leave me alone?" A. J.'s hands landed on her hips.

"You owe me a chance to talk about what happened." He reached for her shoulder, but she shrugged it away.

Obviously, what had happened years ago wasn't over in Rex's way of thinking.

"You're going to be sorry if you don't walk away now." A. J. raised her hands as if to move him from her personal space.

"Ah, come on, baby—"

She pushed. The big guy's face was priceless as his arms rotated in an attempt to regain his balance. She shoved him again, and he fell backward into the pool with a splash, sending a tidal wave of water over the edges.

Marie had to restrain herself from clapping.

A. J. turned on one heel and stomped off. Rex swam to the nearest ladder and pulled out of the pool, water sluicing off him. His soaked clothing clung to every inch of his body. Marie couldn't help but admire the muscles and broad shoulders. He shook like a dog and stared off in the direction A. J. had taken. Then as if he considered it best to retreat, he shook his head and walked away in the other direction.

She wondered what caused their clash. What little she remembered about A. J. and Rex was that they had planned to marry but Master had stopped it. Maybe it was like a Romeo and Juliet tale. Only, why would it stop them now that they worked for the same organization? No surprise that everyone had problems to sort out.

Marie leaned to the side, resting her head on a pillow. What was she going to do about Ryker? He believed he had to protect her from the world. She'd had enough of depending on others. Time for her to pull up her big-girl panties. Most people went after what they could get. Her parents had sold her to a monster for drug money. Master used her for his perversions. She just didn't understand what Ryker got out of *helping* her. If he climaxed whenever they had sex, she would say it was for relief, since he never slept with any of the women in the Sector.

Besides, she didn't want Ryker trying to protect her and placing himself in danger. She never wanted to be a hindrance.

Lying to Ryker had been hard. She'd left out one thing Liam had said. He'd warned her about the Wizard's obsession with capturing her and killing anyone who got in the way. No one would be safe around her until Ryker stopped the one responsible for creating the drug.

Once they returned to Sector and she talked with Doc, she'd take back as much of her life as she could and protect Ryker the only way she could. By separating herself from him. By no longer needing him. She would find other ways to satisfy the drug's flashback.

Why was her heart feeling like it had shriveled up and died?

CHAPTER SEVENTEEN

Marie squirmed on the exam table as Doc listened to her heart. She reminded herself she'd come to him for an answer. She had few secrets the doctor didn't know about, in regards to the scars and damage her body had sustained since she'd been given into Master's care. He'd been the only doctor she'd ever remembered seeing and he'd treated her several times when Master became overzealous in reaching his satisfaction.

"Your heart is steady and strong. That's good." He stepped back. "Any chest pains or dizziness?"

She shook her head.

"We took samples of your blood immediately after Ryker brought you in and compared it to the other women. There are similarities, but yours is more aggressive in melding with your hormones. So you're right. It's different. Maybe the changes are the reason the drug is lasting longer." Doc's cheeks reddened.

He was such a softhearted man, and she understood he felt sorry for her predicament.

"So are the flashbacks causing any other problems?"

Doc cleared his throat. "That's a good question. Let me first mention one thing we're certain of about the drug." He tucked in his lips, concentrating on what he would say next. "It has a powerful sex-drive accelerator. The simplest way to explain it is whenever a person's adrenaline begins to pump through the body, it kick-starts the drug into overdrive. So if you can keep calm and not become excited or scared, you should be able to take care of any problems"—he cleared his throat again—"by yourself."

It made sense. Whenever she'd been in danger with Ryker, her flashbacks happened with regularity. She thought it'd been tied to her feelings for him. A mixture of relief and sadness spread across her shoulders and chest. Between the Wizard's threatened danger and her determination to do without Ryker's *help*, her decision yesterday at Olivia's was the only one to make. She needed to keep her distance from him.

Doc continued. "The extreme reactions you're having from the drug are wearing on your body and in turn your health. I'll give you a prescription for an anxiety medicine that should help you cope, but you can't take it for very long. Maybe three months. After that, it'll quit working without taking larger doses. The stronger it is, the more dangerous it becomes to your health. Just as dangerous as Blossom Flower. But the small dosage might make your life a little simpler until we find the antidote or the drug finally dissipates."

With a hand on Doc's arm, she softly said, "Don't say anything to Ryker."

"Don't say anything about what?" Ryker walked into the room and crossed his arms. He'd reluctantly agreed to stay away while Doc examined her. So she wasn't surprised to see him barge in before they were finished.

Doc opened his mouth and she stopped him. "I'll handle it."

The white-headed man nodded. He turned to Ryker. "Listen to her." He shook a finger in warning as if the leader of The Circle was a child, and then left the room.

She jumped off the table and with nervous fingers smoothed the wrinkles from her soft cotton blouse. A stomp of each foot straightened the legs of her jeans. Fussing with her clothes gave her a little time to focus on what she needed to say.

"Well?"

"Doc said the drug is a little different than what was used on the dead girls. Maybe that's the reason we haven't seen another dead one in so long. Though I hate to think of anyone else going through what I have."

"So you're okay?"

She wanted to blurt out, *No! My heart's breaking!* But what use would that serve?

"Doc said as long as I remain calm, I should be able to take care of my flashbacks." Her chin lifted in confidence. She wanted no doubts that she agreed with the doctor. Ryker's energy and concentration should be centered on hunting down Mulcahy and stopping him. He didn't need to worry about her. Absurdly, he would remain safer that way too.

Ryker's jaw shifted and he nodded in deep thought. "Okay. I see." After taking a deep breath he turned and strode out.

What had she expected? For him to claim he couldn't live without her touch? That he loved her and wanted her for herself and not as a means to give her relief from a stupid drug? Did she truly believe he only touched her to protect one of his people, namely herself? No different than throwing his body on a bomb to shield those around him. If that was the reason he provided his *services*, she didn't want the sacrifice.

The room darkened as she stood there staring at the empty doorway. The bastard! She picked up a box of tissues and threw it against the wall, knocking down a picture of a man's anatomy.

A female nurse ran into the room. "Everything all right in here?"

"No. I just don't understand men. The assholes!" Marie wasn't sure why she was so angry. Ryker hadn't argued with her, hadn't tried to change her mind. It had been for the best.

The nurse grinned. "What's there to understand? The men I know love food and sex, sports and sex, guns and sex, cars and sex—and not necessarily in that order." She chuckled as she picked up the box and picture, arranging them back where they belonged. She was still chuckling as she left the room.

Marie covered her cheeks. The tingling she'd become so familiar with shot through her body. Her jaw ached with the frustration of knowing she couldn't ask Ryker for his help. Taking deep breaths, she headed toward her suite, determined to grab her helper out of the nightstand and forget about the stupid man in her life.

With each step, her feet hit the floor with hard, solid thuds. Before she realized she'd done so, she stopped in front of Ryker's bedroom door. He probably wasn't even there.

Still, she enjoyed pounding on the door. Who did he think

he was? How dare he brush her off as if she didn't matter? She struggled to gulp in enough air. The tingling radiated from her groin and nipples.

The door swung open and her fists continue to pound on his bare chest.

"Marie, what's the matter? Has something happened?" He grabbed her wrists and held them above his heart. The rapid beating beneath her fingers betrayed his calm manner.

"You bastard! How dare you!" Her breath burst between each word.

"What?" He released her and grabbed her shoulders, pulling her inside with him as he shut the door.

"Calm down and tell me what's wrong." He no longer touched her.

She slammed her open hands against his chest. He fell back a couple steps. Eyebrows lifted and mouth hung open, he raised his hands, palms open, showing he wouldn't fight back.

"You fuck me for days and all you have to say is 'I see?'" Her voice broke on the last word from lack of oxygen. The tingling squeezed her torso, heated her face and chest. "You fuck me again and again, bringing me to a fucking climax each time, but do you? Do you even fucking come?" She wanted to regain control of her body and mouth, but she'd had enough of others doing what they wanted to her. It was time for her to take back. There was a freedom to letting her anger take control.

"Marie, I don't—"

"Do you have any idea how demoralizing that is to a woman?" She slammed her hands against his chest again.

A couple more steps back, he reached for her. "Come on. You have to understand—"

"That's just it." She pushed him again. "I don't understand how you could treat me that way after everything we've been through together. When Master made you watch him touching me, I knew you didn't have a choice."

"Marie, I don't want to talk about it."

"You know, *Master*, there are times talking about it makes things better." She slammed her hands into him once more. This time he stood his ground. She could tell she'd finally gotten him angry with that *Master* crack. "Ooh, does that upset you? Don't like being called Master? Afraid I would talk about the time he made you watch him screw me?"

"Talking never solved anything." She was familiar with the mulish look on his face. He refused to heal. Sure. He could control his body, but he refused to come to terms with the fact that he couldn't control everything, just as she couldn't.

"How would you know? You've never tried it." She stepped into his personal space and looked up into his face as he glowered down at her. "I remember when you got the scars on your ass. You probably don't remember, but it was me who doctored them, rubbing in the antibacterial cream everywhere it hurt."

"Yeah. I remember. That was last time I let him fuck *me*." Ryker lifted her by the shoulders to look straight into her eyes. "Is that what you wanted to hear? So are we going to talk about it now? Let's instead talk about how I enjoyed sinking that sword into his stomach and up to his chest. I knew exactly where to aim. He made sure I was trained to be a killing machine and I was fucking good at it. And I would kill him over and over again as I do in my dreams. I killed him for what he did to my parents as much as for what he did to you."

She gasped.

"I deserved what he did to me. I should've saved my parents. But I couldn't let him hurt you anymore. He knew I cared and he used both of us against each other. I would've done anything for you. But I have my limits!"

His eye flashed with anger, then changed to lust. He threw her onto his bed.

She bounced a couple times, causing her hair to fall over her eyes. By the time she brushed it out of the way, he'd kicked his pants off. He stood above her dangerous and fierce with his cock stiff and heavy. The tingling in her body centered between her legs.

She rose to her knees and pulled him by his cock closer to the bed. The heat in her hand expanded as he came nearer. Her mouth engulfed the head, and he groaned. His fingers dug into her scalp as he began to thrust.

Her hands cupped his buttocks, massaging and caressing the scars she'd remembered, and the feel of him excited her more. A finger slid between his cheeks.

"Damn you, Marie." He jerked away from her mouth, making her hands drop from their exploration.

Before she could protest, he pressed her back and climbed on top of her. He lifted one of her legs and plunged into her, stroking long and deep several times, and then he quit moving.

"No!" With her whole body, she pushed him over until she straddled his hips. He had stopped to prevent himself from coming. She was certain.

He rolled her back over. "No. We'll do it my way."

Furious that he planned to take control, she released her temper again. Her fists hammered on his chest and shoulders. She kicked her heels, hitting him along his thighs and lower back.

"Stop!"

She continued to fight him. She needed him to stay and finish it. His temper flared as bright as a volcano erupting. She scratched his back, long rakes down the scars she'd always been careful with before. He shouted his matching fury and began to thrust. Her nails dug into his sides. He began to pound harder. The slapping of flesh against flesh filled the air. The bed pounded the wall. She didn't care that she would have bruises along her thighs and mons. She never wanted him to quit.

He filled her so full until she looked over the edge into pain. She arched her back wanting more. Sweat beaded his brow. He closed his eye and his hair fell across his patch and face. She'd never seen him so beautiful. He picked up speed, hammering into her, his fingers gripping her hips as if afraid she'd escape. She knew with his loss of control he was as near to completion as she was and wouldn't take much more. His large, rough fingers slid up to cover her breasts and then rolled and pinched her nipples. She screamed as she came. When she couldn't take it any longer, she clamped her mouth down on his shoulder and sunk in her teeth.

His roar shook the walls. He lifted her hips and drilled into her hard and quick. Then he stopped. "Marie! Yes!"

Inside her, his cock throbbed so hard with his release that she could feel it and she climaxed again.

She stared at his face. Pain. He desired pain to lose control.

"Now you know. I love it when you dig your nails into me. Pain releases me. The pain, the anger helps me let go." His face twisted in self-loathing.

Ryker stared at the ceiling. Marie's breath caressed his chest as she dozed. He closed his eye for a moment, embarrassed by the tear sliding down into his hair. His patch still covered his right eye, trapping the other tear. She'd seen him without the patch when they were younger and normally he wouldn't give a damn if anyone saw him without it. So he couldn't understand why it bothered him for her to see the white-glazed blind eye. It had never appeared to upset her before. With the explosion of his parents' car, the steel had been so hot when it hit the side of his face that the heat damaged the pupil, iris, and lens. The blankness of the eye caused some people to cringe or stare.

She shifted but her eyes remained closed. He squeezed her to his side.

Why worry about his eye and what she thought? He knew he was ignoring the real problem. By admitting he needed pain to come, he'd allowed her to glimpse at the monster inside of him. Pain. He'd known for most of his life that pain was his Achilles heel. A remnant of living with a dealer of pain. Pain was always connected to what he wanted: food, warmth, and love.

Marie had mentioned an incident he'd wanted to forget but considering the circumstances, he'd done what he had to do. He'd never told her why he succumbed to Theo that night. He'd never told her the last time Theo tried to touch him he'd been sixteen and refused to submit any longer to his perversions. Boys at that age were filled with hope and possessed balls larger than life. Hadn't he known better? Theo was a master manipulator. If he hadn't yielded, Theo promised that Marie would've taken his place. No way would he allow Marie to suffer if he could prevent it. Even at twenty-three, he knew he wasn't strong enough—nor did he have the operatives' support—to overtake The Circle from Theo.

The bastard had made sure Marie walked in on them. Later, he'd sent her to his room to tend his wounds. She'd been twelve at the time, though the sick pervert had thought she was nine. Twelve, nine—it didn't matter. She was too young and good and sweet. The games and stunts Theo had pulled on the two of them had at one time pushed Ryker to act too quickly. He'd planned to kill the old psycho. Before he could put the plans in motion, he'd found himself stuck in a cell at Northern Sector once again.

Afterward, over the years, Theo used Marie as a bribe for good behavior. But each time, another depraved act was added to his nightmares.

And now he was no better than the man who manipulated Marie. He used her for his own satisfaction. That was part of the reason he'd never let go, never allowed himself to climax. But when she lost her temper and dug her nails and heels into him, the pain released his control. Pain was the secret he kept hidden from everyone. He couldn't hide from himself that he was a monster.

He squeezed his eye shut. His breath hitched as he inhaled deeply. Fuck. He'd lost control with Marie.

"Ryker, it's okay. Are you okay?"

That was a switch. Her asking him the question he'd asked her over and over again. "Yeah. Go to sleep and we'll talk in the morning."

She snuggled into his side. Her breath caressed his skin and then she pressed a light kiss on his ribcage.

"Yeah. Everything will be all right," he whispered. He threw an arm over his face. Even if it killed him.

Marie stretched and reached out for Ryker as she opened her eyes. He was gone but his warmth lingered on the sheet where her palm slid, seeking the hardness of his body. She sat up and looked around. She remembered little of the room from that day he'd saved her. The bedroom was the polar opposite of hers. No tasteful landscapes on the wall. Monotone-colored sheets and spread. Blackout blinds without curtains on the large windows. A sleek oak dresser without a mirror faced the foot of the bed. The bareness broke her heart. How could Ryker rest in such coldness?

She heard a flush and water running. When the door opened, she expected to see a naked Ryker. Instead, he wore a dark T-shirt, combat pants, and laced-up boots. He looked tired; creases fanned from his eye and bracketed his mouth. She had a feeling he hadn't slept last night.

"Give me a little while and I'll be ready too." She scooted to the edge of the bed, looking over the side for her clothes.

"No. You stay here." He opened a drawer and pulled out a gun, and stuck it in a holster at the small of his back. After slipping some leather straps over his shoulders, he slipped another gun into its holster. He looked over at her when he picked up a black windbreaker hanging on the closet doorknob.

"I thought you wanted to talk this morning."

"Yeah. It'll take me a few weeks to find the Wizard. We've got some good info that should help." He shrugged into the jacket and then he became still. "Marie, it's not going to happen again."

"What's so different between us being in my bed versus yours?"

"You know that's not what I mean. I'll help you if you need it with the flashbacks, but I can't . . . I won't . . ." He jabbed his hands into the jacket pockets. "Shit."

"I get it." She stood up, taking the sheet with her. "Don't worry. I won't call. Last night was an idiosyncrasy and won't happen again. That's really why I came here."

The smirk on his face infuriated her.

"If you say so."

No softness in his look. She didn't like it one bit. Before she could argue, he cut her off with a slice of his hand.

"It doesn't matter. We agree that this won't happen unless you need a fix and nothing more," he said.

"Agreed." She wanted to bash his head in. Stubborn, arrogant knothead. He acted so cold while she hurt inside. Being mad at him prevented her from feeling sorry for herself. She had to remind herself once again this was for his safety. Bad enough he was going in search for the freak who'd caused this; no need to make it worse for them both.

He stared at her for a second longer as she remained standing with her chin up. Then he walked away, closing the door behind him.

She dropped to the floor, buried her face into the sheet, and cried.

CHAPTER EIGHTEEN

Marie aimed the Berretta M9 at the target and fired the final three shots dead-on into the target. Yeah, her shots hit the bull's eye when she imagined Ryker's face on the target.

"Good job."

She laid the empty gun on the counter in front of her. After pulling off the safety glasses and ear muffs, she faced Jack.

"I've been practicing with it and a few others for the last several weeks," she said.

"I've noticed you've been keeping to yourself."

Jack held her satchel as she stored the weapon and accessories. No need for her to clean the gun here. Later, when she was alone in her room, she would drag out her kit and take care of it.

"Ryker's right. I need to learn several different ways to protect myself. I never want to be helpless again."

He nodded, his gaze following her hands as she placed the ammo into the zippered pockets. She refused to let his undivided attention bother her.

So she reached for the other gun she'd practiced with earlier. It was her favorite. A .38 S&W Special. There was something timeless about a revolver. She slipped it into a separate case and handed it to Jack to tuck inside the bag.

"What's bothering you?" she asked. Jack usually teased or fussed when he was around. The only time he stayed this quiet was when he had a problem and didn't know how to verbalize it.

"They found another girl's body."

"Oh, no." She shook her head. "I'd hoped that nut had decided to leave town for good." Every time she thought of how close she'd come to giving in to Mulcahy, her skin crawled. "Doc had thought they changed the drug formula enough to prevent that from happening again."

Jack closed up the bag and walked with her into the hallway, heading to the elevator. She still lived in the same wing as Ryker. About every other week, a flare-up would become uncontrollable without help, and she refused to go to anyone else. Like it was a business proposition, she left him a voicemail, and he'd show up between thirty minutes and two hours later. He'd take care of her need without shedding his clothes or reaching a climax, just like all the other times before that one night. She'd restrained herself from the temptation of biting him again. Afterward, he would leave and she'd cry, swearing next time she'd hold out longer. Yet as soon as the flashback engulfed her body, she'd punch in his number, hating every beep as if the tones mocked her.

Though she had a regular sex life with Ryker—no way could she call it making love—little had changed in her life. She still worked at improving her self-defense skills, and in the evening, she practiced with different weapons. Jack had given her the initial lessons but she'd improved at such a fast rate, she only needed the occasional pointer from the operative on duty at the firing range. She'd found she had a knack with handguns—her aim true and her eye sharp, hitting the target more often than not.

While Charlie continued to work with her on her patterns in taekwondo, they decided to branch out a little. So she taught Marie how to handle a knife, pick locks, and make homemade bombs—a little side hobby of the mechanic's. If Ryker ever found out about the bomb lessons, he would kill her friend.

She glanced at Jack after pressing the Up button. "There's more?"

"Ryker and his team were investigating a lead on an island in the Florida Keys. The info they received led them to where they believe Mulcahy was hiding. They're certain Mulcahy stashed the Wizard there. Gunfire was exchanged with some of his goons."

Jack stepped into the elevator with her. She held her hand out for her bag. He reluctantly released the straps. He leaned against the wall and crossed his arms, the short sleeves showing off his tattoo.

Marie had always admired the Celtic art on his arm, though she could never imagine having someone use a needle on her—beautiful or not—no less, pierce parts of her body besides her ears. She returned her attention to his face as she clutched the bag to her chest.

He looked at her as if he was judging her mood before telling her bad news. The loop on his brow glinted beneath the light, giving him a sinister cast, and the one centered on his bottom lip made promises of a different kind that would never have anything to do with her.

His gaze fastened on hers. Every nerve in her body tightened until she was certain her head would explode if Jack didn't hurry and spit it out. Something had happened to Ryker.

They stepped out of the elevator.

In a blur, she dropped the bag and pressed a knife against Jack's throat. "Asshole! Is he alive or dead?"

She had to get on her tiptoes and press her body to his, but she wanted to make a point that he needed to quit torturing her. He knew how much she loved Ryker despite their strained relationship.

"You know, you've been hanging out with Ryker too much," he said between gritted teeth. He held his hands out to the sides.

"Quit being a smartass. You're making me understand why he wants you dead so bad. I'm not playing around." Oh, God, if Ryker was dead—

She inhaled. She didn't want to finish that thought.

"He's alive. For now." Jack pressed a finger against her wrist, moving the knife away.

Relieved but still angry with how Jack handled the news, she stepped back and breathed deeply a couple times, trying to calm herself. Her hand trembled as she slipped the knife back into her sleeve. She snatched up the bag and strode into her bedroom suite, tossing it on a chair. "Where is he? In medical?"

"No."

Marie stopped in her path to the closet for a change of clothes and faced him.

"What do you mean, no?" she asked.

"Mulcahy has him."

She screamed. Fists at her sides, she barely, just barely, held back from stomping her feet. Any other time, the look on Jack's face would've had her rolling on the floor laughing. Between frustration with handling her flashbacks for weeks, dealing with Ryker's stubbornness, and now with Jack's unwillingness to tell her all the facts, it was scream or kill someone. Jack looked better and better as the candidate for the latter.

After taking a deep breath, she closed her eyes for a few seconds. "Jack, if you don't spit out the details and quick, I'll make sure Ryker won't ever have to deal with your sorry ass again."

When she opened her eyes, he smiled.

"What?" she asked. What was wrong with the man? Didn't he realize how close he came to dying? She'd become quite efficient at knife-throwing.

"Only a few months ago, you'd have never said anything like that. I like seeing the self-confident Marie. Watching you throw a temper tantrum is so much better than when we pulled you out of Main Sector. You were scared of your own shadow." Jack's smile changed to a wary grin. "Okay. Quit looking at me like you want to slice me up and feed me to the hogs."

She opened her mouth and raised her fists, ready to scream again.

"Wait! Please. Or my ears will start to bleed. Mulcahy said he would release Ryker in exchange for you."

"Are you sure he's still alive?" No hesitation in her decision. And no way would she ever trust that deviant. Any man who distributed a drug that enslaved women to their baser desires and sold them to scumbags needed to be shot. In the groin.

"We intercepted a picture he sent to Liam's cell phone. He has apparently learned Liam betrayed him. In the picture, Ryker's tied to a chair and Mulcahy is holding yesterday's Atlanta paper."

"Yesterday's and you're just now telling me about it." Every terrorist in the world knew to use the most current paper to show a hostage was alive. Of course, there were ways to fake that too.

"You can get as mad as you want. We had to check several things out. His location was hard to find. We both know Ryker doesn't want you involved in another operation. So far, the two you were in went belly-up."

"Like I care what he thinks. It's not like The Circle didn't have its share of failed missions before I decided to get involved." She refrained from the temptation of screaming *and* kicking him in the groin. "Tell me your plans to save him and keep me out of that bastard's hands. Then let's go. Time's a-wasting."

By the time The Circle's large helicopter started for Florida, Marie wanted to choke Jack. She struggled to keep her temper in check when he slumped in the seat across from her and acted so calmly. Sprinklings of white fur covered his black combat pants and jacket. When he noticed where she was staring, he brushed at his clothes.

"Kinky knew I was leaving and went crazy. I would shave her if it wouldn't get her sick." He shrugged and picked a few more off to have them float back onto his clothes.

Marie leaned over to a built-in shelf and unhooked a roll of duct tape from inside. Holding one end of the tape, she pulled it out and wrapped it around her fingers with the stickiness facing out. Using her pocket knife, she cut it from the roll and slipped the tape from her hand, handing it over to him.

"Use this to pick up the fur or it'll drive you and me crazy."

He stuck three fingers into the donut-shaped tape and patted his palm across his thighs and chest. The fur stuck to the tape and he made pretty good leeway in seconds.

The moment was so surreal. Here they were on the way to save the leader of a multi-billion-dollar organization and the second-in-command was worried about cat fur on his clothes.

Jack continued to pat at his clothes as he said, "The Orlando Sector's commander will meet us on a private landing strip and then in about four hours we'll meet a boat near Miami. The Circle's island is about forty-five minutes from that point. We'll stay there and prepare for taking over the island where they have Ryker. I've been told it's about two hours from there."

"Boat? Island? Islands are surrounded by water." Her face washed cold.

"Right. That's why they're called islands. You knew Ryker had received a lead about the Wizard being on an island." He squinted at her. "You don't know how to swim, do you?"

"No." Sector had a pool that off-duty operatives used, but she never thought she would need to know how to swim. Goodness, they lived in the mountains, and she couldn't see herself diving into a cold lake with fish and other slimy creatures. The fear of drowning terrified her.

"I thought we'd take the helicopter all the way to the island."

He remained quiet.

She sighed. "It's too noisy to land without drawing attention, and they could blast us out of the air."

"Bingo."

She closed her eyes, leaning her head back. Well, she had several hours to come to terms with what she was willing to do for Ryker.

They landed in Macon to refuel, and in no time, they arrived near the Orlando Sector at The Circle's private airfield. Three large black Hummers with engines running waited with several operatives standing around them. Two wore drop rigs, wicked-looking guns on their thighs, and two others held M27s across their torsos as they eyed the surrounding area for intruders.

The lead operative for the local Sector stepped forward and greeted Jack.

"Everyone's in place and ready for your orders." Dark sunglasses glanced her way and returned to Jack.

Marie had a feeling the man didn't miss much. With his high and tight haircut and held-back shoulders, he oozed military training.

Jack pulled out his sunglasses from a shirt pocket, slipped them on, and nodded at the vehicles. "Which one?"

"The second one."

Marie followed him to the largest of the three. All black? Could they be any more obvious? But what did she know? She climbed into the back while Jack slipped into the front passenger seat.

"It's about time you two showed up." Charlie sat behind the driver. A door opened and Tom slipped in. He'd flown them in. She flashed a grin at the man. "I thought I'd fry out in this heat waiting on you guys. The sooner we're done, the faster we can return to the coolness of the mountains." She winked at Marie.

During the last several weeks, she'd avoided talking to Charlie about Liam. Since he was one of the lead operatives in The Circle, it was not unusual for him to leave on assignments for months at a time.

Had Charlie heard about Liam's betrayal and his possible elimination? No. Charlie wasn't coldhearted. Though her smile was a little stiff, the wink said she was her usual impudent self. News of Liam's upcoming death would break her.

Truth be told, Ryker had hoped no one had found out about Liam's betrayal in the hope of ambushing Mulcahy and the Wizard. Maybe when they saved Ryker, Marie could talk him into reconsidering. Everyone deserved a second chance.

At the same time, she wanted to warn her friend. But what good would it do at this point? They needed to concentrate on getting through the next few days alive. Mulcahy had crossed over the line of reason when he took Ryker hostage. Too many of the operatives owed him their lives. If Master had still been in control, half of them would be dead by now. Between the rougher-than-usual flight and expected boat ride in the Gulf Coast, her stomach roiled each time she thought about it.

"We should arrive at The Circle's island by ten tonight." Jack talked over his shoulder as he sat in the front near the driver. Before she could open her mouth to ask, he added, "All day tomorrow, you'll take scuba diving lessons. Then we'll leave a couple hours before sunrise the next day."

"Scuba diving lessons? Have you already forgotten I don't know how to swim?"

"Don't worry. I have a solution. For now, you'll learn the basics."

He'd lost his mind. Learn how to swim *and* scuba dive?

"Don't you think we need to hurry? At this rate, when we get to him, he'll have been there for seventy-two hours."

"They won't kill him. He's too valuable alive. Anyway, we need the time to get everyone in place. Rushing in could kill him for sure."

Yes. He was valuable, but was Ryker worth her facing her worst fear? Being in a tub or shallow water never bothered her. But being in a boat or having water above her knees . . . well, the fear was real.

She closed her eyes and hoped her stomach would settle down. Determined to get a grip, she thought about the last time Ryker had helped her with a flashback. After he'd pulled out, she'd rolled over and pretended to fall asleep before he returned from the bathroom. She hated how weak she felt and acted around him. Then his hand had caressed her cheek and smoothed her hair as his deep voice whispered, "Don't worry, I'll take care of you."

She leaned her cheek against the passenger window and sighed. He was worth it.

As they travelled down I-95, Marie stared at the flat land without really seeing it. Various automobiles and trucks passed them in a blur while the Hummers maintained the posted speed limit. The Circle operatives were well aware that to be pulled over for any traffic violation would cause irrevocable delays in their mission. Needless to say, they would have problems explaining the firepower on their persons and stored in the Hummers. Then the locals would call in the federal government, and all hell would break loose, causing The Circle to call in favors from senators they'd rather use at a more advantageous time.

She'd always scoffed at how people said they could sense whether a loved one was still alive or in harm's way. Deep inside, she felt Ryker needed her. That Mulcahy wanted Ryker to suffer in revenge for Marie turning him down.

A tingling feeling shot from her groin to her nipples and blasted warmth across her face. Damn. Double damn. She didn't need this now. She pulled out a thin orange-brown bottle from her pocket and twisted off the cap. Throwing her head back as she tossed the pill into her mouth and swallowed, she hoped it worked fast. No way could she take care of her problem privately. She hated the side effects of the medicine Doc had prescribed her. The only way to describe how she reacted was simply to call her a bitch. Yesterday when Jack had told her about Ryker, she'd just taken a pill.

At first, she could take one every other day whenever Ryker was away. Now it averaged one a day. Half of the three months Doc had given her to use them was over. By the time it was through, she wouldn't have any friends left, and Doc would need to find something stronger. That was, if she didn't kill someone before then. She really needed the antidote.

She leaned the seat back and closed her eyes. Maybe by the time they arrived in Miami, she would have her flashback in control. As it was, she didn't really have a choice.

Jack laughed at a remark Tom made about a passing low-rider with bass thumping, causing even the heavy Hummer to vibrate.

His deep chuckle rippled down her torso.

No!

No matter how sexy he sounded, she needed Ryker. Just the thought of going to another man was not debatable. No other option. So that solved it. She would save his butt, and he'd better show his appreciation slow and hard and often.

Ryker jerked on the bars again. He was no James Bond with Q fortuitously equipping him with a toy to escape the cage in ten seconds flat. And considering that when he woke up over an hour ago he didn't have a stitch on, his chances of finding something helpful were nil.

The cage sat midway between a bank of windows and a mammoth bed in a wide room. The windows looked over a white-sand beach and bluish-green water. Certainly a far better sight than the room. His first thought on awakening was, who in the hell threw up Pepto-Bismol everywhere? Pink walls, pink drapery hanging from bedposts, and pink bedding that included matching satin sheets and pillows.

Even his fucking cage had a coating of pink enamel. He pulled on the door again, hoping the lock would give. Pink paint chipped off as it clanged with each tug.

He stopped. Someone was talking on the other side of a pink door. The pink glass doorknob turned, the door opened, and the person strolled in.

Damn it. He knew there was a reason Liam never cracked and gave him the Wizard's real name. He knew he had missed something important. How stupid and narrow-minded could he be?

"Hello, Ryker." The sugary sweet voice caused him to shudder inside.

CHAPTER NINETEEN

"Letitia." Ryker squeezed the bars as he stared at Liam's ex-wife. Why had he never thought of her? All of it made sense. The woman was a genius and had worked in a pharmaceutical lab as a research scientist straight out of college. No one could make Liam believe she was a cock-chaser even after she disappeared with her lover seven years earlier. "You're the Wizard."

"What a horrible nickname. I've always detested it. As if I would wear a pointed hat and purple robe." One darkened eyebrow lifted. "I must say you've grown into a fine looking man, scars and all. That black patch actually gives you a romantic flair. Give you a puffy shirt, tight pants, thigh-high boots, and a rapier—I would have a real live musketeer in my bird cage."

Ryker looked up. The bars at the top curved up to a point. Damn him, if he wasn't in a bird cage.

"You were all skin and bones back then, but now . . . oh, my . . . how you've filled out."

Her gaze drifted down to his groin. A flash of disappointment darkened her face.

"You should be hard and ready for me."

What had she hoped? That he would be turned on by the cage and her see-through teddy? The pink froth barely held in her manufactured breasts and ended at the beginning of her thighs. Maybe most men would be moved by such a display. She'd kept in shape fairly well for a forty-five-year-old woman. Last time he'd seen her, she'd worn her blonde hair in curls down her back. Now her hair, stopped at chin-level, was straight and a platinum color.

As she crawled onto the bed, he caught a glimpse of the pink thong dividing her cheeks. She stretched, thrusting her chest out, and rubbed her nipples. "I remember how you used to follow me with your eyes. If Theo hadn't been such a control freak, I probably could've been your first." She cut her cold blue eyes toward him. "Your first girl, that is."

"I was an infant when you were a girl," he said, ignoring her attempt to rile him.

Letitia's eyes narrowed and lips flattened as she moved off the bed.

He worked at hiding his satisfaction from that blow. What purpose did it serve in making her angry? He'd half expected her to march across the room and slap him.

"Real men aren't afraid of women with experience." With her bottom lip stuck out, she jiggled across the room and pulled a pink robe from behind a partition made of flamingos, and slipped it on. She didn't bother tying it. "You're no fun." She glanced at a clock on the nightstand and then at his groin. "No. No fun at all. But that's okay. You'll be begging me to help you in a few more minutes."

Her smug little grin bothered him.

What the hell—

The tingling started in his legs and arms and travelled like fireworks toward his cock.

Fuck, no!

He shook the bars. "You, bitch!"

"Uh-uh-uhh. Watch your tone." Making sure to stay out of his reach, she stopped a few feet from the cage. "To answer your question, no. I've been working on a new formula for men. I should've known you can't give the same drug to a man as you can a woman. Two different hormones involved. It was really a shame what happened to your men. I heard you had to put them out of their misery like two rabid dogs."

The tingling hardened him to the point of pain. He sank to his knees, trying to regain control of his body. His back bowed as he thrust his hips out, trying to find some type of relief. Marie had told him about the symptoms, but he had no idea. They were worse than he imagined. How had she stayed sane?

He tried to concentrate on what else the bitch was saying. If not for his head being connected to his shoulders, he believed it would've floated off.

"Mike has been good to me. Gave me the best lab money can buy. Set me up on this beautiful island. He even brings me a new man to test and play with." She leaned her head to the side, eyeing him as if he was a puzzle to be solved.

"I'm not your play toy," he said between gritted teeth.

"But there you're wrong. You're whatever I say you are. The new formula has a few added kicks built-in it for men. And for women, I guess you could say." Her smirk didn't bode well for him.

He struggled to remain calm. Twice he had to force his hands away from his cock. Concentrating on what the woman said, he focused his eye on her and closed his fingers around the bars. The urge to place his fingers around her neck and squeeze helped to control his desire to jerk off. He remained on his knees as his weak legs wouldn't move.

"We haven't given this drug a name yet. Mike named the one for women Blossom Flower. He said that's what a woman's ya-ya looks like when we're all horny and ready for some fun. All open and pink and moist. Maybe he'll call this one Steel Arrow. Isn't that what your penis feels like? Like you have a thick arrow pointing to what it needs? Or maybe he'll call it Piston Primer. Oh, no, I know. Morning Glory." She laughed as her gaze caressed his cock. "He'll love it. Perfect. Of course, the flower does wilt after the sun comes up." Holding her stomach and laughing, she shook her head. "While with this one you can go a long time without losing your erection. That is, if your penis doesn't explode."

"You sick bitch."

"Ah, but you like it. Don't worry—this drug doesn't last as long as the women's. So you'll require additional doses. Besides, if we want to use you for servicing others, we have to let your penis rest every few hours. Mustn't damage it."

She cupped her breasts, and Ryker groaned. His body refused to obey him. Every fiber of his being strained to look away, but her lush flesh tempted his fingers as much as his cock did.

"Having a *hard* time there, buster?" She cackled.

His chest moved in and out like a marathon runner ending a race.

She twirled around. "I need to finish my story, don't I? So Mike hears about me and how I was selling the drug to college students for their frigid girlfriends, making a decent living but getting close to being arrested. The drug at that time wasn't illegal—funny thing, they didn't even know what it was—but having the authorities involved would've caused problems. He shows me, after a few trial runs, how we could use it to make a lot more money. He knew exactly what to do with it. With the right connections a person can become filthy rich!" Hands waving above her head, she danced around, her breasts bouncing with each twist and turn.

He groaned again.

"You can guess I'm richer than I ever imagined." She stopped and her gaze fell to a point below his belly button. She leaned over, her breasts barely held in by the flimsy material, and reached out to touch his throbbing cock.

He pressed his hips to the bars. His mind hazy, he forced his attention to the woman who placed him here. If she moved a little closer, he could grab her and find a way to escape.

"Watch it, Letitia. Don't get too close. He'll bite."

She snapped her hand back.

Mulcahy strode into the room and pulled her away from the cage. His hands cupped her butt as he lifted her for a kiss. She squealed in delight and wrapped her legs around his waist.

"I thought you would never get here. I missed you."

"Ha! I'll be seeing how much you missed me."

"I did! You've got to believe me. I was only having a little fun. You can't blame a girl for being curious. I wanted to see if it was as hard as it looked."

"I have a stiff one you can play with instead."

"Oh, Mike, you do."

Ryker blinked and released the bars, landing in a heap. His cock ached against the cool steel floor. Walls swayed and blended together. The bed creaked and colors splattered across it. A giggle echoed in the room. He tried to keep his eye open but the blurring pulled him under and before he passed out, he heard Mulcahy chuckle and say, "I have something special planned for Ryker. You'll find it to be a wee bit entertaining."

CHAPTER TWENTY

Restless, Marie tapped her foot as she forced the turkey sandwich down her throat. She needed all the energy she could muster after eating breakfast at five-freaking-too-early in the morning. Jack had sashayed into the kitchen at six and announced she would receive her swimming lesson in thirty minutes. He had the gall to say he expected her to catch on quickly. What happened to her understanding friend?

She'd done okay. That was for a person scared of water above her knees.

"How in the hell do you expect to help me if you flunk the damn lesson?" Jack stood over her, his usual laid-back attitude gone as his eerily light-blue eyes shot ice at her.

"I told you I couldn't swim."

"But you said you wanted to save Ryker. You know there's a reason for it being called an island, right?"

"Don't be a smartass." She hated to admit it hurt that he was disappointed in her. He'd only wanted her to be happy, and he was as much of a good friend as Charlie. "I can't believe you said that I flunked. I admit I had problems putting my head underwater, but I got better." She lifted her matted strands. "How do you think this got wet?"

"All the splashing you did." He grabbed her hand and pulled her up. "Go and learn how to not panic underwater. You don't have to be a great swimmer. We'll use DPVs to move from the boat to shore."

She raised her eyebrows at him.

"DPVs are diver propulsion vehicles. Long tube-like equipment with propellers run by batteries that can move us in quickly without detection. I'll be with you and all you have to do is hold on and breathe through the regulator." She gave him a blank stare. He shook his head, obviously disgusted with her ignorance. "The device that goes in your mouth and provides air. It's easier than you think." He rubbed the back of his neck. "Listen, they have a few guards keeping an eye out for uninvited boats, but they depend on cameras for most of the security. Charlie will go in first and reroute two cameras, creating a blind spot. We'll go in from there. By the time they realize what has happened, we'll be in control. Keep that in mind, Marie. In one half of an hour you'll be back on dry land and never have to do this again."

"Don't worry about me. I'll do what's necessary." She said it with more confidence than she felt inside. The alternative was unacceptable. No way would she let Ryker down. She could prove to him and Jack that she was operative material.

And that was what she reminded herself the rest of the day with her head beneath the water as her mind screamed inside.

Ryker woke to his hands clutching his cock and pumping. His skin was so hot, he expected blisters to rise soon. Mindless and failing to care who saw him, all thought centered on his release.

"Get him out of there and ready," Mulcahy said with disgust in his voice.

Clanking warned his sluggish mind they'd unlocked the cage, but his fingers refused to release himself. Hands tugged at his arms and fists slammed into his ribs. He roared. The men hauled his body out and began kicking and beating him in earnest. The room faded in and out of focus. A pinch on his arm caused his body to jerk. In seconds, he sank onto the floor again.

He opened his eye in a different cage. More like a box with threads of light shooting across to the other side. It was long enough to stretch out in, but only inches from his face. Hell, someone had placed him in a coffin, though no fabric covered the sides and nothing cushioned the back of his head.

Minutes ticked by as he assessed the situation. The tingling had ebbed but his hands automatically reached for his cock. Instead of skin, he found silky cloth like the shorts boxers worn in the arena. Underneath that, his hips and groin were wrapped in a cotton-type material with his cock thick and stiff underneath. The bindings were slightly uncomfortable. Yet he was relieved it prevented him from masturbating. Hell, he hadn't been this horny since he last touched Marie.

He breathed in deeply, trying to soothe the panic welling up inside. His elbows scraped the sides. Hell, if he wanted to remove the wrappings, he didn't have enough room to move.

He shifted. A twinge in his arm reminded him someone had injected him again. What had they given him? More of the same? It would probably kill him this time.

Someone rapped on the box. He jumped.

"Wake up. Time for you to earn your keep."

What the hell?

A vibration rattled the metal as he heard the whining of an engine. The box was moving. Twisting his neck, he looked through one of the perforations and saw only cement blocks. He guessed it to be a tunnel or hallway of some sort. Then a rumbling sound added to the vibration and grew louder. The whining stopped and then the soft hum of a hydraulic motor running had the box tilting. He slid to his feet. He and the box were upright.

He opened and closed his fists. He wanted to kill whoever locked him in there, whoever shot him with that shit. Never had he expected to be so helpless again. Only he wasn't a weak kid, hero-worshiping the wrong person. Life had taught him a lot and he knew patience always paid off. They would make a mistake. Then their asses were fish bait.

Light streamed into the box from the holes, this time brighter. A little door near his shoulder opened and though he moved to the opposite side, it wasn't far enough and another needle sank into his arm. The drug worked faster than before. The pleasant tingling changed to raging fire in his blood. The need to fuck overshadowed every thought.

The voice said, "The drug will make you fuck or fight. Unless you like men, I suggest you fight. Defeating your opponent will give you the release you need until the next injection."

The lid of the box popped open, and he stumbled out onto white sand in the middle of an enclosed arena, with a balcony about ten feet up encircling the whole place. He could see people talking, drinking, and laughing as they watched his stilted movements. Two large cameras with red lights pointing at him recorded from the ceiling.

Ryker shook his head, trying to regain control of his body. The drug running through his system ramped up the desire to fuck or kill someone. He loped to the wall and tried to find a way to climb to the balcony. The few notches weren't wide enough for his fingers or toes.

A deep voice behind him screamed, "You're goin' to die, motherfucker!"

Marie wished she could say she was enjoying herself. Wind pulled her hair from under the dive hood and plastered it across her face. She tucked it back in. Most people talked about how exhilarating it was to ride in a speedboat at night as they cut through the waves at a forty-five-degree angle. Sure, the thing was beautiful. Long, sleek lines—blue and silver. Forty-one feet of massive power. The boat was a drag racer on water. She'd asked how fast they were going, but no one heard her. The wind blew away the sound before it reached the other person's ears. Anyway, there were reasons the drivers in speedboat racing wore helmets with microphones and other safety gear.

The operative shifted down the speed until they heard only the slapping of the water against the hull, and the up-and-down motion caused her stomach to churn. She swallowed, hoping not to embarrass herself. Her legs wobbled as she widened her stance to ride each swell. The feeling was nothing like she'd ever experienced before, but Jack told her the waves were small compared to the Atlantic side.

If he said so.

Just thinking of anything bigger turned her stomach, but thankfully Jack had had her take a couple capsules of ginger in an effort to ward off or minimize any seasickness.

"Get your gear. Charlie's already in place and about to hit the switch." Jack slipped on his flippers and shrugged on his tank with one of the operatives' help. Another operative was lowering two DPVs that would be used in moving them in quickly toward the shore. The part they would enter was deep up to twenty yards from the shore. Then it sloped up quickly. They would drag the DPVs to shore and then an assigned operative would hide them. If they were successful, Jack would call in the boat to the docks on the other side of the island.

Marie hoped and prayed everything would go as planned. Thinking ahead stopped her from worrying about the next few minutes.

By the time one of the men helped her with her gear and she had the regulator in place, her heart was racing. She prayed the eighteen-hour crash course in swimming and diving did the trick. If she felt any wavering, she had only to imagine Ryker's face and how surprised he'd be by her daring. He might be pissed, but he had to realize her capability to adapt increased her value as an operative. Preferably one who worked on land.

Jack clasped her head and looked into her eyes. "Are you ready?"

She wanted to scream, *hell no*, but instead nodded.

"That's my girl."

Ryker swiped the blood from his cheek onto his shoulder. His patch had disappeared after the first fight. Was this the fifth or sixth time he'd fought in two days? At least, he thought it had been two and no more.

The stench from his own body gave little evidence to the length of time he'd been in this hellhole. A combination of sweat, urine, and blood coating his body and where he lay caused him to gag when they shoved him into the enclosed space. He ignored the aches from bruises and cuts as he concentrated on finding a way out.

He eyed the small opening, trying to see the number of boxes stacked along the metal ledges like toy soldiers waiting for their owners. A couple of them were missing, as they most likely died or were too injured to return to fight. At least, that was what he imagined, along with how he would escape and take revenge on Mulcahy and that crazy bitch, Letitia. Plotting their deaths occupied his mind, stopping him from going insane in the tight, narrow box.

Between the shots of what they now called Morning Glory, he fought whoever they placed in the arena. It was fight or die. The drug shut down the civilized portion of his brain, and he raged like a beast at the nearest target. As soon as he won, they'd pull him down with netting and stick him back into the box.

No food so far, but every few hours, a man's voice encouraged him to sip on the tube inserted through a hole near his mouth. At first, he'd wanted to ignore it, but overwhelmed by his thirst, he caved in. It tasted of minerals and a sick sweetness. If the fluid was drugged, he didn't care at this point. His entire body ached.

Mulcahy and Letitia would make a mistake and he'd be ready. He needed to keep his mind on surviving and getting back to Marie.

The thought of touching her again caused pain to shoot across his cock and down his legs.

He pushed his head back as he squeezed his eye shut. Each time they pushed him out of the box, they promised release. At the rate he was going, if he ever found his cock unwrapped and between a woman's legs, he might hurt her.

Marie's image formed behind his eyelids. He moaned in pain. Every molecule of his body wanted her—wanted between her legs, tasting her lips, her breasts. Shit! He needed to survive. He needed to find some weakness in the arena or in those who captured him each time. If he could convince an opponent to redirect the anger toward their captors, they might have a chance of escaping.

The clang of a metal door opening nearby alerted him it was time to fight again.

"Time for his booster shot. Letitia's calculations so far have been spot-on. What with the energy they're using in the fight, the drug's doing its job. Poor bastards." The man's voice sounded sympathetic, but Ryker planned to kill the owner.

"He's on in twenty minutes. Make it snappy," another man said.

The small panel near his shoulder slid to the side. Although he knew it was hopeless, he tried to move away as the needle pierced his skin. Seconds after the panel closed, the drug spread like fire from his arm across his torso and to his groin. Then—*bang!*—his whole body stiffened in pain. He growled and shook the box.

"You sure it'll hold?" The voice sounded worried as he asked someone whose voice Ryker couldn't hear. "I know, but maybe this time it was too strong. She swore the man needed a stronger dosage."

Heat and desire for relief zinged through his system. Sweat poured down his face. He lived in hell.

Again, he rocked against the sides, rattling his metal coffin. "You better hope I never get my hands around your throat, you son of a bitch. I'm going to kill you and every fucking freak on this island!"

The tingling travelled through his veins. Whimpers escaped even as he bit his lips to hold them back. His eye refused to remain open, no matter how much he fought the overpowering need pulling him into the blackness.

"Come on, Marie!" Jack waited in the water, bobbing up and down, a few feet out, waiting for her to jump off the boat.

Fumbling with her gear, she remained calm, even when she stepped off the side. Before she could panic, Jack helped her grab the handle of her DPV. For the next twenty minutes, she stayed up with him, and along the way she chanted in her mind, *Ryker needs me, Ryker needs me.* No way could she say she ever relaxed. But as time slowed to a crawl beneath the water's surface, the crash course in scuba diving and swimming appeared to be paying off.

They stayed deeply enough not to be seen by anyone from the island watching the surface, but close enough that the brightness from the moon reflected on the water above her.

She did well until she spotted the sleek lines of a shark. Not that she panicked at that moment; she remembered Jack saying nothing would attack. In fact, most creatures were more scared of them. For a few seconds she did fine. Then her heart rate picked up. She began to struggle for each draw of air. She hated it. She hated being such a wimp about stupid water. Chances were somewhere in the recesses of her mind, something had happened to cause her to be so afraid, but nothing mattered at this juncture but returning to the surface.

Out of the corner of her eye, she noticed Jack waving her back, but her overpowering need to breathe fresh air dominated her common sense. At last, she surfaced at an angle but they were too close to the island.

At first, she didn't realize they were firing at her. The splats near her were nothing like what she imagined bullets hitting water would sound like. And the crack of gunfire followed a split second afterward. So disconcerting when the sequence should be the opposite, but the distance and water played with the sound waves.

She gestured to the men surfacing around her to dive again. But it was too late. One grunted and went under. Blood in the water with at least one shark nearby was asking for more.

"Marie!" Jack pushed her away from the growing pool of blood.

In seconds, they heard motors starting up. They were coming for them.

"I'm sorry. This is all my fault." She jerked her arm out of his grip. "Go. I'll tell them it was me and just those who were shot. Go!"

He looked at her and then at the boats coming nearer, the bows slapping the waves as they came at them from an angle so as not to be turned over by the swells.

"Hang in there. I'll come after you and Ryker," Jack said, and then he dove beneath the next wave.

Too many of The Circle's men had died. The horror of those first few minutes she'd live over and over again. They dragged her—protesting, screaming, crying—into the boat. Two other operatives pulled from the water were not as lucky. When they reached the shore, they tossed one operative's body onto the sand. Mulcahy's men wouldn't let her stop his bleeding. The other one they beat to a bloody pulp before dragging him off.

They threw her into a room empty of furniture. The only light came from a bug-coated bulb set behind a grill in the ceiling. Shivering, she sat in the corner, her back to the wall as she faced the door. She still felt them pulling at her wetsuit, the echo of laughter surrounding her as she'd fought strange hands trying to strip off her black bikini. Someone had gruffly ordered them to stop before they closed the door.

Her eyes refused to focus. Was she going into shock? Rocking back and forth helped warm her chilled skin. She chafed her arms and pulled her knees to her chest.

Was Ryker still alive? Had Jack and the other operatives made it to shore? No matter how she tried to comfort herself, she knew the truth. Her stubbornness and silliness in not listening to Jack had killed at least two of The Circle's operatives. It was left to her to save Ryker.

Mulcahy. It had been his voice she'd heard. His interest in her might be the key to helping Ryker. Time for her to take matters into her own hands and be the operative she'd dreamed of being.

By the time the door opened, her tears had dried and she knew what had to be done.

CHAPTER TWENTY-ONE

Marie clutched the white material to her breasts. Mulcahy stood in the doorway examining her as if he owned her.

"The white suits you. Turn, let me see how it looks in the back." He crossed his arms and waited for her to comply.

Inside she wanted to scream and knee him in the groin. But she had a role to play that had begun when Mulcahy entered her cell.

The day before, she'd lied, claiming Jack had forced her to attack the island. Like many men, he allowed his cock to control his brain and believe that because of her small size, she was harmless. And luckily, he'd fallen for it.

So here she was dressed up in a Roman tunic, about to play a part in tricking him to drop his guard even further. In the meanwhile, she'd search for where they locked up Ryker. Once she found him, the next step was to find a way for them to escape.

Hopefully, Jack had made it alive to another part of the island or back to the boat with the remaining operatives. Staying positive was her only option.

"Yes. You have a beautiful back. The long scars make it most interesting. So your newest scar will blend in with the rest. We mustn't have anyone tracking you down." His finger traced the two stitches where her locator had been removed.

She fought the need to step away. Her stomach roiled, hating his touch.

The door opened behind them and drew his attention, saving her from throwing up on him.

"So how's the little whore doing?" Letitia entered the room in a swirl of white. Her tunic had been tailored and pulled tight to show off her acquired breasts and overly ripe hips. With her height, the folds flowed to her feet in seductive lengths. She eyed Marie with distaste. "You say that Ryker taps that? She's so tiny, everywhere. He's so big; I don't see how he could fit it in her." Her nose wrinkled and upper lip curled. "Are you sure he doesn't close his eyes and imagine her as a young boy? He may have acquired the taste from Theo. Of course, the psycho loved them young."

The tall woman turned to Marie. "Does he bend you over and fuck you from behind, little girl?"

"Enough! It only bothers you because Ryker wouldn't take you up on your offer, even when he was drugged," Mulcahy said in an ugly tone.

Any satisfaction Marie received from knowing Ryker had turned the huge woman down was colored by hearing they had shot him up with Blossom Flower too.

"Is he still alive?" She hoped she sounded as if she wanted to know out of normal curiosity.

Mulcahy opened his mouth but Letitia answered. "I guess you could call it that."

She wanted to know what the woman meant, but knew another direct question would be pushing it. So she said, "I thought the drug was made only for women. Doesn't it make men too violent?"

When Mulcahy tilted his head and narrowed his eyes as he studied her, she waited for the accusations. She needed him to remain convinced she didn't care for Ryker.

Letitia shook her head. "That's true but we—"

With a sharp cut of his hand, Mulcahy shut up the woman. "Why are you so interested?"

"One of her disciples shot me up with the stuff, and I know how it affected me. So why shouldn't I be interested in hearing that men have an equal opportunity to know how women feel with the drug in their system?" She stared back and lifted her brows. Inside, she wanted to scream curses at the two crazies standing in front of her.

He chuckled. "Disciples, huh? I do believe she's calling you a devil. You do love to wear red, and those long nails of yours can go deep. Yeah. I think it fits."

Letitia glowered and stomped a foot. "I've had enough. If you get her, I get Ryker."

Hot rage washed over Marie. She wanted to show the insane woman what she'd learned from Charlie and Jack the last few weeks. Her hands clutched the tunic material, and she stepped toward the woman. A noise at the door saved her from ruining her plans.

"We have activity near the docks." Ice's cold, black eyes skimmed over her and returned to Mulcahy.

"Then handle it as I instructed. Obviously, the scenario is being played as I expected. I'm busy here." Mulcahy turned to

Letitia. "Go on and get the show started. Marie and I will be along directly."

"Fine. I believe tonight I get the right to have a little fun with the winner. And we know who that will be, don't we?" With that cryptic remark, Letitia shot her a nasty look and glided out of the room.

Ice closed the door, leaving Marie alone with Mulcahy.

"Winner?" She suspected they were talking about Ryker, but winner of what?

"Ignore Letitia. She's only trying to get under your skin. I had them set up a table so we can dine and watch the games." He clutched her arm, holding tight enough for her to stay next to him, but not to hurt. "Have I told you yet how lovely you look?"

Ignoring him, she said, "You know, I haven't eaten all day and I'm starving." She wanted a crowd of people around her, especially with the hungry way Mulcahy undressed her with his eyes.

"Letitia told me how skinny you used to be when you belonged to Theo. I like you better this way: curves in the right places, your breasts perfect for my palms."

She tensed, expecting him to prove his point.

He merely grinned. Then he nodded. "Let's go." In a showy flourish, he opened the door, bowed, and waved her through the doorway.

Bunching the material into one hand, she held it away from her feet. The last thing she wanted was to trip and give him an excuse to touch her. He led her down a beautiful sweeping marble staircase and then around a sharp turn to a dimly lit stairwell.

What was it with these people and basements? Since her time in one with the creep in Chattanooga, and the cold, sterile one near Cartersville, she'd rather stay out of them. She frowned and glanced at her feet. A strange sensation tingled along the soles. Nothing similar to Blossom Flower's flashbacks. Once they reached a well-lit corridor with twin large metal doors at the end, the vibration beneath her feet became stronger. Then she heard what sounded like an engine with pistons thumping. Just as Mulcahy pressed the thick bar on one door, she realized the sound wasn't mechanical, but hundreds of people stomping their feet in sync and chanting a name.

"Ryker! Ryker! Ryker!"

The rhythm from the excited crowd pulsated through Ryker's cock. Always for the first two hours after the shot, he sported a painful erection. If not for the wrapping protecting his cock and the other contestants being in the same condition, the liability would've gotten him killed before now.

How many days had it been? No watch or clocks, never seeing the sun, he had no way of knowing how long he'd truly been in this hellhole. He guessed four days, maybe more. Only the shots he now craved and the fights measured his time.

"Your turn again," said a deep voice from the shadows.

The door swung open, and he stepped into the arena. Blinking from the glare of the bright lights, he shaded his eye as a dark blur charged him. His opponent attacked with a right uppercut and then brought up a knee to the groin. He missed by fractions as Ryker instinctively twisted his hips and stuck a foot out, tripping the man.

Ryker rubbed his eye. Seconds mattered in who came out of this alive. Just as his vision cleared, the man jumped to his feet and threw a punch to Ryker's stomach.

The roaring and shouting from the balcony became no more than white noise as he straightened and stepped toward the man. The man's face paled seconds before Ryker struck. Fists and feet flew at a furious pace. The thud of flesh hitting flesh satisfied his need for a release even though he preferred another kind. The crowd screamed their approval as he landed solid hits and his opponent dropped to the sand in seconds.

Marie, frozen to her seat, watched the violence below on the sand. She hadn't seen Ryker in over a week. He looked different. His hair was longer, face unshaven, and patch gone. With his eyes wide, one shining white, he looked crazed. Bruises marred his chin and arms. In fact, from what she could see, he suffered from several abrasions and contusions. Wearing only a dingy loincloth, his arms and chest glistened beneath the bright lights. She'd never before seen him so wild and out of control as he pummeled the man. Even when the man crashed to the ground, Ryker continued to hit him. She cringed inside as she struggled to keep her face unemotional. No way could she reveal to Mulcahy the horror she felt on seeing Ryker's violence.

His opponent kicked Ryker hard, sending him back several steps, allowing the man to reach his feet, swaying. Before he could manage another hit, Ryker attacked again with a kick of his own to the man's chest. A loud crunch warned the crowd Ryker had probably shattered the man's ribs. When the man didn't move, the crowd went crazy shouting Ryker's name, clapping as if he'd taken down a wild animal instead of another human being.

"How do you like Ryker's performance? Your old master has been dropping them like flies. That was the most hits I've seen someone get in before he killed them." Mulcahy's cold eyes watched for her reaction.

Before she responded, a wire net shot from the ceiling and covered Ryker, pulling him to the ground. His bellow told of his frustration. Several men wearing soft armor and helmets rushed out and jumped on top of him. Like a feral animal, he continued to fight. They pressed him into the sand until one of them pulled out a hypodermic and pressed it into his hip. His body became limp.

Marie's fingers began to ache. She looked down. Her nails dug into the chair's leather arms. She forced her hands to drop into her lap and stopped their trembling by clasping them. How could this be happening? When would she wake from the nightmare? Every time she thought she'd seen the worst a human could inflict on another, a new perversion turned up.

She barely registered Ice as he stepped onto the balcony and whispered into Mulcahy's ear. The growing smirk on his face bothered Marie, but she had to concentrate on regaining control of her queasy stomach.

The roar of the crowd caught her attention and she looked into the arena. Two more men were fighting. The sickening hollow sound of flesh hitting flesh brought new acid churning in her stomach.

"What do you think of our little games? It's amazing how much people will pay to see one brute kill another. None of this virtual reality crap they can find on the Internet. Video games don't compare to the real thing, although we do make a killing on the Internet with videos of the fights." Mulcahy covered her hands with one of his. "I see that you're bothered by the violence." He leaned toward her, his excitement obvious on his face. She dared not look down to see how excited.

Every inch of her body shrunk from his touch. She wanted to jerk her hands away and run screaming from him. Relieved her flashbacks appeared to be in control, especially around the delusional man looking at her with such sick lust in his eyes, Marie stood, brushing his hands out of the way.

"You're right. I think I need to lie down." The glint in his eyes rushed her to add, "Alone." She needed a little time to find her way to wherever the fighters exited the arena.

"Sit," he commanded. A different kind of interest flashed in those dark eyes. "We haven't eaten yet. Besides, I have a special surprise for you."

What was he going to do to Ryker? Hadn't he suffered enough? He thought he was responsible for his parents' deaths. What would killing people with his bare hands do to him?

Her gaze skimmed the china and crystal laid out for them. With her stomach tossing around as if she stood on the bow of a deep sea vessel, warning her of what would happen if one bite passed her lips, she shook her head.

Afraid of what she was about to see, but too afraid to defy the mad man blocking her way, Marie dropped back into the chair, keeping her gaze on Mulcahy. "I don't like surprises." She peeked over at Ice as he stood next to the doorway with his arms crossed, watching her with cold, emotionless eyes. Even if she found a way past Mulcahy, Ice would stop her.

"Oh, you'll like this one." He nodded toward the arena. They were dragging off the winner of the most recent bout. "I told them to bring him straight to the arena."

A door opened and a man stumbled, falling face-first into the sand.

Damn. They'd caught Jack too. All hope of saving Ryker and escaping disappeared, sucking the air out of the room with it. She forced her lungs to work again without emitting a sound, though inside she whimpered like a beaten puppy. What could she do? Was she up to saving herself and Ryker—and now Jack?

Even from a distance the bruises on his arms and back told her of how hard he'd fought his capture.

A huge man with greasy hair stalked across the arena. Jack's opponent made the mistake of allowing him to regain his footing.

Marie cringed as the familiar thumping of a fist hitting a naked torso resonated throughout the arena. She wanted to look away, yet she watched, hoping that by willing the fight to be quick and Jack successful, it would happen. Seconds later, it was over and they were dragging Jack out of the arena while leaving the other body to be hauled out.

Her muscles loosened and she sighed.

"You know, I've been thinking."

Marie hated the way he paused. She refused to look at him. He would wait a long time if he expected her to prompt him. She was in no hurry to hear what horror he planned next.

"You don't want to play, uh?" Mulcahy grabbed her arm and lifted her to her feet. She blindly stared at the blood-stained sand. "I had planned to let Ryker and Jack fight each other. I've changed my mind after seeing them today. It would be too dangerous to have the two of them in the arena at the same time. The drug can make them unpredictable. A good thing someone offered to take one off my hands for a price. Otherwise, I would need to kill one of them. We must have only one alpha bull in the ring."

She looked at Mulcahy then. He was like Theo, playing his games, manipulating people into giving away their feelings. If she played favorites with either man, what little time they had left in this world would be a living hell. But would life be any better here?

Unsure of what to say or do, she remained quiet. The first lesson she'd learned growing up was to keep her mouth shut and her eyes open. A lesson that had saved her life many times with Theo.

"Let's go see what Letitia is up to. That should help me decide." Not releasing his hold on her arm, they exited the balcony just as the crowd roared with approval at the start of another fight. When they entered the hallway, instead of continuing straight, they turned left into another wing of the massive underground facility. Out of the corner of her eye, she caught some movement. Ice followed quietly behind them.

They reached a large gate. Two burly guards outfitted in the black, soft armor she'd seen earlier stood at attention nearby as a man in a blue lab coat unlocked the bars with a loud clang. Metal screeched as it opened.

"I hadn't expected you so soon. Letitia's with him now, giving him the extra shot you ordered."

Mulcahy's hand squeezed her arm harder. She grimaced. Any bruise he gave her at that moment would be worth it, considering how upset he appeared at the news. But who were they giving the additional injection to? Ryker or Jack?

They walked by a glassed-in lab into what looked to be a storage room. Her steps hesitated as the stench assaulted her nose. It smelled of unwashed bodies and urine with a large dose of despair.

Around a hundred metal boxes lined the ten-foot-tall shelves and several of the boxes stood upright on the floor. From the dime-sized holes stamped into the metal, eyes stared back at her, causing her skin to crawl with the realization that they each contained a human locked inside.

Mulcahy pulled her toward a steel door marked "Authorized Personnel Only" in yellow and black. Still holding her, he opened the door and kicked it, slamming it against the wall.

Letitia leaned over Ryker. With his head, chest, arms, and legs strapped to an examining table, Ryker would be unable to stop her from doing whatever she wanted. She had a hand beneath his loincloth and a knee on the table, and was about to crawl over his defenseless body.

"Get off me, you fucking skank!" Ryker said between gritted teeth.

"No one's coming to your rescue. While Mike's fucking your little whore, you're mine to play with until I've had my fill. Then we'll take turns cutting pieces off you. That is, if you don't die in the arena before then."

Marie resisted the urge to scream, but for the first time in a long while, she had the desire to kill. By touching Ryker, that woman became the walking dead.

Chapter Twenty-Two

Ryker's arms and hips ached from the numerous shots they'd given him. It only added to the contusions he'd received from his opponents' hits and jabs. Now with Letitia treating him as her own private sex toy, he wanted to grab her by the throat and squeeze.

Hatred and lust swamped his brain. Not since the last time Theo had restrained and used him had Ryker wanted to kill another with his bare hands.

"Bloody hell, get off the man. You can take him back to your room later." Mulcahy stopped close enough to the examination table for Ryker to see his hand gripping Marie's arm. She was beautiful with her hair piled on her head and ringlets brushing her cheeks. The white gown made her look like one of those women on Greek urns.

Her green eyes flashed with anger. She jerked her arm from the asshole and pushed Letitia. "Are you deaf and stupid? Get away from him!"

Letitia stumbled off the table, clutching a chair to regain her balance. She stood straight and thrust back her shoulders. Fury reddened her face as she towered over the small woman. "Don't you ever touch me again!"

When Letitia pushed out a hand to knock her to the side, Marie grabbed it and with surprise written on everyone's faces, the taller woman's body flew through the air, crashing hard into the floor.

"No. Bitch. Don't touch me." Marie reached for the Velcro straps holding Ryker down.

"What do you think you're doing, my darling?" Mulcahy ignored the unconscious woman at his feet.

"He can't . . . You can't—" Tears streamed down Marie's face.

Ryker understood what was going through her mind. Tying them down for punishment was a favorite of Theo's. He wanted to tell her to stop crying, that everything would be okay, but his compassion would only give Mulcahy more ammunition.

"Oh, yes, I can—and will."

Fruitless as it was, Ryker fought the straps as he caught the look Mulcahy gave him.

The gun in the man's hand pointed straight and steady at Ryker. "I had planned to let him live a little longer, but I don't like how you have such a soft spot for him. I don't like how you look at him."

Before he squeezed the trigger, a scream echoed into the room, followed by gunfire and shouting. Mulcahy moved out of Ryker's field of vision.

"What the bloody hell have they done?" The screaming became louder as a man opened the door and ran at them brandishing a long knife. "Marie, stay here. I'll deal with you and Ryker later." Mulcahy shot the man, and then using the knife he sliced him open as if for good measure. Then he disappeared into the crowd, firing and slicing along the way.

Standing frozen, she stared at the chaos outside the pane of glass.

Although she was the most courageous woman he'd ever known, all the bloodshed and trauma she'd been through would affect such a sensitive soul. From what little Ryker could see, the acts of barbarianism on the other side could send her into shock.

Needing to get her mind on something else, he said, "Marie. Get the straps."

She blinked a few times and reached for the one at his right arm. As soon as she pulled the strap away, he jerked the others from his head and left hand as she worked on his torso and legs.

She asked, "What's happened?"

Ryker eyed her while he massaged his numb legs. Though she moved with purpose, as if seeing the slaughter on the other side of the glass didn't affect her any longer, her shaking hands matched her trembling voice.

"I had inside help setting up a disturbance. It appears he decided to release all the fighters."

Just as he sat up, Ice slipped into the room.

"Took you long enough," Ryker said. "Is there a way out of here?"

"If we leave now. I have a boat ready. Can you make it?" Collin's top operative looked cool and in control. His brother swore the man could be trusted.

How ironic was that? From what he'd seen, the man was good at his job and had done his best to protect Marie—when he could without raising suspicion. Ryker didn't trust his brother, but he had no other option.

Ryker tested his legs as he held tight to the examining table. The booster shot the bitch had given him swirled in his veins. His vision became fuzzy and his head felt like a balloon about to float away. His fingers gripped the edge of the table harder and he waited for his head to clear as all the blood flowed to his groin. He didn't have time for this.

"He's been working for you all along?" Marie's tone hinted at her disbelief.

Ryker concentrated on piecing the words together so he could answer. "No. Yes." He shook his head. Damn it, whatever booster the bitch had given him was blurring his mind more so than usual. "He works for my brother. So technically, he works for me." Her confused look was no surprise. He hadn't told her what he and his brother had agreed on back in Georgia. It felt like a hundred years ago.

"Time to go. Or it's never. Mulcahy's rallying his guards." Ice waved them over to follow.

Marie's soft touch on his arm jolted through his body to his hard cock. He jerked away. The hurt look on her face penetrated his cotton-filled brain.

"Don't touch me for a while. I'm not sure how much control I have. The drug—"

Ice interrupted. "Let's go!"

"Follow Ice. I'll be right behind you." He didn't want Marie out of his sight—more out of fear that someone would take her from him, than because she looked like a goddess in that white dress. When he got a look at her back, his knees almost gave out on him. He could see the dip in her waist where her buttocks started. Heat infused his body. He wanted to touch her badly. Then his gaze noted a red, swollen area with three delicate stitches beneath one shoulder blade. The asshole had cut her and taken out her locator. When he got his hands on Mulcahy, there wouldn't be enough left to bury him. For now, he needed to concentrate on getting her to safety.

Only twice did a guard or unfortunate inmate get in their path as they wound their way through a passageway. The pleasure Ryker felt in mashing in their faces and breaking their arms didn't compare to what he really wanted: Marie with her legs spread.

Another hot surge gripped his body. *Keep your mind on getting out of here first, you rutting bastard.*

By the time Ice slapped open an emergency exit, sweat covered every inch of Ryker's body. Instead of the outside, they were in a dank cave. Several yards later, they ran up steps carved into rock that twisted and turned with a strong salt-laden breeze hitting their faces. Instead of coming as a relief to his overheated body, the breeze caressed his skin. Moisture trickled down his face. At first, he thought it was sweat, but when he wiped his face he realized it was tears. Fighting the urge to throw the woman before him on the ground and fuck her brains out was killing him.

They finally emerged into a small grove of trees. Pushing their way through, they came out near a cliff overlooking a snow-white beach. A few yards away, a Sea Ray boat anchored near shore bobbed in the water.

"Here." Ice knocked off a pile of dead fronds covering a canvas bag. "You both need to change into these. It'll make your time in the boat tolerable." He tossed the bag to Ryker.

Inside, he found the typical clothes of tourists: loud-colored shirts and khaki shorts, and at the bottom, flip-flops.

"You're kidding, right?" Ryker held up a large blue pair with two fingers.

"A tourist wouldn't be wearing combat boots in a boat in the middle of the Gulf." Ice pointed between two palms. "Follow the trail along the ledge and it'll come out on the beach. I've got to get back before they realize you're gone. When they start searching for you, I'll help Jack escape."

He was right about the clothes. Although Ryker wasn't sure how to hide his blind eye.

"What about a weapon?" Ryker dug into the bag, checking between the clothes.

"They're on the boat. Be sure to look in the side pockets. The odds and ends will probably come in handy." Then the man disappeared into the shadows.

Ryker unzipped a side pocket and pulled out a compass. Another pocket yielded two pairs of sunglasses, and next to them, a couple of baseball caps. The last pocket had wipes and a bottle of mosquito repellant.

Hmm. Three out of five were useful. Not many mosquitoes with all the wind and waves. Ice had better left some guns and ammo in the boat. Floating around the Keys with drug runners and other low-lifes without a weapon only asked for trouble.

"Here. Put this on." He pitched the sack of clothes to her. His fingers trembled as he touched the material wrapped around his hips. Leaving on the loincloth and the binding around his cock would probably be best. He couldn't take a chance of being naked even for a second around Marie. They needed to get out of there, quick.

He turned his back and leaned down to step into the shorts. A wave of dizziness struck and he stumbled. Marie grabbed his arm.

His breath left his body for a second and heat shot though him, all the way to his cock, hardening and lengthening it in need. He dropped his shorts at his feet. The need to get away forgotten, he jerked her toward him and covered her mouth. His tongue stroked hers, filling her mouth as he wanted to fill a hotter place of hers. Hell, he never knew how sensitive his tongue was until now. Walking her backward, he stopped in the shadows.

"I'm sorry. Ah, hell, I can't wait any longer." His harsh voice sounded like someone else's. Damn it. He didn't want to hurt her. For days he'd suffered, needing relief. When they locked him in the box, he'd dream about her, sinking into her, stroking her, taking them both over the edge. She was here: soft, warm, alive. He'd always had a soft spot for her. Other women were easy to resist. Maybe that was why he'd survived in the arena—all that need directed to killing instead of fucking, as she wasn't available and she was the only one he wanted.

Her face softened as she nodded her acceptance, her understanding.

He pushed her into a pile of leaves, onto her hands and knees. His shaking hands bunched up the skirt of her dress and pulled off her thong.

"Part your legs," he growled.

Without waiting for her to comply, he spread her knees. Cloth ripped as he yanked off the loincloth. Her gasp warned him to go a little slower. He fumbled as he hurried to unwrap his cock.

"Oh, my, I never thought . . . but that's sexy," she whispered as she looked over her shoulder.

He hesitated for a few seconds. The thought of her finding it sexy gave him thoughts of many scenarios they could play out, with more time and the proper setting.

Then his hands cupped her cool buttocks and opened her a little more. She glistened with her excitement, ready for him. In one long thrust he entered her. He exhaled, fighting the needed to drive harder into her. She whimpered.

"Are you okay?"

Her body shook and as he started to pull out, she said, "I'm okay. It's just so funny—I've missed hearing you ask me that. I want you. Please don't stop."

Unable to hold back any longer, he took a deep breath and then started pumping his aching cock into her. In seconds, her moistness and heat squeezed and tightened around him in her release.

He adjusted his hold, cupping her breasts and lifting them out of her dress. He clasped them for better leverage, squeezing and easing with each stroke inside of her. Then he continued to thrust with quick jabs as he tugged her nipples. He wanted to feel her come again. His desire to come in her drove him to keep going.

Yet, no matter how much the drug in his system screamed

for him to let go, he couldn't. Release waited and burned in his groin. So close.

Her low moan warned him. Heat bathed his cock as each contraction and release pulled him a little closer to the edge.

He caught her as she went limp, panting. His cock pulsed but remained tight with need.

"Sorry. I need more." He flipped her around and hooked his arms behind her knees.

"I can't take more. All my energy is gone. I can't. Please." She closed her eyes.

"You can." He needed her to want it. Otherwise, he wasn't sure if he could keep his mind on escaping. Look where the drug had gotten him so far. No more than a few yards from the exit and he had to stop to take her.

His fingers opened the pouty flesh between her legs as his mouth sucked and tongue lapped at the sweetness. Her hips arched and rotated as she whimpered. He pressed his thumb into her wetness. When he suckled on her clit, she stuck the side of her hand into her mouth to stifle a scream. Before the first wave hit, he pinched the hard nub.

"Ow! What are you doing?" She dug her elbows into the leaves and glared at him.

"I'll make sure it's even better." He wanted to be inside her when she climaxed once again.

Moving between her legs, he pushed her knees toward her shoulders. Without giving her a chance to argue, he sank into her heat. His thumb flicked the tender knot. She gave a sweet moan.

"You're a cruel man." She bit her lower lip.

"Yeah." Without slowing, he leaned over and continued to pound into her. He leaned further and drew in the offered nipple. He stretched the nub with his teeth.

Her hands dropped to his buttocks, pulling him closer.

Her eyes, half closed in satisfaction, stared back at him from beneath smoky lashes. He watched her as he eased his wet thumb into her tight hole where his balls slapped with each downward thrust.

Soft eyes widened in surprise as her nails dug into his flesh. When he pumped his thumb as he did his cock, she came for a third time. The waves massaged his cock, strong ripples moving all the way to the tip.

She scraped her nails down to his thighs. Pain boiled over and he bowed his back, grunted, and finally climaxed. He continued to move until the last ripple left their bodies.

For the first time in days, his mind cleared. Their heavy breathing slowed after a few seconds. He slipped out of Marie, his penis limp and sore as she must be after he'd used her so roughly.

He looked at her, expecting to see tears and disgust at his lack of control. Tears pooled in her eyes and she appeared exhausted, but she wore a smirk. She tucked his hair behind his ear. The gesture was so gentle and caring. If they'd been alone, he'd strip her naked and fuck her underneath every tree on the island.

Helping her to her feet, he stepped back and nearly stumbled over the canvas bag. Her hand came out as before to help him regain his balance.

He lurched away from her simple touch. The hurt on her

face bothered him, but they'd delayed long enough. He didn't want to admit that her touch had brought a new surge of need racing through his body. His skin tightened everywhere on his body until he wanted to scream. They didn't have time for another go-around.

Besides, if he kept at her like he had, they both wouldn't be able to walk before long.

Using every bit of control he possessed, he took a deep breath and said, "Don't touch me until we're away from the island. I thought once would be enough, but the drug is playing havoc with my libido." He caught the understanding in her eyes. "Yeah. I guess you would understand."

After he slipped on the shorts and buttoned up his shirt, he glanced at Marie.

The tight-lip expression on her face as she zipped her shorts—her shirt already buttoned—told him whatever was going through her mind, understanding or not, she was unhappy about it.

The desire to comfort her had to wait. They had lost too much time. He hoped his delay hadn't ruined their chance to escape the island. No way would he allow Mulcahy to touch Marie again.

"Follow me." He headed for the beach. First he'd see to her safety and then he'd be back to take out that bastard Mulcahy.

Marie followed Ryker through the palms and prickly bushes as they came closer to the beach. She wanted to cuss out Ice for providing flip-flops instead of sturdy tennis shoes. Every time her feet sank into the deep, loose sand, ants covered and stung her feet.

She hated bugs, especially ants. No matter how quickly she picked up her feet, one or two would get her. She hated feeling helpless.

A silent sigh escaped. Who was she kidding? The helpless feeling was from allowing Ryker's attitude to bother her. So what if he was back to not wanting to touch her again? She'd done what she'd promised him months ago; if the situation was reversed, she would help him as he helped her with the flashbacks.

Even after having mind-blowing sex, he rejected her simple attempt at helping him regain his balance. Though she understood what he'd told her, it didn't make it any easier to take. And no matter how she told herself over and over as they walked toward the beach that he wasn't responsible for his actions—who knew what kind of drug Letitia had shot into his body?—she still hurt from the rebuff.

Nevertheless, they were still in a dire situation.

Helpless. She was helpless. Maybe she needed to stick with her office job in the Crypt. Her plans to save Ryker had failed. Sure, he was alive—but instead of her finding a way to save him as she'd hoped, he'd already had a man inside waiting for the right moment.

No one would be at their best—physically or mentally—after the last few days she'd had. She blushed as she watched Ryker continue to make steady progress through the undergrowth. How rough had it been for her compared to Ryker?

What in the world?

Suddenly it hit her: for the last twenty-four hours, she'd had no flashbacks. Did it mean the drugs Doc gave her had deadened the reaction? Or had the drug just worked its way out of her system? One fact was she'd wanted Ryker for Ryker and not because of a flashback.

How ironic, considering that now Ryker was dealing with a similar drug.

They'd finally reached an area near the beach, and they scooted down a bank onto the white, sandy shore.

Ryker walked into the waves.

"Wait!" The cool waves bathed her burning feet. She fought the urge to scream and run out of the water.

He turned, his forehead wrinkled.

"I can't swim. Well, not well enough in those waves." If it was the last thing she ever did, when she returned to Sector, she was taking swimming lessons. Something better than the crash course from the other day.

His shoulders slumped. The cap shaded his face. Would she see disappointment?

"Go! I'll hide and you can send someone back to get me." A burden. That was what she was to him. She had to quit pretending she would be anything else. When she returned to Sector, she would never make trouble again.

She glanced off to the side, gauging which bushes would be best to hide behind. Then someone clasped her waist. Startled, she lifted a foot and stomped on an instep.

"Damn it! I'm carrying you to the boat. There's no way I'm leaving you here." Ryker shifted her until her cheek rested against his shoulder. "Be still. Once I reach the boat, grab hold of the ladder and pull yourself up. You can do that, right?"

"I'm not a weakling. I just don't know how to swim—that is, well enough."

The water came to his chest, soaking her too. The up-and-down motion of the boat on the waves caused her to miss a few times until she timed the wave to help her reach the ladder, stumble up the steps, and fall onto the floor.

Just as Ryker pulled up on the ladder and came over the side, landing on his back with the canvas bag cushioning him, Marie heard the popping sound of guns firing. One bullet tinged against a metal rail near her.

On the cliff overlooking the shore stood two black-clad guards, and more poured from the tree line. They had found their exit.

"Stay down!" Ryker turned the key in the ignition and the motors caught on the first try. He slammed the gears down and the boat's bow lifted out of the water.

Marie caught the edge of a built-in seat to stop her downhill slide on the rough, thin carpet.

After about a minute, she lifted her head and looked over the side toward shore. The beach was getting smaller by the second. She breathed deeply. Maybe everything would be okay now. Ryker could send in his people to take it over once Jack and Ice were off the island.

He continued to drive the boat at full speed. Each slap of the hull on the waves jarred every sore joint in her body. She eased onto a cushioned bench and stretched out.

"Rest! I'll let you know when we're in the Florida Straits."

Ryker shouted above the noise of the motors and the wind. She heard him rummaging in the canvas bag.

　　She was so tired. Her eyes closed and a smile loosened the tightness around her mouth. Ryker's usual grumbling reassured her he was safe. They'd pulled off a miracle and escaped. No way could Mulcahy get them now.

Chapter Twenty-Three

"Fuck! Fuck! Fuck!"

The first thing Marie noticed besides Ryker cussing up a storm was the quietness of the boat. No motors running.

"What happened?" Bruised and stiff, she moved carefully, placing her feet on the floor.

"I'm not sure." He lifted a panel on the floor and then closed it. "Go over there and sit. Keep an eye out for any boats. I need to look at the motors."

She had no idea how long she'd slept, but with the contrasting sensation of feeling rested and aching all over, it could've been anywhere from minutes to hours. But surely they'd travelled far enough to be safe. Right?

Though she'd travelled by boat to reach the island, the silence of the engines and the bobbing in the waves frightened her. She clasped her hands together to stop the trembling. What a chicken! No matter how far out of her element, she would prove to Ryker she could hold her own. Taking a few slow, deep breaths, she looked at the moving horizon. The least she could do was keep watch like Ryker had said.

"That's just fucking great!" Ryker kicked the boat. He had a hood opened in the back as he looked at the engines. Though she had no idea what she could do to help, she walked over and peered around his shoulder. The strong smell of oil and gas brought her hand up over her nose.

"See that?" He pointed to a bunch of black hoses and wires. A stream of liquid oozed from a small puncture. "I guess we can count ourselves lucky that one of the bullets only nicked it." That was when she noticed the hole in the fiberglass side.

"Is that gas?"

"Yeah." He moved away and began opening and closing cubby doors.

"What are you looking for?"

"Duct tape. That should help save the rest of our gas, but we won't have enough to get through the strait even with the Gulf Stream's help." He grunted and pulled out a silver roll from underneath a cushion.

"Are we going for another island?" Being on an island again, even if it was land, didn't hold the same appeal as it had at one time.

"Not exactly. From what I can tell, we can head northeast and hit shore in about two hours. We might have just enough gas." He bent over and tore small strips off the duct tape, tightening it to the hose on each side where the gas leaked. Then he rolled the tape around and around the strips to hold them in place. "That should do it."

He shut the hood and returned to the controls. The engines didn't start. He jabbed a couple buttons, shifted the gears until the boat vibrated and roared to life. Then the engines settled down to the usual loud hum.

Ryker didn't say a word about how worried he was, but Marie noticed the grim look he gave the water.

She watched him for a few minutes. The bruises on his arms and chin appeared darker. Beads of sweat on his forehead warned her that he was fast approaching the limits of his body's endurance.

"Do you think I can drive the boat?" she asked.

Forehead creased, he looked at her for a moment and returned to staring straight ahead. "Yes. Why?"

She rolled her eyes and bit her lip to keep from saying something sarcastic. No one thought clearly after going through the traumatic experiences he'd survived.

Being careful to keep her feet apart to maintain her balance, she moved next to him and placed her hand on his arm.

"Go and lie down, close your eyes, and I'll drive. You need some rest. If I see anything or have a problem, I'll wake you."

He opened his mouth to argue.

"Please." She pulled at his arm. Her hand slid down to the steering wheel.

"Okay." He sat the compass on the ledge above the wheel. "As long as the needle points to true north in this direction"—he pointed to a spot a few marks to the left of the N—"and the boat keeps heading north-northeast, you'll do fine."

Without another word, he rubbed her cheek with the tip of a finger. She caught his hand and placed a kiss on his scabbed-over knuckles. For a moment, they didn't move or say a word—only looked at each other. Then he lifted her, placing her in the seat as he scooted past.

A few moments elapsed before she dared glance back at him. He'd dropped the cushions onto the floor and stretched out with his ankles crossed and his hands behind his head. He was sound asleep.

Checking the clock on the control panel, she decided to wake him in two hours unless she spotted land first. She refused to consider that they would run out of gas first. Luck had to be on their side now. She checked on him one last time. His scarred face relaxed as he slept. They deserved better luck. They were due.

Marie had never experienced the darkness of a moonless night in the Gulf. The stars twinkled brightly in the sky but did little to help her see more than a few yards. With no lights on the boat, she'd slowed it to a crawl. The dangers of running into a sandbar or another boat crossed her mind, but she'd never expected to just run up on the shore. Actually, the motors churned up sand first, before she realized they'd found shore. The awful sound of metal hitting shells, bending and fighting whatever it dredged up in a grinding stop. She tried to push it into reverse. Saving the boat was top priority. They may need to follow the shore until they find civilization, as the possibility of walking miles wasn't at the top of Marie's list of fun times.

With no house, condo, or hotel lights to warn her how near the boat was to shore, she understood what had caused her to drive it so close to the sandy beach. What would Ryker think?

"What the hell!" He jumped to his feet and reached around her to shut off the engine.

"Sorry. It was so dark. One moment we were hitting heavier waves, then the propellers hit bottom." What little she could make of the land assured her it was land and not a sandbar. "There are no lights. Are we on an island?"

"Maybe. Maybe not. We'll find out in the morning. For now, jump over and make your way to the shore. Once I move the boat out a little and release the anchor, I'll be with you."

Marie looked over the side. What could be waiting for her to enter the water?

"I'll stay here until you're ready to go," she said.

"It'll be easier for you now. I can't swim and carry you too."

Where was her backbone? He was right. She could tell that the whiteness of sand was only a few feet from the boat.

While she contemplated her cowardliness, he stuffed the canvas bag with several items from the boat and tossed it onto shore. Then he opened a small door next to the captain's chair. "Here. Use this." An orange lifejacket landed at her feet.

She wanted to kick it to the side. After all she'd been through lately, the short distance of unknown water should be a cakewalk. Taking a deep breath, she grabbed the preserver and slipped it on, easing over the side. The water reached her waist. She concentrated on putting one foot in front of the other. In no time, she stood shivering on an abandoned beach, watching Ryker prepare the boat and anchor it a few yards away.

Ryker dove into the water and in seconds walked onto shore like a scarred Poseidon. His wet cotton shirt plastered to broad shoulders and well-defined pecs reminded her how much she enjoyed running her hands across such contours.

He stooped to pull out their hated flip-flops and tossed hers near where she stood. "Put those on. They're better than nothing." Next, he pulled a small bottle from the bag. "Put your hand out." She held her hand out and he turned it palm up.

"What is it?"

"It's Jungle Juice, mosquito repellant. A little bit goes a long way. Rub it on your skin but don't touch anything plastic, like your flip-flops. It'll melt it."

She jerked her hand back, expecting the stuff to burn.

"Don't worry. It attacks plastic—not flesh—but still you don't want too much. It's the best thing to keep mosquitoes away."

That was when she noticed the buzzing and other sounds behind her. She looked off into the blackness, where she could just make out lots of bushes and a thick stand of trees.

As she rubbed the lotion on, she glanced around, not seeing but a few yards, and everything appeared black and gray. Another shiver raced down her back. Was someone watching?

"How far from a town do you think we are?" She already had a suspicion what the answer would be, but she asked anyway.

Ryker pulled out a beach towel and handed it to her. With one of his own, he ran the cloth over his hair and then unbuttoned his shirt to swipe at his chest.

She wrapped the towel around her shoulders, sat in the loose sand, and hunched over and shuddered.

He eyed her for a second and then dropped to her side. Before she realized what he'd planned, he pulled her into his lap and folded her in his arms, adding the warmth of his body and towel. Heat seeped through her chilled skin. The summer evening was still warm but the last few days had caught up with her. She snuggled her face beneath his chin, touching her chilled nose to his warm neck as she inhaled the unique smell of Ryker.

"It could be forty or a hundred miles. In the morning, we'll see what we can do and where we might be. I checked the tank before I left the boat. It's almost empty. We may have enough for about five minutes or just enough to crank up the engines." He slipped his warm hand beneath her blouse and rubbed back and forth across her ribs. She snuggled a little closer. "I'll pull out the tent Ice packed for us and we'll get a little sleep before sunrise."

When she shifted to look up at him, he added, "Yeah. I know what you mean, but Ice can pack a mean bag. If only he'd placed a satellite phone in it. Then we could alert our people. But electronics are a little more dangerous to supply."

Marie understood. Compasses and bags of dried food and mosquito repellant were easy to sneak out of a compound, but a satellite phone would set off alarms.

"We'll pitch the tent a few feet back. High tide will be in about the time the sun comes up. We don't want to be washed away."

With the incessant humming behind her, she was glad they had the tent to protect them from insects.

By the time he set up the small tent and doled out the dried jerky, she was dying of thirst. They had a couple of jugs and a six-pack of water. He'd warned her to drink sparingly as the Glades didn't have many places to replenish safe water.

She ran her tongue over her teeth. She hoped Ice had placed a toothbrush or two with a tube of paste in the pack. Maybe she could talk Ryker into sparing a little water to brush her teeth.

"Marie."

She rubbed her eyes and then looked over to where he stood in front of the tent. He pulled back the flap.

"Take your beach towel into the tent and stretch out on it after you take off your clothes." Each word emerged darker and harsher as he said it. His good eye almost shined like a predator sensing its prey.

A delicious, warm fever rushed down her back. He'd fought the drug for most of the day.

"The drug they gave you. It wasn't like mine, was it?"

"Why do you say that?"

"Your men. The ones you told me about. The ones who turned into animals after being given the drug—Jack said you had eliminated them."

"Jack talks too much."

"Well, was it the same stuff?"

"No. They developed a new one called Morning Glory. It takes booster shots to continue in the system."

"That you know of."

He nodded.

"But you're feeling whatever flashback they have."

He nodded again. His gaze remained on her.

"Okay. You helped me. The least I can do for you is return the favor." She threw her towel in the tent and bent down to slip inside.

"I'm sorry."

She twisted to look behind her. "Quit saying that. We didn't ask for any of this. And it's not like I don't enjoy it. You're real good at it."

He snorted and shook his head.

She stood. "What's that sound?"

"What do you mean?"

"The sound of disbelief. Haven't your other lovers told you how good you are?"

His gaze shifted away from her.

"Ryker?"

He sighed and turned back to her. "Lovers? No. No lovers." He understood she wasn't talking about Theo. She never could call what Theo did to him loving.

She headed back into the tent and stopped again. Tilting her head, she looked up. "What do you mean, no lovers?"

His broad hand stroked his scarred face. "Women are scared I'll hurt them."

"So you used prostitutes."

"I really don't want to talk about it."

She chewed on her lip. Something about this conversation wasn't right. Then she remembered Jack telling her how hard Theo worked them in the Northern Sector. They never had R&R and weren't allowed to go anywhere without another operative with them. Theo directed Ryker's every move as he trained him to be the best. One thing about Theo was he never shared.

She moved to stand in front of him.

"Am I your first?"

He slowly turned to her. His dark gaze searched her face. "You're my first woman."

CHAPTER TWENTY-FOUR

Marie flinched from his bitter tone.

"I see. You're determined to hear it all. You've already seen it. You know what I was to . . . Theo." Every word he said cut.

He was right. Theo had set it up for her to see. She'd been so happy to have a new friend. Though Ryker was much older than her, he treated her like she was special and worried about her happiness. He'd made sure The Circle's cook fixed at least one item at each meal that she liked—to fatten her up, as he would tell her.

Theo had found her in Ryker's room during a thunderstorm. She'd explained how the thundering had scared her, and Ryker only comforted her until she calmed. He appeared to understand, but when Theo's latest mistress informed her that Master wanted her to come to his study, she'd been afraid of being punished. He wasn't known for being patient. When she arrived, the study door was closed. She'd been instructed to go inside and wait. As she carefully opened the door, the rhythmic thumping caught her attention before her gaze found the source. Bending at the waist across Theo's desk with his jeans and underwear at his knees, Ryker gripped the far edge as their master thrust from behind. Ryker stared at her as if he'd been waiting for her. Such despair and shame filled his gaze and pulled at his mouth and scars before she could back from the room and ease the door shut.

Looking back, Marie understood Master wanted her to see Ryker being used as she would be soon. But she never understood why.

"Marie. It was a long time ago."

Adjusting her eyes to the present, she looked up. "Why did he want me to see that?"

"The next morning after the thunderstorm, Theo told me he'd decided to bring you into his bed. The sick son of a bitch believed you were nine, but he didn't care. He hated the thought of anyone getting to you before him. He never once understood the concept of caring for someone without expecting sex in return. I did the only thing I could think of to stop him." Ryker sighed. "The last time he'd tried that, I was sixteen and determined to make him stop. So I threatened to cut his cock off if he touched me again, and it had worked for several years. Until you. When he caught you in my room, it didn't matter that I never touched you, that I only treated you as an older brother did a little sister. He perverted it. He wanted to punish me because I had your affection, and he knew I cared for you. There hadn't been anyone to look out for me but him since my parents died. Theo had already destroyed any tender feelings I had for my brother, even when I thought he was dead. "

How sad and horrible to lose his parents and then to be taken into the home of a pedophile, a pervert who taught him to hate his own brother. She wanted to comfort him, but the way he held himself from her, she knew he'd reject her touch. For now, he needed her to listen and do no more.

"We came to an agreement. He could use me, if he promised to wait until you turned thirteen before taking you to his bed. I had hoped to find a way to take over The Circle by then, but he was smarter. He made sure I languished in the Northern Sector for eight years before I could return."

"You knew I was twelve. After the life I lived with my parents, I could've handled it."

"But he didn't know. He expected people to be too afraid of him to lie. In the meanwhile, I'd hoped to find a way to save you before the four years were up."

She thought about lying to him and letting him believe Theo had waited. She couldn't do it. Theo had loved to twist the truth to his advantage. She refused to do the same. "He lied."

"Damn him! He took you after he had me hauled off?"

"Not exactly. But he took me three years later. Though I was fifteen, he thought I was twelve."

"I'm sorry. I tried."

"Ryker, it was probably because of you he waited as long as he did," she whispered. Moving closer, no longer able to hold back, she placed her hand on his chest and stood on tiptoe to kiss his cheek.

"Marie—"

"Shh!" She placed a finger on his firm lips. "That was a lifetime ago. Come to bed." She turned and entered the tent.

Ryker watched Marie slip into the tent. His gaze travelled the horizon over the Gulf, the stars dividing the water from the sky. A slight turn and lightning bugs danced above the bushes inland. Only the sounds of buzzing insects and waves hitting the shore assured him that they were alone. He should rub on more of the mosquito repellent and keep guard.

His hands began to tremble. His fingers blurred. He squeezed them into fists.

With all the horrible memories, one thought always saved his sanity over the years: if he had the opportunity to kill the bastard who abused him and Marie, he would take it. And he had. When he slid the sword into the man's gut and the blood gushed over his hand, a powerful relief engulfed him. The words he whispered into Theo's ear as he heard the man take his last breath were often his mantra leading up to that day.

Go to hell knowing that Marie is mine.

"Are you coming?" Marie's voice, low and promising, broke him away from his gruesome thoughts. All those years of fearing he would turn out to be like Theo came crashing down on him. No. He couldn't use Marie like that. Shit! He was no better than Theo, using her like he had for months. He ducked into the tent, prepared to apologize for his treatment of her on the island and before.

Naked and on her side, she smiled. Elbow bent, her hand held up her head as she waited for him.

"Here. I'll help you." Her fingers deftly unbuttoned the shirt. When she started on the snap of his shorts, he stopped her.

"Marie, the drug has nearly worn off. No need to do this."

His cock stretched and hardened as he wanted to lick and bite every square inch of her soft skin. Though he wanted to leave her alone, he ached. She was every good dream he'd ever had in his life.

"Don't you realize it has gone further than taking care of our physical needs? I swam underwater for you. I braved sharks in the water and on land for you. I care about you deeply. Don't you understand I have a huge crush on you?"

All the air left his body. Was she delusional? Had she been sniffing too much insect repellant?

"Don't look so shocked. I believe everyone at Sector knows but you. At least that's what Charlie told me."

He forced his lungs to inhale. He wanted to tell her he had more than a crush. That he loved her beyond life, but she deserved so much more. "We've been through a lot, especially the last few months. You're under a lot of—"

"Shut up and kiss me."

Arms open, she waited. He covered her mouth, moving his head to rub their lips together as he filled her mouth with his tongue. He thrust hard, alternating between stroking and sucking on hers. He pushed at his shorts until his cock popped free. Her hands wrapped around his length and squeezed.

She leaned her head back and gasped. "Wait. I want . . . I want you in my mouth."

All his willpower directed toward not coming with those words, he nodded. Kicking off the shorts the rest of the way, he picked her up and flipped her around as he laid back.

"What are you doing?"

"I want you in my mouth too."

He spread his legs as her breath tickled his cock. Her knees rested next to his shoulders. His hands pressed her buttocks down, making it easier for his mouth to reach the sweetness waiting for him between her legs. His tongue swiped her from clit to anus. The smell of woman and earth had him hard as the poles holding the tent up. He licked, sucked, and ate at her moist center and the hard bead at one end.

His pulsating cock parted her lips. She bobbed her head, taking as much of him as she could. Every time her lips reached the cap, she sucked, smacking her lips as if she tasted sugar. He fought the urge to pump into her mouth and down her throat. When her fingers lifted his balls, rolling and licking them while they were in her hot mouth, tears came to the corners of his eyes as he strained not to come.

He spread her folds wide and drew on the nub while he dipped two fingers into her, coating them as he swirled his tongue over the taut bundle of nerves that swelled some more. Then he rubbed the moist fingers around the nearby tight opening. Her legs began to tremble. She knew what he planned to do next. He sank those fingers into the small, tight, hot hole and pushed in and out quickly, going past the second knuckle.

Her mouth released his balls and they drew up. Panting, she didn't hesitate in filling her mouth with his cock. She humped his face as wave upon wave shook her body.

Before he could stop himself, he rolled over and jabbed his cock down her throat, needing the release only her touch could give him. His fingers continued to work her ass as he ate her sweetness. Small fingers gripped him and jerked as her nails bit into his tender flesh and her body continued to climax.

Her hands wrapped around the base of his length stopped him from choking her. When the waves eased up, he nipped at her clit and the waves began again. Then she scraped her teeth across the sensitive cap. He climaxed, pumping until too weak to do more than move them onto their sides.

She suckled and licked at his cock as he did the same to her clit. With two fingers still deep in her, he finally slid them out after the last tremor eased. Her soft, warm breath tickled his limp cock. He inhaled the sweet scent he would never forget.

Before they dozed off, he moved until her head rested comfortably on his chest and his arms held her tight, their heartbeats slowing until they both fell asleep.

CHAPTER TWENTY-FIVE

Marie used the dogwood twig Ryker claimed could be used to brush her teeth. At this point, anything would help. She ran her tongue across her teeth. Wonderful. It did work.

She brushed her hair—he'd found a brush in the bag—and avoided looking at him as he washed up in the salt water, shirtless with his shorts riding low on his hips. Fanning her warm cheeks, she knew the feeling wasn't from the sun topping the bushes and trees to the east. Never in her life had she'd been more embarrassed than when she woke up with her hand on his stiffening penis. By the time they'd untangled their arms and legs from each other, and pulled their clothes on, her face had been so hot, she was certain blisters would bubble up.

Bad enough that she'd enjoyed their oral satisfaction so much she'd become light-headed. A gasp escaped as the image of Ryker's mouth less than an inch from her mons flashed though her mind. Nothing sexier. The man knew what to do. And his dark five o'clock shadow—and even his one eye of amber and other of white—added to his dangerous look.

"Marie!"

She stood, tossing the brush into the bag, and looked at Ryker. Kicking up water, he ran toward her, waving his arms, indicating the dense bushes and trees behind her.

Movement in the water caught her attention. Of all things she could imagine, she hadn't expected Jet Skis in the middle of nowhere. Six of them were speeding toward the shore in their direction. The riders looked as if they had wings. She edged backward. No. Those were M16s strapped to their backs.

"Run! Head into the trees; I'll be right behind you!"

She grabbed the bag and headed for cover.

The further she ran into the bushes, the softer the ground became, and then her feet splashed into water. Praying she wouldn't come across any snakes or other wildlife that would make her scream, she headed toward the trees. As she reached the stand, she heard splashing behind her. The trees were so close to each other and their roots so thick and bunched together, she jumped on top and climbed over one to another until she could turn and see if Ryker had made it.

He wasn't in sight, but she spotted three of the men running toward another stand of trees to her right. Had Ryker lost sight of her and headed into another direction?

"Marie!" Ryker said in a loud whisper.

She jumped and turned, her hand over her racing heart. He stood on roots a few yards away, a gun sticking out of the band of his soaked cargo shorts.

"Where did you get that?"

"It was on the boat. I have only one magazine for it." He handed it to her. "Keep this with you."

"What about you?" She looked down at the small Beretta, so similar to the one she'd practiced with over the last few months.

"I'll be fine." He pulled out a wicked-looking knife. The curved black blade and razor-sharp edge ending at a point were not made for show.

"The boat?"

He nodded, his gaze searching the trees surrounding them.

Someone shouted, "They're not over here!"

"What should we do?" She wanted to grab his hand and run, but by the way he held the knife, it appeared he had a plan.

"Climb." He pointed his thumb up. "Then stay put until I come to get you."

Above her, the thick limbs grew in every direction. When she looked back at Ryker, he was gone again. Not wasting any more time, she looped the heavy bag over her shoulders, placed the gun in one of the outside pockets for easy reach, and scrambled up. She'd never had the opportunity to learn how to climb trees as a child, but she quickly figured it out. Twice, she placed her hands on bugs and almost screamed, catching herself with a small squeak.

By the time she reached a branch high enough to feel safe, breathing hard, she pulled out the gun and checked the magazine, full with fifteen rounds. She wedged a shoulder to the trunk to keep her balance. One look down and she quickly jerked her gaze up. Maybe she'd climbed too high. Then she heard gunfire. En masse, birds took to the air, drowning out any chance of her hearing the men.

Oh, please don't let them kill Ryker. He should've kept the gun.

A few more minutes seeped by, and then more gunfire and a scream.

The quietness of the woods surrounded Marie. No birds chirping or the incessant buzzing of insects broke the silence.

Then she heard the crack of a twig. When she looked in the direction of the sound, nothing was there. Then there they were: two men edging in between the trees, their rifles pointed ahead and ready to fire. Would they look up and see her? Would they fire, shooting her out of the trees like a squirrel? She lifted the pistol and aimed. How good had she gotten? Shooting at a paper target was different from a moving, thinking human being.

Realizing she'd been holding her breath, she opened her mouth to take a deep, quiet lungful of air. Then a hand covered her mouth as she was hauled against a broad chest. Before she could scream or raise her gun, her body registered something about the touch and heat. Ryker.

"Shh," he said close to her ear, barely making a sound.

She nodded. He released her as the men walked by, eyeing their surroundings but never looking up.

Being careful not to shake the limb, she twisted a little to look at him. Sweat covered his pale face. Was he sick?

"Are you okay?" she mouthed.

He swiped his forehead with the upper sleeve of his shirt and then nodded.

Why was he lying? She ran a hand over his chest and down his sides. He flinched from her touch. When she examined her palm to see if the wetness was blood, only dirt and clear moisture coated her hand.

When she glared at him, he rested his head on the tree trunk and stared at the foliage above them. She pinched his thigh.

"Damn it. You're going to make me fall."

Somehow his face became whiter with a bit of a green cast around his mouth. Then she remembered. He hated heights. She knew why he sat there in the tree, fifteen feet off the ground. Her safety was more important than his fear of heights.

"I'm sorry."

His gaze met hers. He gave her a lopsided grin.

"Don't move. Stay here." His lips brushed her ear. Then he was gone again.

If they ever got out of the Everglades alive, she would make certain to never leave Sector again.

For now, she needed to help. But the familiar feeling of helplessness engulfed her. She hated it. Every move she imagined trying would endanger Ryker further. So she sat on the limb, letting her ego have a rest. His words at Sector came back to her. If she stayed at Sector she wouldn't need to learn how to protect herself. Problem was she wanted to protect him too.

Talk about being a hindrance in the field—she was a disaster. Maybe they'd allow her to do some investigative work online when she returned to Sector.

More birds took off in a flutter of wings with new gunfire breaking the unnatural silence.

Marie fisted the gun but moved her finger from the trigger. In her nervousness, she could easily discharge the gun without thinking and alert Mulcahy's men. Stiff from sitting on the limb for so long, she leaned a little to the side, bend-

ing and popping her back. Oh, hell. She hoped the cracking
sound didn't carry to the ground.

A large grasshopper jumped from one leaf to another,
shaking twigs in a nearby bush. Nothing else moved. Even
the wind had died down.

She leaned back against the trunk and closed her dry eyes.
Tiredness melted her body to the rough wood.

A bird chirping on a nearby branch woke her up with a jerk.
She scrambled to regain her hold, almost dropping the gun.
Her heart pounded with the close call. A breeze caressed her
arm, the air several degrees cooler. What time was it?

Ryker? While she dozed, was he out there bleeding to
death?

Unable to wait any longer, she placed the safety on the
gun and stuck it in the bag's side pocket. Taking her time, as
quietly as possible, she worked her way down the tree while
keeping an eye out for Ryker and any sign of the others.

Once she reached the ground, she headed in the direction she'd heard the gunfire. A few yards later as she edged
around a thicker stand of trees, she found a footpath. Following alongside of it—the beaten ground showed regular
use—she stayed alert. Twenty minutes later she came to a
large sawgrass marsh. Several yards away another stand of
trees framed a shack. Weathered board exterior, it looked to
be a hundred years old and empty.

She remained still. A creepy feeling warned her to be patient. Then she caught movement at the opposite end of the
building. Someone opened a door and walked inside.

Was it strangers willing to help or another threat? Had Ryker found more trouble than he could handle and left her in the tree, believing she would be safer?

She looked at her mosquito-bitten feet. No one in their right mind would walk in a snake-infested marsh with only flip-flops on. She stooped to take a closer look at the sawgrass. Each blade had what looked like little teeth on it. Well, that explained the name. No way could she walk, dressed as she was in shorts and flip-flops.

How could she reach the shack without being seen and getting cut up? The end of the house opposite the door didn't have a window, and the marsh butted up almost to the pilings supporting the shack.

The sky had darkened in the time she studied the only way to get a peek inside. She would have to come from the front between the cypress trees standing guard near the marsh and shack. On the other side of the bulging roots, she spotted another trail. The only way in.

Taking a deep breath, she stepped back into the shadows and waited for the sun to sink a little lower.

CHAPTER TWENTY-SIX

"You really think we didn't expect your people to try to rescue you?" Mulcahy's pleasure in recapturing the leader of The Circle was obvious from his sneer.

Strapped to a straight-back chair in the middle of the dingy one-room shack, Ryker wiggled his fingers and toes to bring back some feeling. The plastic ties bit into his wrists and ankles without mercy.

If Marie stayed in the tree until daylight, she would be safe. By then he would be free and his fist pummeling Mulcahy's face. Or dead and the asshole satisfied that they had split up.

"So where did you put the locator?" He'd suspected as much when the Jet Skis showed up. From the toothy grin Mulcahy gave him, he knew for sure. No way in the large vastness of the Gulf could they have found them without help.

"Does it really matter?" Mulcahy stopped in front of his chair. With one arm across his chest, holding the elbow of the other, he tapped a finger against his thin lips. Then he tilted his head and stared hard at Ryker. "Why would you leave

Marie to fend for herself? You obviously love her. Her feelings appear to be mutual. She tries to hide it, but you should've seen her face as you fought in the arena. I had a hard time holding back the laughter. She's a terrible actress and lousy operative. You should find her another job. Wait. You already have one for her, don't you? Warming your bed."

Ryker's whole body shuddered inside. The need to smash the man's face almost caused him to lose control. The bastard thought he'd won. For now. An opportunity would come and when it did, Ryker would make sure only one of them walked away alive.

One of the men lit a kerosene lamp sitting in the middle of a rough-hewn table positioned against a wall. The dirty windows above it no longer glowed from the late evening sun. Just a few more hours and maybe Marie would be safe. From the way Mulcahy eyed him with such hatred, Ryker felt certain he either planned to kill him and dump his body in the marsh or take him back to the island to be killed.

"A job you would love to take over." Ryker lifted a shoulder to swipe off the blood from his busted lip. He glanced over at two of Mulcahy's men. At least their faces looked as if someone had used them for batting practice. Damn. It stung like hell to smile.

"Ha! So right." Mulcahy's bitter laugh filled the room. Then his gaze lifted above Ryker's head. Someone caught his attention. "What's your problem?" He snapped.

"I heard something outside." The man cleared his throat. "Maybe I better go see."

"Do you think?" Mulcahy glared and jerked his head toward the door. "Stevens, go with him."

"Top of the food chain you got there, Mulcahy." Whatever he did, he needed to keep his gaze anywhere but on the window. Hell, he prayed Marie remained in the tree and that the noise had come from an alligator. Chances were slim that one of his operatives had tracked him down.

The man sneered. "I had expected to find Ice or Jack with you. They disappeared about the same time as you. Doesn't matter. If I ever see either of them again, they're dead. I'm tired of messing around. You and your organization wouldn't stay out of my business. What's a dead woman or a handful to you? You've probably killed more than that in a week. Maybe that's where I went wrong. I should've paid you to stay out of it or hired you to kidnap the women. Money is what motivates people like you." He pulled another chair from the table and sat with his legs crossed at the knees.

"Some things money can't buy."

Mulcahy leaned to one side to pull out a knife from his pants pocket and flipped it open. "I wonder how well you'd fight in the arena without your remaining eye." He ran his finger lightly up and down the blade.

If he'd hoped for a reaction, the idiot was mistaken. Ryker ignored the screaming horror inside of becoming blind. He didn't want to give Mulcahy the satisfaction of seeing him scared. Even if he survived, his usefulness to The Circle would come to an end. So losing his sight wasn't an option. Compared to his brother, Ryker possessed more brawn than brains. He'd come to that realization soon after taking over The Circle. But after the first several missions failed, he'd quickly learned to listen to others. He was teachable.

"Where's Letitia? Have you already killed her?" Ryker asked.

"Kill Letitia? The woman is like a cat. She has nine lives. Considering how reckless she is, she's probably on number six, the vindictive, licentious bitch. But no, she's too valuable. So be happy she remained behind on the island. She would love nothing better than to geld you." He chuckled and threw the knife between Ryker's feet. The thin blade quivered as it pierced the wood floor. "Her 'test subjects' destroyed her lab. So it will be a few months before she can make up new batches of Morning Glory and Blossom Flower. Then we'll start selling it. We've already sent out samples to several countries. I'm surprised by the number of people in the U.S. who want to test it. Supply and demand. That's what rules the world. Much can be learned from OPEC."

Mulcahy nodded toward the man looking out the window. "Jones, go see what's taking them so long. No, you stay here, Santiago. Enough people will be tramping around outside." The remaining guard leaned against the wall with his arms folded. Despite the man's relaxed pose, Ryker could tell his lanky frame hid toned muscles brought about by extreme training. Not the average guard.

"What? Are you afraid to stay here with me alone?" He doubted any amount of taunting would see Mulcahy letting him go and would most likely get him another beating, but he couldn't resist smarting off. Now only if he could find a way to grab the knife and cut his ties. Then before the asshole knew what was coming, the handle would be sticking out of his chest.

As soon as the door behind Ryker closed, a scream ripped through the air outside the window, followed by several shots.

Mulcahy picked up the knife and headed for the door.

Fingers clasping the chair's arms, Ryker threw his body to one side, falling into Mulcahy's path, knocking him off his feet. Assured by the sound of the knife skittering across the floor, Ryker waited˜little else he could do while on the floor like a turtle on its back˜for what would happen next.

"You son of a bitch! I should've killed you and let Letitia be dammed!" As Mulcahy regained his feet, the door burst open.

Unable to twist around, Ryker watched Mulcahy's face for some idea of what was happening. The man's eyes widened in bemusement, and he remained still.

What happened? Were they hauling in Marie? Had they hurt her? Ryker shifted back and forth, trying to get the chair to move. He stopped when he heard the voice he dreaded.

"You've been watching too many movies, Mulcahy. You'll be on the floor dead or bleeding out before you even reach the knife. So do you really want to take a chance?"

Desperate to hide her nervousness, Marie held the pistol with both hands. Jack told her often enough that whenever she entered a hostile environment, the situation needed to be controlled within the first two minutes or all hell would break loose. She hadn't expected the rawboned, dark-haired man in the corner eyeing her with such interest. And Mulcahy's confused look irritated her to no end. What was his problem? Did he believe she wouldn't shoot?

With her attention split between the stranger and Mulcahy, she hated ignoring Ryker tied to a chair and helpless. Out of the corner of her eye, she watched as the chair began to rock. Ryker's struggling relieved her worries about whether or not she'd arrived too late.

"Marie, my men will return any minute." Mulcahy stepped a little closer. "If you want you and your lover to live a little longer, you'll put that gun down."

"Stay right there." Deep inside, she wanted him to keep moving. Nothing would make her feel better than to shoot the man and throw his body outside for the alligators and snakes.

She got her wish. He dove for the knife. As she squeezed the trigger, the other man leaped toward her. All hell broke loose as Ice and Jack charged in shooting. Explosions fired off over her head as she landed on her side with a limp body resting on top. Her head slammed into the floor. Men shouted and footsteps rushed out of the room. The other guard had escaped.

Her vision blurred from the blow. She looked a couple feet away at Mulcahy. His unseeing eyes stared wide in surprise. She'd killed him. He deserved it, but she'd never killed anyone before. The nausea nearly engulfed her. She felt like she was floating in another dimension, as she watched the blood pool near his body and slip in between the wooden planks.

"Fucking hell! Get these ties off me!" Ryker's voice echoed. "Marie!"

The room dimmed. She closed her eyes and smiled as she drifted into the darkness. He was alive.

Marie opened her eyes. Ryker's beautifully scarred face leaned over hers. A new black patch covered his right eye. She was in his lap, her cheek pressed to a hard bicep and his arms wrapped tight around her.

The whoop-whoop of helicopter blades caught her attention.

"How did you get Spirit into the marsh?" She craned her neck. Out the window, miles and miles of waving grass and cypress trees moved beneath the travelling helicopter.

"We didn't. I carried you back to the beach and we loaded up there." He swept a few strands of hair from her face. "You've lost a lot of weight. When we get back to Sector, I'm going to feed you pancakes and ice cream every day."

"With maple and chocolate syrup?" The ends of her lips tilted up though she tried not to smile. From the concerned look on his face, she wanted to keep a straight face.

"Both, on it all, if you want." He grinned back.

She licked her swollen lips and blinked to clear her eyes. Everything came back to her. When Mulcahy had scrambled for his knife in the split second she'd squeezed the trigger, she'd had an epiphany. She'd never told Ryker her true feelings, and if they died in the middle of the Everglades without her having a chance to express them, her life would be wasted. Taking a chance with her heart was worth finding out the truth.

"I have something important to tell you."

"Shh. Doc flew down from Sector and is waiting for us in Orlando. As soon as he gives the okay, we'll head home." His thumb rubbed across her chapped lips.

She cupped the side of his scarred face. "I have more than a crush. I love you, Arthur. Surely you've realized that by now."

Not since she was a kid had she called him by his given name.

His thumb stopped moving and he stared at her. She swore he stopped breathing. Was he trying to find a kind way of letting her down?

He released a sigh and said gruffly, "By God, you better. You took twenty years off my life when you burst into that shack. If Ice and Jack hadn't been seconds behind you, I . . . I . . . ah, hell! I love you more than life."

Warmth and strong arms surrounded her as he lifted her to meet his mouth. The gentle kiss brought tears to her eyes. All the pain and suffering this man had endured, and he still knew how to be tender and loving. She grabbed two handfuls of hair and tugged hard as she opened her mouth wider, wanting more of his taste and to swallow his groan of arousal.

He clasped her wrists and moved her hands to her waist. "Wait until we have some privacy. Otherwise, the fellows here will get more of a show than they've already had."

She looked over her shoulder. Ice, slouched in the opposite seat, appeared to be asleep. Skin bruised and his light eyes shining with fever, Jack, stretched out across two places, glanced at her for a second and winked.

Blushing, she smiled and closed her eyes, burrowing into Ryker's embrace.

"I can wait."

He squeezed her and grunted. The thick, hard cock pressing against her buttocks warned she wouldn't have long to wait.

In an effort to take her mind off sex, she asked, "Did I really kill Mulcahy?" She cringed. Not exactly the direction she wanted to go, but she needed to know.

"I doubt those girls' parents care who killed the man partly responsible for their daughters' deaths. Just know you did what was needed. You've proven you have what it takes to be a Circle operative." He squeezed her and leaned his head back, closing his eyes.

Despite being drawn and pale, he looked wonderful to her. Her fingertips glided over his beard-roughened chin and cheeks. She never remembered seeing him as anything but clean-shaven. This gave him a more dangerous image than usual. She liked it. Maybe she could talk him into keeping a moustache and goatee. No matter, he would look good to her.

An old saying came to her mind. *Pretty is as pretty does.*

Mulcahy had been a handsome man, but so ugly inside. Shooting Blossom Flower into those girls so they would do his bidding and make him rich, he had no compassion for the many lives he destroyed. What type of childhood would create a monster like him?

"What are you going to do with his body? Does he have family?"

Without looking at her, Ryker said, "Family? I have no idea. We don't have to worry about it anyway. No body."

When he didn't say anything more, she tugged on his hair. He opened his eye and glared at her.

Ignoring his feigned irritation, she asked, "What happened to the body?" Did she really want to know? Yeah. Otherwise, she would have nightmares, believing he was still alive.

"Let's say the alligators were well fed today."

Her stomach churned. Well, she had asked.

"What of Letitia? We need to make sure she can't make any more of those drugs." Marie's finger carefully traced the bruises and cuts along Ryker's collarbone. She remembered the night in the tent. Even in the dark, she'd seen the painful wounds left from fighting in the arena. He would most likely have many more scars.

She suspected there was more to the story about the drug—Morning Glory—that had been forced on him than he would ever tell her.

He sighed. "They reported before we took to the air. She wasn't on the island. No trace of her."

"No! You have to find her. She'll do it again! We've got to stop her before she kills more people." Marie struggled to sit up.

"Shh! We'll find her." He pulled her tighter and kissed her forehead. "First, we'll go home. You need to recover. Then we'll plan. She won't be hidden long. The woman loves attention too much. It'll be her downfall."

"Ryker." She touched the spot he kissed. "We need to talk now."

He looked at Jack and Ice. "Not now."

"Yes. Now."

"Okay." His face went blank.

Poor baby. He thought she was about to give him bad news. Maybe in a way, but he really needed to understand her feelings about their new relationship. Yes. A real relationship, not just her hero-worshiping him.

"I've decided field work isn't for me. My run of luck has been all bad. I think I'd rather do most of my work from Sector. Not in the Dungeon, but as a handler."

He released his breath. "Okay."

She fought the grin wanting to burst on her face. "And I want you to quit protecting me."

"That's not going to happen." His chin tucked in as he prepared to argue.

"No negotiation. I don't want you bossing me around every moment of every day."

"I don't boss you."

Jack emitted a sound between a chuckle and a cough. When Marie looked at him, he hit his chest with a fist. "Freaking allergies."

Ryker snorted.

Her attention returned to the hard-headed man holding her. "You do. We'll talk more about that when we're alone."

He muttered, "That's what I had wanted to do in the first place."

"I'm not going to marry you." She might as well get it out in the open.

"I don't remember asking you."

She lifted an eyebrow and stared at him in disbelief.

"Damn it! You're not playing fair." He swiped over his mouth and stubble.

"You've got to be kidding me." She giggled and punched him in the arm.

"Ow!" With a crooked grin, he winked at her. "But you'll marry me when I ask, right?"

"We'll see. A girl has to leave her options open."

"Looks like I'll need to stay on my toes around you."

"You betcha." She clasped the sides of his head and pulled his mouth to hers.

CHAPTER TWENTY-SEVEN

The brilliantly colored dresses swirled by as Marie stood to the side. She moved a little closer to where the air conditioning tried to cool the overcrowded ballroom. The gilt-framed mirrors reflected rainbows from the dancers and the crystal chandeliers above them. Over two hundred of The Circle operatives and service personnel laughed and ate with abandon. An unheard-of event: The Circle giving a party to celebrate their leader's marriage to one of their own.

Marie laughed. A week after they returned, Ryker had demanded she marry him. When she said no, he'd stomped off, slamming the bedroom door. Several days later, he ordered her to accept his proposal the second time. She merely crossed her arms and stared at him until he walked away, pulling at his hair in frustration. On his third try, he fell to his knee and politely asked her to be his, and she said yes. From the surprise on his face, he'd expected failure. She was glad to put the fellow out of his misery. For that matter, she'd been miserable too. Why she thought he needed to ask her properly, she wasn't sure. Maybe she deserved a little romance after the ordeal with Blossom Flower.

A month later, they got married, and here they were celebrating with all their friends. Even Collin and Olivia attended the ceremony with one of the orphans they'd adopted, a one-year-old girl with auburn curls and mischievous dimples. If they hadn't known better, everyone would have sworn she was the couple's own flesh and blood.

"I've never seen you so happy, Marie." Olivia stood beside her, while her husband held their sleeping daughter to his shoulder.

"I am. And the same to you. She's beautiful." The thought of two dangerous people tenderly caring for such a tiny person . . . it was hard to believe. "You named her Emma after Collin's mom, right?"

"Yes. I could only think of saint names, and Collin stopped me and said he wanted our child to have his mom's name." Tears came to the woman's eyes. "*Our child*. The man surprises me every day. I'm so fortunate."

"We do owe their parents a lot. They brought up two boys who went through hell and still kept their humanity."

"Yeah. Enough of the mushy stuff. I see your new husband wants your attention. And Collin is giving me that look. He hates for Emma to be up so late. He gets cranky when he doesn't get a nap." Olivia hugged her and then grabbed her husband's arm as they headed toward the doors. The two grown-ups stumbled as they stopped to pick up the little black patent shoes falling from their daughter's feet.

Marie laughed with delight.

"It's not nice to laugh at those who dance like a bear." Ryker nodded toward Rex as he stopped beside her.

The new second-in-command stepped on the toes of his partner, Nic Savage. Nic gazed up adoringly at Rex. At six-foot-five, he towered over the small woman. She was actually an inch taller than Marie, but with her pixie-cut black hair, she looked even shorter.

At first, Marie felt uncomfortable around the big man, but his roar hid a soft heart. She was surprised to realize he no longer trailed after A. J. After seeing their argument at Collin and Olivia's country home, she expected the couple to work things out. Nic was nice enough, but . . . she couldn't put her finger on it. As improbable as she had thought it when she'd first met the woman, A. J. turned out to be a good friend. With Charlie leaving to work with Jack at the new OS facility in Atlanta—Liam had been sent to the Northern Sector as punishment until Ryker believed he learned true loyalty—Marie had been at loose ends until she started training with A. J. A person never knew when she would need to use a gun and knife again. Though she still worked behind a computer monitor, she loved being a handler, and Sal said she was a fast learner.

Ice had disappeared. Though Marie had overheard Ryker and Collin talking about how he was probably tracking down his wayward half-sister, they only hoped it had nothing to do with them still not finding Letitia.

Yet, her destroyed lab revealed that there was no known antidote for the drug. But with the new anxiety medicine Doc had prescribed, the drug was losing its control, and he estimated within a year they both would be free from any aftereffects.

Marie covered her mouth. She had to say, hers and Ryker's love life hadn't slowed down. They'd embarrassed Jack several times when he'd walked into Ryker's office unannounced.

Jack. She missed him. When Collin had visited not long after they returned from Florida, he and Ryker had argued. She learned that Ryker's brother planned to hand over the OS to him within the next few months. In the meanwhile, he'd expected Rex to control the specialized newly returned branch of The Circle. She'd remembered Ryker mentioning it before, but hadn't realized to what extent.

"Baby, are you all right?"

She loved how Ryker showed his affection for her without worrying what others thought.

"I'm glad Jack could make it."

"Humph." Though Ryker trusted Jack with the OS, part of the motivation of his new position might be wrapped in how far away he was from her. Yet, tonight Jack stood on the other side of the ballroom and A. J. danced in his arms. They were laughing hard, and the glares they received from Rex told a lot.

"I think Jack better be careful. His brother doesn't look too happy with him right now." She glanced back at Rex. "For that matter, A. J. may need to keep an eye on Nic. The woman is shooting daggers at her. Obviously, she doesn't like Rex paying attention to A. J. Those four appear to have some problems to work out."

As the music stopped, the dark-headed woman pulled on Rex's hand when he made a step toward the jolly couple.

"Brothers can be a pain in the ass." Ryker downed the last bit of his wine. "Want to dance?"

"I would love to." She handed her glass over to a waiter walking by and hooked her arm into Ryker's. The next song was a slow one. He enveloped her in his arms. "Thank goodness, you're not as tall as Rex. You would look like a bear dancing too."

He laughed, and everyone turned to stare in shock.

Ryker grinned, not caring what others thought. If only she knew that he would dance to any tune she wanted. He loved her more than his own life. She'd already proven how valuable his life was to her back in the Everglades.

"How soon can we leave the party?" she asked, tugging hard on his goatee.

"Ouch!" He instantly hardened. "Right now, if you want."

"Good. I want you."

"Are you okay?"

She shook her head. "You really need to learn to say three new words."

"I'm all yours?"

"Close."

He grinned, knowing she never got tired of him saying it. For that matter, neither did he.

"I love you?"

"Those are the ones, but with feeling," she teased.

"I love you, Mrs. Marie Ryker."

"Aww, now that's more like it."

"Yes, ma'am."

He knew who was mistress of his heart.

ACKNOWLEDGMENTS

Goodness, where do I start? To Wendy Lee, whom I wish much success in her new endeavor. Chelsey Emmelhainz, who thankfully has a sense of humor and isn't freaked out by my peculiarities. Nalini Akolekar, who guides me with a calm and kind hand. To my beta readers, who continue to help me: Candi Moody and Terri Nguyen. To my family, who harass ...uh...encourage strangers to buy my books: Gayle Pirtle, Greg and Wanda Reese, Patsy O'Dell, Rita Dunaway, Kim O'Rear, Evelyn Shaw, Daniel Ray, and of course, my daughters, Candice and Audrey. To my mom and dad, whom I love. To my husband, who is cooking his own meals while I write and diet.

See how The Circle began . . .

As the top assassin at The Circle, a shadowy group of mercenaries, Olivia St. Vincent can hunt down anyone. She's been trained since she was a teenager to kill without feeling, to interact with men without love. But when she's kidnapped by the enigmatic leader of a rival organization, she learns she's been lied to for years. She never worked for the good guys.

Collin Ryker believes the sultry woman he's abducted knows more than she's telling about The Circle and its plans for complete domination. Over time, as they work together, Olivia's tenacity and vulnerability captivate him. But if he isn't careful, Collin will fall into the biggest trap of all: caring for a woman who can betray him to his greatest enemy.

Read on for an excerpt from the first Circle novel,
CIRCLE OF DESIRE,
available now from Avon Impulse!

CHAPTER ONE

Olivia St. Vincent typed the ammunition data into the keypad on the sniper rifle and then nestled her cheek against the stock's custom-fit pad. She waited for the information to be processed and her target to come into view.

Keeping her attention on the boardwalk outside the open window, she caressed the silencer attachment and sighed. Powerful and lightweight compared to others, the rifle was her favorite and the only one of its kind. She wasn't sure how The Circle got their hands on the prototype, and she knew better than to ask. She'd used it twice in the last eleven months and had no complaints.

She inhaled the fresh salt air coming in and watched the few early joggers trotting along the boardwalk next to Elliot Bay. Almost the whole length was visible from the empty fourth story apartment. A strong wind picked up and splattered water off the windowsill onto her hands and the rifle even though she sat a good three feet from the opening. She grabbed a soft cotton cloth and stroked off the liquid. It had rained for ten days straight since she'd arrived in Seattle, and only twenty minutes ago had it stopped. To the north, a break in the clouds showed deep blue sky. A miracle. Good grief, she couldn't wait to get back home to Atlanta.

One moment, she was running her fingers across black metal, enjoying the bumpy finish. In the next, she was aiming at her target, taking a deep breath and then releasing it, relaxing, holding her trigger finger steady. He'd crossed the street and started down the boardwalk. Five foot eleven with a well-proportioned torso, he always wore the same dingy sneakers with orange Day-Glo stripes.

She squeezed her eyes shut for a few seconds and inhaled. Time to concentrate on the job. The Circle had given her orders to eliminate him, and she was programmed to follow. Later she'd hear he was a child molester or a killer like herself. Why she should care one way or the other, she wasn't sure. Maybe knowing helped her sleep at night. Not that it would matter otherwise; she was a killer and good at what she did. She never really had a choice.

She waited as he'd jogged a little past the half-mile mark. His feet pounded in a steady rhythm as the early morning light glistened on shifting muscles. Like clockwork every day, he hit the pavement at sunrise, jogging down the same area. Only thing about predictability, it could be deadly.

The area around him was clear, no one nearby. He turned down a short pier. Only a few feet more and he would be at the mark. She cleared her mind and inhaled, holding her breath for the fraction of a second. She squeezed the trigger. The jogger's body continued straight ahead, propelled by the bullet's trajectory, and then he toppled off the edge of the pier and splashed into the water as his god-awful shoes tumbled across the boardwalk. Perfect shot. That was why they sent her.

Once she pressed a couple buttons on the gun's microcomputer, she scooted away from the tripod and stretched with arms up, bending her back, getting the kinks out. Her back popped. After an hour in one position, it was no wonder her body protested, no matter how much she worked out. She shook her head when the image of the body landing in the water tried to resurface. Think of the good she carried out. Her job eliminated those who preyed on the weak. She performed as a tool for the greater good.

Yes. That was it. She was a tool.

Thinking of tools, she smirked at the gun. The usual brutal recoil dampened by the hydraulic system always surprised her. The rifle worked like it should with little firing signature, a thump of air and only a small amount of flash at the end of the barrel. The suppresser did its job. Unless someone stared directly at her open window and caught the small flare, nothing gave away her location.

Damn! If she'd been a man, she would have a hard-on now. She loved her gun. Objects she could control. People were a different factor.

As she closed the window, a warm breeze caressed the fine hairs on her arm. She shivered. Yeah, she was ready to relieve the pressure that had been building up inside. Playing the waiting game and finishing the job always sent her seeking the only outlet from all the tension. Others used alcohol or drugs to forget for a little while what they'd done. Sex with an anonymous handsome stranger was her drug of choice. Someone clueless about what she did for a living. Someone who held her as she used them for release.

She looked out the window at the crowd gathering at the end of the pier. She jerked her gaze away. Concentrate on anything but the finished job. Think of the gun she loved to control. Think of the power she held. Think about sex. A strong, hard, hot male body always helped. Think about getting away and planning the next job.

She reached out and caressed the two marks she'd made on the butt of the rifle. *Time for a third.* Her fingers shook; tears threatened her composure. Drawing her hand into a fist, she took a few deep breaths and then with well-practiced precision broke down the rifle and placed the sections into her luggage. Another tremor started at her hand and vibrated down her torso, before she knew it her whole body shook. Why couldn't her body cooperate? She'd done worse, been worse. Taking several more deep breaths, she closed her eyes and imagined a swing on a long porch, pushing against the wooden floor with a bare toe. Back and forth. Finally, the shaking stopped, and she swiped at her forehead, surprised by the sweat she found there.

She glanced at her watch. Time to get her act together and pick up speed. By the time the authorities responded to a passerby's 911 call, she needed to be on the road, heading to I-90 and Denver. Unless someone noticed the spray of blood before he landed in the water, they would be clueless that he'd been hit by a sniper until they dragged the body out of the water.

Inside ten minutes, she sauntered out of the fingerprint-cleaned apartment, pulling a rolling safari-chic suitcase behind her while clutching a large tote on her shoulder. The black linen pants, tailored black silk blouse, and auburn hair piled on top of her head shouted business trip.

The clouds in the blue sky had separated allowing the sun to peek between the breaks. Emergency vehicles zoomed by and their echoing sirens bounced off the buildings. They headed toward the boardwalk further down the street as a small crowd pointed at the water.

About the time she walked the block and half to the parking deck and threw the luggage into the trunk of her rental, her cell phone vibrated.

"Yes, sugar booger." She loved irritating the hell out of her handler.

Jason Kastler thought he was God's gift to women, and she took every opportunity to remind him his good looks were good only for one thing, to play a Romeo, an operative who seduced women for information. Whenever he walked into a room, women watched his every move as if he was a walking sex toy. He hated it when she reminded him that men stared too. With his sun-kissed blond hair, vivid blue eyes, and six foot six frame, he needed someone carving off his massive ego.

"Sugar booger? Christ, woman, can't you be the least bit respectful?" His growl revved her engine.

Good looking *and* an orgasmic-inducing voice. It really was a shame. She could use him at the moment, though it would never happen. He liked to be the one in control. One thing about her, she always relished being the one on top.

"Respect is earned, doll. The job's done, and I'm heading to my next assignment's location. I already have a plan. Should take me a couple months to set up. I just need to scout the area," she said, ready to move on.

She tossed her purse to the passenger side and then slammed the driver's side door. Wasting no time, she had the cell phone plugged into the radio's speakers before cranking up the car. The state of Washington had a hands-free cell-phone law and ironically, considering her job, she followed all the traffic laws. The last thing she needed was to be pulled over for a minor infraction and be caught with the sniper rifle and numerous other weapons hidden on her person and in the rental.

"Change of plans . . . Theo wants you to return to the office. We have a ticket waiting for you at the airport." He was smiling. That light tone shouted his enjoyment in frustrating her.

She shut her eyes for a moment, anxiety curled in her stomach; he knew how much she hated flying. Not counting the up and down of the plane, the arranging for her arsenal to be shipped across country without her was a pain in the ass. The roar of the plane's engines didn't help the defenseless feeling.

Being ordered off an assignment by Theo was a bad sign. She avoided any face-to-face with him as much as possible. Hell, she'd worked hard for her freedom and for the last couple of years he rarely required her presence. So this meant something bad. Last time he'd made the demand, it had taken her a week to recover. He wasn't an easy man to please, and she no longer cared about satisfying his perversions. From the orphanage to the streets to Theo's control, there was always somebody waiting to use her, to take advantage of her. No more. She wouldn't go back to being that girl, begging for kindness and love. She squeezed her eyes closed, blocking out the images. No more. She dreaded being that needy little girl again. Tears welled up, threatening to spill.

Inhale. Exhale. Worrying wouldn't help. She struggled to regain her usual calm, steady façade. She took several more deep breaths, hoping it stopped the feeling of panic engulfing her. Pressure applied by her fingertips on the corner of her eyes pushed back the tears.

Olivia knew it was useless to argue. Operatives never won arguments against Circle handlers; disagreeing too much could be unhealthy. People had been known to disappear.

"Okay. Tell me which airline." She took another deep breath.

As he spit out the instructions, she turned the car toward a local UPS store and made her plans. Two hours later she boarded the plane, and all her weapons, including her gun, were on their way in several parts to her home in Georgia.

She settled into her first-class seat. After questioning the flight attendant, she learned the plane was full for the non-stop flight to Atlanta. She hated it when the seat next to her was used. No elbow room. Not that she was tall—a mere average height of five foot five—or big—roughly a hundred and twenty pounds. She didn't like strangers rubbing against her and often took the window seat, not for the view since she usually pulled down the shade, but so she could lean against the wall of the cabin, putting as much distance between her and the next seat. First-class seats were wide enough she could even pull her feet up beside her, but she always loved more room.

Pretending to stare out the window, she waited for the rest of the plane to load. One drawback to first class was having every man and woman file by, staring at those seated in the more expensive rows. Bloody hell, wouldn't they hurry up? She hated the closed-in feeling, the helplessness, the sitting and waiting, the curious looks. Couldn't the freaking flight attendants help the tourists place their handhelds into the overhead compartment, so everyone would quit staring at her?

Closing her eyes for a few seconds, she mentally shook herself. What good was it to be short tempered, bitchy? Sure, crowds made her uncomfortable. Too many people pressing in, too many staring, guessing at what she did for a living. Was murderer written on her face, her clothes? She hated feeling like this. Add in her unexpected meeting with Theo, and she was certain she would go crazy.

When she was about to scream in frustration, the last person walked through. Whoever had the ticket for the seat next to hers hadn't arrived yet. Maybe she'd be lucky, and the seat would remain open. She rarely slept well the night before a hit, and it would be wonderful to stretch out.

The attendant pulled on the door and stopped when someone shouted from the walkway.

Olivia dug her nails into the armrests. Shouting always grated across her nerves. She always expected the worse. Had she screwed up and the local yokels or the big boys were after her? When she heard laughing, she realized whatever happened didn't involve the law. People rarely laughed when the authorities showed up.

"Sorry, my flight was late coming in. I almost didn't make it," a deep voice said.

She looked up. Oh, yes, this was what she needed. The man was a good six-one, possibly two, and the Armani suit showed off his wide shoulders perfectly.

He glanced toward the empty seat the attendant pointed to and then he looked at her. Those mysterious dark eyes punched the breath out of her. Set in an angular face with a small dimple in the chin, his eyes appeared almost amber, glowing with such a life force. His lips etched full but still masculine and begged to be licked. Oh, she liked the look of those lips. His nose was manly, not crooked from fighting but not a picture-perfect narrow one either.

Yeah, she liked the package in front of her. Now if she could remove the wrapping to see what lay underneath. Her body had been humming ever since she'd completed her mission. With those gorgeous eyes and his athletic body, she was more than willing to put him through his paces.

Maybe being stuck on a plane for five hours wouldn't be so awful after all. This stranger she wouldn't mind touching or have him touching her. She reached out and introduced herself.

"Hi, I'm Olivia Roth."

"Joe Murphy." He held her hand for a second longer than necessary.

Her grin spread wider. Oh, yeah, this was going to be a whole lotta fun.

By the time the tires bounced and rolled on the tarmac at Hartsfield-Jackson Atlanta International Airport, Olivia already had Joe inviting her to dinner that evening. She felt primed and ready to give her new friend a good time. Since taking a stranger home with her was out of the question, she worked her wiles until he told her he was staying at the Marriott Marquis.

Then she remarked, "Isn't that a coincidence? I'm staying there too." She liked how his eyes glimmered when she said that. To him, she was a lone woman on a business trip, easy pickings for a one-night fling.

She ducked into the women's restroom at the airport and called reservations. The Marquis happened to be her favorite hotel, and they had room. When she stepped out, her gaze zeroed on Joe, leaning against the wall nearby; his eyes drank in every inch of her. Oh, yes, he was exactly what she needed.

They shared a cab, laughing and talking all the way to the hotel's check-in counter. As they walked toward the elevators, he mentioned wanting to visit one of the restaurants below street level. She smiled.

They would never make it. Though she detested strangers brushing up against her, she didn't mind using one to release her tension, to forget what her job entailed. Her body using his throughout the night until he fell exhausted from her demands. And she had many demands.

Oh, yeah, a beautiful thing about being a phantom in the world of assassins, at the end of a mission she could enjoy a little downtime with a good-looking man. No one in the world knew what she did except her handler and Theo. She'd always been careful.

Leaning against the glass wall of the elevator, she stared as the lobby became smaller. A few more years and she'd kill Theo and disappear.

One corner of her mouth lifted as she looked from beneath her eyelashes at the man next to her. "I'll be waiting for you at seven-thirty." She felt like the spider waiting for the fly.

The knock came at seven-thirty on the dot. She liked how his amber eyes flared when she opened the door and waited with one hand on her hip. Her deep sigh brought that burning gaze to her breasts.

She'd dressed—better yet, undressed—specifically to push all thought of food from his mind. The lace-and-mesh deep ruby nightgown brought out the red highlights in her hair that flowed down her shoulders and made her skin appear a creamier white. Her full breasts tested the strength of the well-placed lace. Masterfully applied makeup emphasized the green of her eyes and the fullness of her dark red lips. Her bare toes peeked out beneath the edge of the gown and a fragile tinkle rang from her anklets, drawing his attention to her long, long legs as the slit at the side opened and closed with her every movement. She knew how to rein in a man's interest.

"I like a woman who knows her mind," he said in a low voice. His lips lifted, allowing only a flash of white teeth.

She stepped back and without hesitation he walked in.

"And I like a man who knows what he wants." She closed the door and leaned against it. With deft fingers, she locked it with a double click behind her.

"So no dinner." One dark eyebrow lifted.

"A man who picks up on the subtleties."

His body grazed hers as he moved closer and looked

down, a grin flitted across his lips. "You look beautiful," he murmured. "Damn, you smell good." He inhaled, his eyes half closing as he brushed his thumb across her bottom lip. "You feel good too. Smooth, soft, hot."

Though she enjoyed being called beautiful, she knew better. Makeup and clothes could hide many defects and she was an expert at it. Yet she appreciated a man who would lie to get what he wanted, especially when she had done the same.

"For you. Hot for you." Her eyelids heavy, she leaned toward him.

He slid his hands down her arms. His gaze travelled a burning trail across her breasts. "Luscious."

"What a sweet talker." Her nimble fingers pulled at his tie and worked the knot loose until she had the silk material in her hand and tossed it over her shoulder. Then she started on his shirt.

His hand clasped her wrists before the second button made it through the hole.

"Wait," he said softly.

Her shoulders drooped. She wanted to forget about what she did today. Hell, to forget what she did for a living just for a few hours, to immerse all her thoughts in a hard male body. She took a deep sigh, causing her breasts to lift high enough to catch his attention again and remind him of what waited. Did he really want to chitchat? Patience wasn't one of her virtues.

She hoped to survive her nine a.m. meeting with Theo tomorrow and still go on assignment. And that could be any-where, maybe Denver as she'd been originally scheduled, or even somewhere on the other side of the world, far, far away from Theo. What a lovely thought.

Anyway, the memories she made tonight would help her live through the time she spent with Theo or at the least make them bearable. She puckered her lips and looked up at him beneath her eyelashes, pretending to pout.

His heated look confirmed it worked.

"I have to taste you," he whispered, his lips brushed her cheek.

"Yes, sir," she teased. Before she could raise her face, he wrapped his arms around her and lifted her to his mouth. His tongue thrust against hers, tasting, stroking until her fingers dug into his back.

Whoa! The man knew how to kiss.

He lifted his head.

She liked how he tasted of whiskey and male heat. She wanted more. She tried to push him away but he grabbed her arms.

Who did he think he was? She preferred to be the one in control. Before she could show him how she felt about his manhandling, his lips fanned small bursts of hot air against hers as he said, "I couldn't resist a sample. I wanted to see if you're as spicy as you look."

Her skin heated and stretched so tight she thought she would burst from need. The man did have a way with words.

"And?" She rubbed her breasts against his hard chest.

"Another taste. Just once more." His mouth covered hers. He sucked in her bottom lip, and then his tongue dove into her mouth, taking what she offered, taking all he wanted.

Whenever she tried to meet his tongue with her own, he thrust harder, opening her mouth wider, dominating the kiss and her response, showing her what he liked and giving her an idea of what else he expected from her. He decided on the rhythm of their kiss and she was surprised by how much she enjoyed letting him have the lead. Her body softened as he took her breath away.

His fingers gripped her butt and pressed his groin to hers. She leaned into him, letting him hold her weight, letting him have control. For a little bit.

Yet his kisses weren't enough. She wanted to see and touch every inch of him. Despite how wonderful his mouth felt against hers, she pinched his hard abdomen. Not enough to hurt. Just to draw his attention away from the kiss for a second.

"Bed?" she suggested with hope in her voice.

Her libido was on overdrive, and his kisses had been like gasoline on a smoking fire. That was her excuse for letting him get away with caveman tactics so far. She always liked being in control, but there was something about the way he held her, kissed her, touched her, made her want more. He dropped one wrist and held the other, leading her deeper into the room and toward the bed. She followed, taking in his broad shoulders and the way his hair met the back of his neck.

Happy that he was finally getting down to what she wanted, she purred.

She stepped in front of him and reached for his shirt. "Let's take some of your clothes off. You're overdressed in my opinion." She wanted to see what was hidden beneath his expensive suit.

Without a jacket, would his shoulders be as broad? Would he have defined muscles? Exotic tattoos? Scars? How far down did his tan go? How big and hard was he? She rubbed a hip against his groin. Oh, yes, he was hard. Men were easy to manipulate when sex was involved. And she was grateful.

He stopped in the middle of the room and looked at her. His face turned brooding as his eyes darkened and searched hers. The hot kisser from a few seconds ago had vanished. She wasn't sure what he was looking for, but she shivered in excitement. She liked being the center of his attention. The businessman had disappeared, and in his place was a dangerous and lethal man. Danger proved to be the strongest aphrodisiac. She knew that for a fact. He looked ready to throw her on the floor and fuck her to death.

Death by sex? Now that would be the way to go. Lust slapped her libido into higher gear. She stepped back to recover her breath. At the same time, he clutched a handful of material at her shoulder and with a flick of his wrist tore the gown in two.

She gasped. "You son of a bitch!"

Chill bumps popped along her arms and across her chest. She wanted to believe the tingling was from the cool room. She knew better. She liked it rough, only that gown was her favorite and an original. With a fluid turn, she brought her leg up and he caught it, stopping her dead. Uncertain of what he was up to, she knew she needed to think fast, as only an expert in martial arts could stop her kick. Going with the momentum of her leg, she twisted her body midair and brought him down with her.

Instead of knocking him out or at least dazing him, he

smoothly flipped her onto her back and seized her wrists, pulling them above her head. She kicked and bucked, trying to loosen his hold as he dragged her onto the bed. His knee jabbed her stomach, and she lost her breath. Before she could recover, something cold and hard clicked around her wrists. Handcuffs? He'd handcuffed her?

She blinked. "What the hell?"

"Shhh, Olivia. It will be over quick," he whispered in her ear.

With his knee still in her stomach, he held her cuffed wrists with one hand while the other unbuckled his belt.

"No you don't, asshole. There's no way I'll let that happen now," she said in a steady, angry voice. At the moment with her hands useless and his body pinning her down, her words were all hot air, but she wasn't about to give up.

He chuckled.

Heat flooded her cheeks. He actually thought she was funny. She bit the inside of her mouth. He may control her body, but she needed to rein in her emotions. She needed to think clearly about the situation and a way out.

"Un-cuff me," she demanded.

He placed a finger on her lips and shook his head. "Don't raise your voice. I would hate it if you forced me to neutralize any unwelcome visitors."

She would never endanger an innocent, no matter what he thought. Too many variables could go wrong. First rule she learned in The Circle was You're on Your Own. Second rule, Protect the Innocent. She would handle this man and anything he dished out.

Wait. What did he say? Neutralize? Well, crap! No regular Joe off the streets talked like that. She needed out of this jam.

She peeked at the door.

And she would find a way to escape.

Whatever he did was nothing compared to what Theo could do to her.

Normally, she could protect herself as she had enough experience to keep the upper hand. But this guy was different from the others she'd picked up for sex. His toned body appeared to come from more than regular gym push-ups or daily runs. Few men could stop her like he had. Well, damn, she'd picked on the wrong one this time. Her recklessness had finally caught up with her, all because she wanted him so much. His soft voice and perfect manners had misled her.

She tilted her head and watched as he fastened the handcuffs to the bed frame with his belt. No hesitation. As if he did it every day. He shook her arms to test the hold. She was as good as stuck until he unlocked them or she found a way out. He acted as if she was merely a job. Was she?

"Who are you?" she asked.

He ignored her as his gaze travelled a heated path to her chest. He straddled her thighs, keeping her legs flat on the bed by using his weight. His hands rested on her collarbone for a second and then skimmed down, dipping and massaging areas as if he was searching or maybe testing for something. When his hands cupped her heaving breasts and squeezed, she groaned, hating how good his touch felt. Unable to resist, she arched her back, wanting more of his firm touch.

He dragged his callused palms over her sensitive nipples before slipping down her waist; taking his time as his eyes savored every inch of skin, his fingers continued with their examination.

He was examining her!

Was he looking for a locator maybe? Only another operative would think to look for one. The Circle embedded the device beneath the skin of those considered unpredictable. Luckily, she'd been deemed trustworthy, a small benefit from being Theo's former mistress. Then again, she never understood how they could use that as a gauge, considering how much she hated him.

An operative? Well, that explained a lot.

He lingered a moment at her hips, brushing his fingers across her shaved mons and then continued to her knees as he slid down and resting his weight on her feet. Her body bowed, trying to stay in contact with those strong, rough hands.

"Damn you. I don't have a locator on me."

Why not tell him the truth? He would realize it soon enough. But then again his hot gaze tempted her to lie and suggest a certain wet place to look.

She'd never been as turned on in her life. He moved onto the bed and jerked her legs apart, and she gasped. Open and wet, she throbbed in answer to his stare.

She kicked and he quickly clasped her ankles. His gaze returned to her mons. She wanted to tell him to go to hell, yet his hungry look sent heat skimming over her body. She liked his attention.

"And you would never lie to me," he quietly said.

She ignored his sarcasm. Deep inside her sex-hungry brain, his hands had slowed during the examination and wandered into areas less likely to hide a tracking device. The change told her he was rethinking his strategy. He wanted her despite his original intentions.

His fingers dipped and traced where she'd hoped he would venture. They retraced their path, returning to her breasts to pinch the tips. She gasped again. The electrifying tweak brought a flood of moistness between her legs. His fascination in her body was appreciated by her own. She couldn't catch her breath, and she didn't want him to stop.

"Obviously you're a man who won't take my word for it." Unable to catch her breath, the words emerged nearly indistinguishable.

The handcuffs rattled and began to cut into her wrists. For heaven's sakes, they weren't even fur lined. He needed to learn no one treated her this way, even if it did turn her on. In the end, if she lived, he would learn not to mess with her in this way. She would stake *his* life on that fact.

She looked down and noticed the nice long bulge beneath his slacks. Good. She hated to believe he possessed more control over his body than she did.

Why wasn't he doing anything more? Tuned and ready, she wanted everything. He was pissing her off. What was he waiting for?

"Ah, come on. No need to play around," she said. Release one of her hands and he'd be waking up in the Chattahoochee River. "Let me go, and I promise you'll be surprised. I can take you places you've never been. . . ." She fell silent.

Stupidly she'd forgotten to arrange for a gun to be delivered to her room. For some reason she'd trusted him. See what she got for trusting a man?

If she'd been standing, she'd stomp her foot. Not a blink

or look from him to indicate one word had registered. No longer did his hands probe and test but instead heated and rubbed to bring pleasure. His eyes followed every inch he touched. He mounded and then squeezed her breasts with the right pressure. She inhaled deeply. Then panting, she groaned and arched into his touch again. Lord of Mercy, his hands felt so good. She wished she could control her reaction. The man wasn't human; not a drop of sweat touched his forehead, while she wanted ... no ... needed him badly. Her fingers dug into his belt as her body moved with each stroke. She hated feeling powerless.

He ignored her as his eyes remained on her heated body. Then he looked away for a second. When his gaze returned to her, she caught the conflict burning in their depths. He wasn't sure what to do next. Nice to know he was human after all.

Her own flaw of needing to be touched had brought her here. What about him? What did he really want?

Being angry and still aching for him drove her crazy. He thrilled her, excited her with the unexpected. Yet a part of her wanted to kill him.

He finally moved back. Seconds passed as his gaze remained on her. Like a bird caught in a cobra's stare, she stared back.

"Fuck it," he said in that deep, soft voice as he yanked off his jacket, tossing it to the other bed, and then rolled up his sleeves.

Her heartbeat picked up speed again. The sleek muscles on his arms showed how strong he was without being bulky. Just the way she liked it.

Then she noticed where his gaze lingered, radiating

enough heat to scorch her, and she forgot everything. His stare centered on the vee of her legs. In a graceful move, he stretched out at the foot of the bed, and his arms wrapped around her legs before she realized what he intended. He pushed her heels almost to her buttocks, opening her wide, and then his mouth covered her.

Her back bowed off the mattress. His wicked tongue dove into her and licked the taut nub already throbbing for attention. His teeth scraped sensitive skin as he moaned with her. Two thick fingers jabbed into her wetness and worked in tandem with his tongue.

Each firm thrust of his fingers and tongue wound her body tighter. When he sucked on the knot of nerves, she gasped. There wasn't enough air in the room. She couldn't breathe. She'd never had a man go down on her like she was a honey jar, and he wanted every last drop. The sounds of his sucking and licking excited her as much as the act itself. Her hips rotated and thrust against his expert tongue and fingers. Her nipples hurt from being neglected, pointing high and stiff.

She squirmed, wishing she could free her hands to soothe the aching tips. As if he'd read her mind, a broad hand moved up and rolled and tugged one nipple and then the other, pushing her over the edge. She released a long high-pitched moan. Oh, hell, she'd never climaxed so fast or so hard. Limp, she opened her mouth and took gulps of air.

He moved up just enough to rest his cheek against her stomach, his stubble caused her muscles to flinch. His heartbeat throbbed against her thigh as his short breaths tickled her sensitive skin. Good. His treatment of her had pulled him in too.

She waited for him to take her. Though he'd done a good job bringing her to the better side of satisfaction, she still felt a light humming in her body. She knew that meant she needed more.

Then his tongue glided from her belly button to her clit. Her hips reached for his mouth. Holy crap! It was as if she'd never climaxed. Her body hit second gear with the needle in the red. She wasn't sure if she could take another one like that. Wasn't he ready for the real deal?

He shoved himself off the bed and stood, shrugging his shoulders, pulling them back as he rotated his head. She heard joints popping. He stretched as if he'd finished a job and wanted to get the kinks out. Then he wiped her off his chin and looked her way with glittering eyes.

She groaned. Oh, shit, he was so damn hot.

He turned away from her.

Shock sent a shiver through her. Was he finished? She admitted his technique was different and a little constraining for her taste, but she wanted more. She'd gotten a glimpse of his groin. Hell, yeah, she hadn't been the only one wanting more. The impressive bulge against his trousers promised he had the right equipment needed to do the job. But first things first, he needed to let her go.

"Okay. You've had your fun. Un-cuff me." She jingled the handcuffs.

He picked up his tie and slipped it into his jacket as he sat next to her on the bed.

"No. I don't think so. Not yet," he said in his usual soft soul-sucking voice.

Heat travelled down her torso and centered on the area

now tender from his enthusiastic treatment. She liked how he didn't raise his voice. She'd liked it on the plane, though she'd thought it was from wanting to keep their polite conversation private. But she now realized it was normal for him, if she could call him normal in any sense of the word. What man didn't take what was freely offered?

"What do you want?" She narrowed her eyes at him.

When he kept quiet and lifted his chin, she kicked out. In a lightning quick move, he caught her ankles and then threw his torso across her knees. In seconds, he had her feet fastened together with his tie. A snap of his wrist brought a sheet off the other bed, and he wrapped it around her feet. If she'd planned to kick him again, the cushion would make it no more than a nudge.

"Enough already," she protested. "Who are you?"

He continued to ignore her. Her stomach tightened, and she swallowed to keep the fear down. Was he an operative out for revenge? Had she killed a friend or a brother of his? Which organization was he with? Blinded by lust, what had she missed?

"Who do you work for? Who are you?" she asked once again.

Those eerie amber eyes caught hers. "I'm your worst nightmare, Ms. Olivia St. Vincent."

A chill swept her body. He'd called her by her real name.

CARLA SWAFFORD lives in Alabama and is married to her high school sweetheart. A third-generation storyteller, she loves every shade of romance and the many paths taken to find that special someone.